Jagged Crossfire

Omicron Annihilation

Stephen L. Thompson

Jagged Crossfire

Books by Stephen L. Thompson

The Crossfire Series

Colorado Crossfire
Believer's Crossfire
International Crossfire
Israeli Crossfire
Spirit Crossfire
Faith Crossfire
Chinese Crossfire
Texas Crossfire
Dark Crossfire
Island Crossfire
Jagged Crossfire
Violent Crossfire
Russian Crossfire
Nuclear Crossfire
End Times Crossfire
Revelation Crossfire
Gates of Hell Crossfire
Assassin's Crossfire
Albatross Crossfire
Global Crossfire
Far East Crossfire

The SFO Series

Station Force One - Onset

Jagged Crossfire

The Crossfire team must help stop an evil threat by terrorists who seek to destroy Israel and the United States of America.

-   Stephen L. Thompson

Jagged Crossfire

Published by
Stephen L. Thompson
Facebook.com/CrossfireNovelSeries

ISBN- 978-1-943879-09-0

Published in the United States of America

Foreword

To my Christian readers –

The Crossfire series of action/adventure stories include depictions of violence which are unusual in Christian literature. It would be nice if there were no conflict or violence in our world. But we live in a time when evil is increasing instead of diminishing, when some men seem to be controlled by selfishness, madness, or evil forces. When the enemies of decent mankind are bent on subjugation of other men and women, righteous men and women must stand against evil. Please remember that the yoke of oppression is not lifted by prayer alone. God is our shepherd and we are his sheep. As long as there are wolves about, God will use some of us as sheep dogs to defend the rest of us. These stories are about people like that and the forces they fight against. The stories describe violence because it occurs in the real world and it is active in the lives of all people whether they recognize it or not.

To my non-Christian readers –

The Crossfire series include depictions of spiritual warfare and spiritual activity with which the non-Christian may not be familiar. These stories describe the realms and activities of both God and Satan because they are real and active in the lives of all people whether they recognize it or not.

Steve Thompson

CHAPTER ONE

The night sky in the rural area near Badingen, Germany was full of stars. The land around the remote building was as dark as the night. The only light available was from the stars. Not a ray of light leaked out of the building from a crack or filtered through screened windows. It was completely dark even though the hour was early evening. Yet, there was movement and deadly intent.

Mark Connelly breathed slowly and quietly. His attention was riveted on his scope picture on the silenced M-107 .50 caliber military sniper rifle. The view he had was impressive through the U.S. Army's AN/PAS-13 thermal weapon sight. He was perched on a small elevation on a hill above the entry path and far enough away from the building so he could oversee the building and the escape route. At the moment he was watching the three mercenary security guards believing that they were invisible as they protected the Omicron building. Mark's job was to ensure that the guards didn't see or interfere with the on-going Crossfire operation.

Mark, a former U.S. Navy SEAL team leader, had taken his skills and adopted them to the streets after leaving the military. His six-foot, two-inch tall frame and muscular build occasionally made it hard to fit into tight spaces but was handy the rest of the time. In the frozen dark he smiled to himself. His wife and most other women considered him to be fairly handsome and occasionally charming.

Mark was happy that his desire to "rid the universe" of scum and predators had taken a major leap forward when he met Jack and Laura Malone in Denver thirty months ago. His hard work at all levels of anti-terrorist work had dovetailed into their drive to fix the world for God.

Working with the Malones he had met a female Mossad agent in Houston, Texas. Sarah Cohen had led the three of them on an operation in Israel which involved the poisoning of the world. Taken by her honesty and beauty, he truly admired her abilities in the spy world. The feeling had been mutual and they had married a year and a half ago. Mark was eternally grateful that his involvement with Sarah and the Malone's Christianity led him to a relationship with Yahshua and the hair-on-fire life he was now involved in daily.

Sliding his scoped rifle to the right Mark could see Jack, Laura, and Sarah. The three were silently climbing the west wall of the building using the sunken fire escape ladder that extended from the first floor roof to roof over the fourth floor.

As he watched, Mark evaluated the others. Jack was the tallest of the group at six-foot, four-inches but at 175 pounds he was lighter than Mark by almost forty pounds. His blonde hair and jade-green eyes gave him a cultured, professional look that matched his old life as President of his own company, Technology Alternatives in Denver, Colorado.

Mark knew Jack had spent over ten years as a martial arts instructor and that training showed in the way he moved. While Jack was tough he had come from a civilian background. Mark understood that Jack knew both Mark and Sarah were tougher and had said so several times. Still, Jack was a fast learner and with his walk with Yahveh he was quickly becoming effective in combat.

On the climb to the roof the night air was cool and the sounds of a distant jet flying five miles high drowned out any noises Jack made as he climbed. He reached the top of the ladder and carefully looked over the top of the roof. There was a single sentry walking across the roof. Jack waited until the man was on the far side of the roof looking the other direction before he pulled himself onto the roof in one silent movement.

He quickly moved five feet to his left. Hiding behind an air conditioning tower he continued to watch the sentry through the grills of the tower as the man reversed his course and slowly walked toward the west wall. It was obvious that this man wasn't a low-paid security guard with little or no training. He was intelligent, alert, armed, and looking for any sign of an intrusion.

Jack carefully removed a dart gun from a holster on his left side and took a two-handed stance. As the man walked past him and looked out over the west wall Jack carefully aimed and fired a dart into the side of his neck. The man slapped his neck thinking he had been attacked by an insect. Realization of what really happened came to him just as the drugs shut down his mind. He collapsed backwards and dropped to the roof surface.

Laura and Sarah quickly climbed up onto the roof and helped carry the sentry to the area near the stairwell entrance. They didn't bother to tie him up because the drugs would keep him out of it for the next two to four hours. Still, Jack watched Sarah as she let her fingers caress the handle of the Cold Steel Tanto combat knife she had sheathed upside down to the left side of her arm harness. She had told Jack that her Mossad training had been very emphatic that you don't leave an enemy alive at your back. Still, Jack had shown her that indiscriminate killing was a sin and not a smart move. Shoving the mental conflict out of her mind she moved to be close to her fellow warriors.

Jack watched the two women. Laura and Sarah were similar in build with Laura being blonde-haired and a couple of inches taller than Sarah. Both women were classic in stature and would be called beautiful in looks and spirit. Sarah was more focused due to her military and Mossad backgrounds. Jack internally smiled because he knew that Sarah knew to let Laura lead when the spiritual world was involved. He recalled when Sarah was converted to the Christian faith. It had been dramatic when her friend and boss had been killed saving her and Laura in Israel. Yahshua had brought David Zahavy back to life and restored him to full health.

Jack covered Laura as she used two meters to check the door and frame for alarms. Not finding any they opened the door and quietly went down the stairs. As they neared the bottom of the stairs Sarah stopped them with a raised fist. The landing for the stairs was brightly lit and there were two cameras pointed at the landing area. One of them covered the stairs to the roof. Sarah took out a silenced .22 automatic and carefully shot the cable off of the camera facing the stairs.

Staying out of sight of the second camera they quickly moved through the landing area and into a long hall. Their target was the third room to the right.

Jack found the door locked but overcame the lock quickly with a hand held lock picker. He put the probe of the picker into the lock and squeezed the large lever on the front of the handle. The picker ratcheted twice and the door was unlocked. Jack put the picker away and opened the door.

As he stepped into the room he heard Mark's voice in his combat communications earpiece. "Move it guys, they're on to you. The three guards in front just high tailed it into the building."

Jack looked at the two women and pointed at the door. As they moved to defend the door he quickly walked to the cabinet they had identified from their Intel on the site. Breaking the locking handle on the cabinet with a twist of his wrist he opened the doors. Quickly scanning the disks inside he gathered twelve of them together and put them into a pouch and placed it in his backpack.

Going to the door he didn't see anyone there yet. Nodding to Sarah he stepped into the hallway followed by Laura with Sarah bringing up the rear. Sarah pulled the pins on two smoke grenades and pitched them down the hall toward the elevators. They hurried back to the door to the stairs as the dense smoke filled the hall. A "ding" announced the arrival of one of the elevators and Sarah repeated her pin pull-pitch routine but this time she sent two flash bang grenades down the hall. The three warriors ran through the landing and up the stairs as the flash bangs went off.

Almost to the roof Jack heard a sound he didn't like. The wup-wup-wup of helicopter blades was audible through the closed door to the roof. He keyed his microphone and asked, "Mark, what do we have in front of us? We're at the entrance to the roof."

Mark came back, "Hold one."

Mark sighted on the rotor gearbox on the chopper hovering off of the roof. The thermal weapon sight gave him a ten-power magnification and he could be very precise. Squeezing the trigger he rode out the recoil of the huge .50 caliber round. The 1500-grain boat-tail slug covered the distance in less than two seconds and smashed into the machinery with a massive impact. The effect was more damaging than Mark expected. The huge slug not only smashed the gearbox but released the main shaft of the rotor. The rotating wing was suddenly freed of constraint and went upward. At the same time the helicopter dropped to the roof of the building with nothing to slow it down.

The chopper only fell twenty feet but it hit with such a hard impact that the tail rotor, which was still turning, smashed into the roof and rebounded upward. This action tipped the chopper over the edge of the roof. There were faint screams as the chopper fell the four stories to the ground and smashed into a concrete wall and staircase and the aviation fuel exploded.

Inside the stairwell the raiders were shaken first by the impact of the chopper with the roof and then again by the explosion. Mark's voice came back, "All clear."

Opening the door and seeing nothing but a damaged area with parts of the helicopter still bouncing on the roof, the three warriors skirted the damaged area of the roof and raced to the west wall. Seeing that the area was still clear, they grabbed the outside of the ladder and slid down three floors to the bottom. Jack was grateful for the metal-reinforced gloves they were wearing because controlling their rate of fall with their hands could have been painful otherwise. As it was his hands got really warm.

The ladder only went to the roof of the first floor of the four level building. Running to the scaling ropes they had left attached they quickly climbed back down to the ground and ran to the hole they'd made in the security fence. Climbing through the hole they ran for the woods. Half way to the trees Mark said, "Get Down!"

All three of them dove to the ground and covered their heads. Mark had fired an M136 AT4 fin-stabilized 84mm High Explosive Anti-Tank (HEAT) warhead which whooshed over their prone figures and took out a speeding Humvee with an M-60 machine gun in the turret. The explosion also killed several foot troops running after Jack and the women. When the fireball died out there were only six troops able to pursue the trio.

Getting shakily to their feet they faced the on-rushing troops. Because they were going in light they didn't have any rifles, only handguns. Laura went to one knee and fired steadily at the six mercenaries running at them. She knocked one dead off his feet. The boom of Mark's .50 caliber brought down another one. Then the two forces merged and it became hand-to-hand. Jack knocked the handgun out of the hand of the man firing at him as one bullet went over his right shoulder and the next tugged at his body armor on his left side. The merc threw a vicious backhand with his left hand which Jack blocked with his left arm while he drew his Tanto Master blade with his right. The merc used the power of the block from Jack to extend his distance. As the merc reached down to pull a knife out of his right boot Jack slammed the Tanto into the top of the man's head permanently turning out his lights.

Sarah ducked under the barrel of the M-16 her merc was firing at her and drove a six-inch blade into the man's groin below his body armor. As he screamed and dropped his rifle to clutch at his groin she drove a full power, right hand knuckle punch to the man's left temple, the crunch signifying that the fight was over.

Laura was outclassed by the big merc facing her but she was praying and leaned back out of his grasp and snap kicked him in the groin. It didn't completely stop him but it did slow him down a lot and make him bend over. Laura brought her left elbow down on the back of his neck and something snapped. The man fell to the ground and didn't move.

The remaining merc saw his fellow mercs dropping and flicked his M-16 to three-round burst. He started shooting as fast as he could regardless of who was in front of him. Laura fell backwards while Sarah dived forwards under the incoming rounds. Jack hauled his recent opponent up in front of him as a bullet sponge to absorb the rounds headed his way.

Mark's .50 caliber round snatched the life away from the shooter. Then things were quiet. Jack looked around and tipped his head towards the woods. After retrieving their knives, the women took off running with Jack behind them watching their back track. Reaching the woods they quickly worked their way to the hidden van. Six minutes later they saw Mark coming from the other direction. Getting in they drove away into the night.

CHAPTER TWO

As they drove to the private chalet which, in reality was a Mossad safe house near Berlin, Jack asked Mark. "That was some reception. Do you think they knew we were headed there or is that the general state of their preparedness?"

Mark had been thinking about the massive response their incursion had engendered. "I don't think they laid this position out as a deliberate lure to get us to attack it. If they had, we would have been toast. I think it was a standard reaction to any intruders, but especially to intrusion by the Crossfire Team. They almost had us there." Mark remembered the three black-clad mercenaries that had dropped in to wish him a good evening. Their bodies were stacked together below his sniper's nest. "It's very close each time we come up against the people the Omicron Cartel hires to protect themselves. These are the highest paid, most professional mercenaries available on the market. They're pulling out all the stops to trap us since they can't find us."

Jack nodded, "That reinforces my idea that they have something very bad planned and are making every effort to keep it secret. Do you think we'll get anything off of these disks?"

Mark's lips tightened, "I hope so. We need Intel to combat this organization. Linda Wu says that their lackeys are spending millions trying to find out where we are, what we are doing, and when."

Jack looked into the back seat where their wives were attending to their wounds and hurts. "I think it's time we skip some levels and start trimming this group down from the top."

Mark nodded.

Jack made a left turn into the driveway to a small courtyard in front of an enclosed building. He looked at it sourly. He turned and looked over his shoulder. "I got the wrong place."

Retracing his path he found where he was supposed to go left and had gone right instead. Then he found the right place. Jack pulled into the small courtyard of the safe house and Mark hopped out to close and lock the gate behind them. A young, athletically-built Oriental man met them in the court yard. At five foot ten inches, Charlie Wu looked unimposing with his ageless Asian features, black hair, and quiet brown eyes. Looking at him one would never know that he had been one of the top Chinese Internal Security agents only three and a half years ago.

Charlie smiled at them and held out his hand. Jack handed him the package of disks and he headed back into the house. After a quick debrief of each person was recorded and filed, the team went for hot showers and some sleep.

Around eight a.m. local time, Laura went to the kitchen to make some breakfast and found Jack, Mark, and Charlie sitting at the kitchen table with cups of coffee and worried expressions. Looking at her husband she quipped, "Is the world ending today, or what?"

Jack smiled a small smile. "Maybe the world as we know it."

Mark got up and went to get Sarah as Laura got herself a cup of coffee and sat down at the elegantly finished table next to Jack. When Mark returned with Sarah he also brought Linda Wu. Jack once again considered her. Linda was a classic Asian beauty with a petite figure and a demure attitude. Jack knew that a person would have to know Linda very well before they could detect the fiery dynamo that existed inside of her. She was Charlie's wife and match. She, like Charlie, had been a top Chinese security agent in the field when they first met.

Together they had found Yahshua and left China for a life in the west. Joining forces with the beginnings of the Crossfire Team they left their own investigative agency and went full-time with the team. Jack had been aware of Charlie's advanced computer skills and the new computer center at the fortress, which Charlie had helped design, exceeded anything his imagination could of conceived of two years ago and kept him very busy. This field trip was a welcome break in his routine but he still worried about all the things he had to do back at work.

Glancing at the concerned faces around him Jack decided to cut to the chase and tell them the heart of the matter. "Charlie was able to de-crypt the information on the disks we "liberated" last night. There are a host of operations that Omicron is fielding against us, and others, detailed on these disks. Could this be one reason that the disks were so well guarded?"

He got up and paced as he pulled the concepts together. "The primary efforts against the Crossfire Team are influence direction and active search and destroy. The Omicron Cartel has been infiltrating the governments of the world for the last five years. They have contributed heavily to many politicians and are now asking for a quid-pro-quo for their money. They can't hound us and try to imprison us like the Senator did a couple of months ago but they can do their best to isolate us from any support or cooperation at any level of the government."

Jack shook his head. "They have so little regard for the people in the world that they aren't attempting to mold public opinion against our team. They are calling in markers to force Senators and Representatives to force the President and the Military to not cooperate with us or else they will vote against anything the President tries to do. They are also infested in the Congressional oversight committees which control the purse strings to the military. It hasn't been brought to our attention as yet

But we will soon be told by the President or General Miles that we are on our own until the situation is resolved. They will have no choice but to isolate themselves from the Crossfire Team or face a virtual shutdown of the government which will result in chaos. That would allow the Omicron Cartel to make large strides in controlling even more of the functions of our government."

Mark smiled at the group. "We started on our own and we can still function without the governmental help. Omicron can't do anything about the fortress or our ability to fight them."

Charlie shook his head. "You're right about the fortress but they are in the process of quashing our authorization to hunt them down in any country and prosecute them. In the next week it will be a dead issue and we will be a group of citizens unable to fight them on an equal basis and possibly banned from many other countries. Sort of like China, right Honey?"

Linda smiled but didn't reply.

Sarah said, "We still have David and the Mossad's help."

Mark shook his head. "I'm afraid not, spylady. According to the information on these disks, they are putting extreme pressure on the Knesset to force the Mossad to distance themselves from our activities. One of the key elements is the censure of David Zahavy." Sarah's face reflected the anger she felt.

Jack added, "With this level of pressure I doubt that we will have the use of any of the alphabet agencies or Miles Marauders. We will have to find a way to determine their agenda and stop it all by ourselves. Let's get back to the fortress."

Laura smiled, "Well then, I think we need to pray for guidance now, and on the trip, right?"

Mark made an observation as they prepared to seek divine guidance. "You know, we have a strong base in the fortress, one of the most powerful computer systems on the planet, a dedicated crew, our own transportation and delivery systems, not to mention some of the most highly advanced weaponry in existence. But, the thing that sets us above the Omicron Cartel is our dependence and relationship with the creator of the universe. We can't lose!"

Laura smiled at the timely, upbeat analysis. She began their prayer time. "Dear heavenly Father, we seek you in love and ask your will in these matters..."

CHAPTER THREE

David Zahavy was considered one of the best tacticians the Mossad had ever produced. His activities and operations were taught to agents throughout the land. His recent ventures with the Crossfire Team had saved the Jewish homeland multiple times from nuclear holocaust and bio-hazard. He had an honored history as an agent, controller, and director. He was also requested to leave the agency immediately and quietly because it would be in the best interests of Israel.

Having been warned by Sarah by phone two mornings earlier the action didn't take him by surprise and he accepted the censure without comment.

A handsome man of thirty-two years of age impeccably dressed and cultured he was the proverbial steel fist in a kid-leather glove. He was versed in field work and operations and had taken life as required.

He knew that he was at the top of his game and that he could find work with any other agency in the world. But, he had prayed and knew what Yahveh wanted him to do with his life at this point.

Removing his belongings from his office and turning in all the required forms, identifications, and equipment he exited the headquarters building and quickly lost himself in the crowd. Arriving home he found his wife and two children waiting for him. An associate had called ahead to break the news of his termination from employment.

His wife of eight years had never gotten over his acceptance of Yahshua and being a Messianic Jew and had been quietly arranging her affairs so that she could leave him and take the children. David was quite intelligent as befitting his career field and had known about her preparations for several months. This too was not a real surprise. He had taken steps to make sure that she would be financially comfortable and the kids would be well taken care of in his absence. He also knew that his wife was leaning heavily on both of the children to attend temple and see him as a heretic to the Jewish faith.

It hurt him to see the look on his son and daughter's faces as they left but he knew that time would show them he had done the right thing. If she hadn't decided to divorce him he would have put them in greater peril by their association with him involving his next career move. He was sure that his wife would quickly revert to her maiden name which would further distance her and the kids from any actions taken against him.

Just to make sure, he had asked a trusted friend at the Mossad to keep an eye on them

As soon as they had left the house, David went to his secret safe and withdrew the money and credentials that he had stored there. A good agent is always ready to assume a new identity at a moment's notice. He carefully altered his appearance and gathered anything he knew he'd need. He had already shipped most of his personal effects and clothing. Looking around the house for a few minutes he left his regrets on the floor and shut the door for the last time. The house and its contents were already sold.

Catching a late flight out of Tel Aviv to the U.S. he studied the files he had accumulated from the Mossad concerning the growing threat of the Omicron Group. Several hours out of New York he called Sarah on the Air Phone in the arm of his first-class seat.

Sarah answered with "Shalom aleichem, David" (literally: "Peace be upon you, David"). David's response was, "Aleichem shalom, Sarah." ("Upon you be peace, Sarah").

"Well, David, did they come down on you as we expected?"

David laughed quietly, "Yes, I was pensioned immediately. I'm on the way to Denver, do you know of anyone who might want to use my services?"

Sarah said, "Wait one." She looked at Jack, Laura, and Mark with a smile. "Know anyone who wants to employ the services of a slightly used ex-Mossad director?" Over the phone she heard David say, "I heard that."

Jack looked at Mark and Laura, they nodded. Jack reached over and took the phone from Sarah. "David, it's unanimous, you would be a welcome member to the team and we look forward to your help. We see it as our gain and the Mossad's loss."

David was composed when he replied even though there were tears in his eyes, "I thank all of you. I expect to report to work within the next twelve hours."

Jack handed the phone back to Sarah. She asked, "David, how are Ruth and your children taking the news?"

David smiled wanly, "Ruth has been upset with me ever since I became a Messianic Jew. When she heard about the termination, she left me and took the kids. It's actually all right at this point because I've known for the last few months she was making preparations to leave. Anyway, since I'll be joining your team they will be safer if they are not associated with me."

Sarah commiserated with him for a few minutes and promised that they would be there to pick him up at DIA when he arrived in Denver.

The remainder of his flight was routine, as was the interconnection from New York to Denver.

Six hours and forty minutes later David stepped out of the flight line exit to be embraced by Sarah and welcomed by Jack, Laura, and Mark. He had been to the fortress before so it's unique construction and defensive capabilities were no surprise to him. What was a surprise is that his clothing and belongings were already prepared in his own suite at the fortress. He was impressed by the preparations made for him by the members of the team.

Jack gave him a new guardian disk that would identify him to the NOVASTAR2 defense system throughout the fortress as a member of the team. He realized the blessing that was and the trust in him that it represented for everyone there.

Jack and Laura left the suite leaving Mark and Sarah to help David get acquainted with his new home. After an hour of discussion and additional information about the high-tech fortress, the Connelly's left him so he could get some rest and get over any jet lag he had.

It was four hours later when he walked into the kitchen and met the second newest member of the team, Alexis Taggert. She had just poured a cup of coffee for herself and when she saw David she tipped her head in a silent question. David smiled and nodded.

Alexis brought both cups to the table and took a seat next to the ex-Mossad man. David for his part thought that she was one of the most beautiful women he had ever met.

They chatted for a few minutes about mundane things like the weather and the decor before Mark walked into the kitchen and spotted them. Walking over he smiled and introduced them to each other. David was almost as impressed with Alexis's credentials as a SpecOps operative for the NCS as she was with his recent career and accomplishments. She had heard of him and even studied his tactics. As she sipped her coffee she regarded the dapper man as somewhat of an enigma in the future.

CHAPTER FOUR

Laura came into the War Room and sank into her chair at the circular table. She was encouraged to see David and Alexis at the positions that had been set up for them. Doing a quick head count she went around the circle to her right. She counted Jack, Mark, Sarah, Su Li, Alexis, and now David. Charlie Wu and his wife Linda were there in virtual positions from the computer center three floors above them.

Nine presently active and nine more on call as needed. She ran the list of names of the people they could count on that weren't there right then. She thought of Sensei Grady, Victor Chamberlain, Tim Carson, Stan and Debbie Hargrove, Steve and Larry Malone, and Carol Nolan. That made seventeen in total. Seventeen warriors stood against the vast resources of the Omicron Group. Oh! She hadn't listed the most important members of the team, Yahveh and Yahshua. That made their forces far greater than the enemy.

She spoke quietly but her voice was picked up by the auto-ranging microphones and was heard at conversational level at each of the other nine positions. "I have been praying for guidance concerning our fight with the Omicron Group. While I haven't had a visit, vision, or direct command I have a strong leading that we are to carry the battle to them. I also feel that we will get invaluable help from some of our earlier efforts. Which ones I am not clear on, but, we will be helped greatly."

Mark spoke up. "Let's review what we've got so far. We know Satan's forces are deeply involved with these characters, as shown by the destruction of all the members of the meeting in the chalet by the demons. We also know that we have penetrated to the fifth level of the organization with our capture of Ms. TA and Mr. Beta. Jack remembered their recent battles where they had captured and interrogated the two fifth-level directors of Omicron. The disks we liberated indicate the direction of their efforts towards us."

Jack picked up the thread of conversation. "What we don't know is what their agenda is, who's behind it, and what resources they have of their own other than mercenaries. We need to get a handle on the top level of this monster and behead it. Then we can work our way down until we hit the street people." Jack knew his honesty and passion came through as he discussed the people that had tried to kill them several times.

Sarah looked at David, "Any chance we'll still be allowed information from the interrogation of Mr. Beta by the Mossad?"

David smiled, "Not from the Mossad, officially. But I still have personal ties that aren't official. I'll let you know when I hear anything." David felt the buzzing of his personal cell phone and pulled it out of his pocket. Looking at the calling number he flipped the phone open and said "Shalom".

He listened for a minute and smiled. Looking over to Jack and Mark he asked, "The information you wanted on Mr. Beta is waiting outside the front gate of the fortress. Judah Maritz and Aaron Jacobson have come in person with the information."

Mark smiled, "Let them in Charlie."

In the computer center Charlie ran all the ID scans and other protections and then let the vehicle into the parking space of the fortress.

Mark had taken the elevator up and met the two men as they exited their car. After a short discussion he took them back to the War Room. They shook hands with David and the rest of the team and sat down in the gallery seats near the round table. David requested they speak English for the benefit of the other people there.

Judah spoke first, "We finished the interrogation of Milton Warrow or Mr. Beta and were pleasantly surprised with our findings." He looked at Aaron, "We aren't very confident in the communications between the Mossad and Mr. Zahavy at this time so we thought it best to bring the information in person."

David frowned, "I doubt that the firm was too pleased to let you two leave to confer with me."

Aaron answered, "Actually, Mr. Zahavy, you are still held in high regard at the Mossad, unofficially. But we didn't ask permission, we both resigned and left the firm. We're hoping you could use our talents in your latest endeavor."

Judah smiled a crooked smile. "Also, you promised to teach me about Yahshua and the spiritual world. I didn't want to miss that opportunity."

Laura, as usual, was quiet and in prayer. She spoke up at this point. "David, I believe you could use two talented operatives at this time, don't you? I feel that Yahveh is just as much in favor of their supporting you as He was when we asked about you and Alexis. Also, I see the hand of God in the timing of this personal response to Sarah's question as to the possibility to our getting information on Mr. Beta, don't you?"

David smiled a small smile, "Who am I to argue with God? I'll leave the details of your employment up to Mr. Malone but please, give us the information you were able to retrieve from Mr. Beta."

Aaron stood up. "Since Milton Warrow realized that his group was out to kill him he decided the only way to survive would be to help the Crossfire Team take them out first. We didn't believe that he was on our side in any sense, only that he would do anything to save his hide. Still, since he was actually cooperating with us it was easier all around, especially on him. We did the usual debrief and found the seven levels of planted memories that seem to come with this group."

Aaron gestured at Judah, "Actually, Judah suggested a path that gave us the major breakthroughs with Mr. Beta. He suggested that we avoid searching for Omicron operational or personnel information and work with his casual life instead. Since he was wrapped up in Omicron it would probably involve them anyway. It was amazing. It was like a back door into his world that didn't butt heads with his programming. We've decided that the programming of the upper level Omicron people is being done by two Chinese psychologists skilled in this type of mind bending."

Linda Wu interrupted from the computer center. "That would be Lei Chong and Tzu Wo. We ran across their efforts in China when we were working with prisoners."

Since he couldn't locate Linda Wu, Aaron asked the air, "Are there any special techniques or flaws in their programming that you know about?"

Charlie spoke up. "We weren't in on their operation, only witnessed the effects on others. But, I will take it as a task to find out those things for you."

Jack steered the talk back on track, "What did Judah's method provide us?"

Aaron smiled, "The names of two of the four members of level 2. We also discovered the important fact that there is only one man on level 1. Also, there was something odd about the way Mr. Beta thought of the top man, sort of with a mixture of awe and admiration mixed with an intense fear. Very strange concept for one of the man's most significant social contacts, but one he's never met."

Mark nodded, "But, it makes sense. Why not one person with total control and direction to maximize command functions? The person would probably be very charismatic and impressive."

David asked Aaron, "Did you get any location information concerning the two names you got?"

Judah laughed, "Yeah, we did. You won't believe it but both of them live in the U.S. One of them resides in Chicago, Illinois and the other one in New York City."

CHAPTER FIVE

As the meeting continued, Mark asked the number one question, "What is their goal and what do they expect to get out of it?"

David answered, "They seem to be aiming at full control of the population of the civilized world through the reigning political structures. In the U.S. that would be the Congress rather than trying to take over like a military force. Their efforts have been to control world governments and to affect policy. I can't see that there would be any other goal than complete control of the world. They are just trying to do it through perverting the legal processes so that they get their way politically rather than trying to dominate by war and conquest."

Laura sat up in her chair. "But they were willing to destroy the United States and Britain and let the Eastern factions run the world. How does that tie into a world domination scenario?"

Jack spoke out, "I think they were just trying to use one group to eliminate two of their biggest problems of democracy. I doubt that they would have let the Eastern powers rule unless it was as a puppet government with the Omicron Cartel running the show from behind the stage."

Mark frowned, "But, to what end?"

Sarah slapped her hand on the table. "I think we need to arrange a discussion with one of the men that Aaron and Judah have unearthed so that we can get a better handle on the real thing. We could sit here until Hades freezes over talking about "what if" and never know if we are on the right track."

Alexis uncrossed her long legs and swiveled towards the dark-haired woman. "Okay, which one do we grab and how do we do it so that they don't get wise to the snatch?"

David smiled, "I say we go for the man in Chicago and do a sleight of hand op on his routine so that no one gets wise to our intentions. We can't do another op like the one on Ms. TA. Too much coincidence and they'll know what we are doing.

Laura looked puzzled, "What's a sleight of hand operation?" Mark laughed, "Remember the old TV show, "Mission Impossible" or the movies of the same name? We scope out the target's daily movements and routines. Then we pick the time and place and grab him and drain him of information. Afterwards, we make it seem to him, and others, that he just got drunk, or did drugs, or something like what he would normally do. The Sleight-of-Hand job refers to the magician's trick of doing what you need to do in plain sight but so that no one notices what happened. It's complicated and somewhat risky but if it works right, we're in, get what we need, and get out without anyone catching on."

David swiveled around in his seat. "Okay Aaron, who is the target and where do we find him?"

Aaron took out a folder and scanned it. "The man's name is Howard Vortmer and he lives in an exclusive high-rise on Chicago's gold coast.

That's a strip of buildings on the lake shore north of the city. He has offices in downtown Chicago and a country club he owns in a very exclusive western suburb. I've got a lot of research we did on him but it is in Hebrew and it will take me a day or so to translate it to English."

Charlie spoke out of thin air. "Aaron, I'll be there in a few minutes. I think Crayton can speed up the translation operation."

Aaron looked lost, "Who is Crayton?"

David laughed, "That would be Mr. Wu's computer personae."

A few minutes later Charlie showed up and picked up the thirty pages of Hebrew data. He left again immediately.

Aaron joked with Judah in Hebrew, "I'll bet you that data gives his computer an overload. That's my own personal version and includes a bunch of intuitive jumps which will require a bunch of time to figure out."

Both men chuckled. David just smiled at them.

Laura suggested they break for lunch and gathered up a bunch of volunteers to help as she headed for the kitchen.

Jack had been wrestling with a problem for a while and decided the time was right to get something started. He punched in the code for Charlie's communicator. When

Charlie answered Jack asked him to find the number for Major Gary Danning, the military construction guru that had built the fortress for them.

Charlie asked Jack what he needed to know. Taken aback slightly by the question, Jack smiled to himself and told him, "I think we're going to need additional rooms for the Mossad men and any others that join us and we've just about utilized all of the suites on the second floor."

Charlie told Jack, "Get into the elevator and use your key to select floor five. I'll meet you there."

Jack broke the connection and signaled Mark to go with him. They got into the elevator and Jack did as Charlie told him to do. The elevator did it's sideward, up, and over routine and the door opened onto a new floor that neither of the men had seen before. This floor was hallowed out of granite like the rest of the fortress there was a large community room that had room for twenty conversational groups of six to ten people each.

It was done in the same tasteful decor as the other parts of the fortress and had indirect lighting and two large viewports that showed the valley on one side and the mountains on the other.

The elevator door opened again and Charlie stepped out. "What do you think?"

Mark waved his hand indicating the room and the hallways off of it. "How did you know this was here? Gary Danning didn't say anything to us about it."

Charlie grinned, "He wouldn't, until you asked him. This was the living quarters for the construction crews. I found it after I asked Crayton to detail the mountain for me concerning the fortress. There are three more areas that are accessible from the elevator in semi-finished form for future expansion. Let me give you a quick tour of this place."

They followed Charlie through the community room with its large screen LCD TVs and found a large galley-style kitchen, huge pantries stocked with non-perishable goods and several large freezers and refrigerators. A general set of rest rooms and five individual rooms that could be used for music appreciation, like blasting rap or Bach, prayer, or simply quiet contemplation. Gary had used the granite as a sound absorbing structure element that kept noises in or out. They then toured three of the individual rooms that could sleep one to four people with dressers, nice beds and plush carpeting.

Mark commented to Charlie, "Everything here looks brand new and unused. I thought you said that this was where the construction crews lived."

Charlie nodded, "Yeah, which fooled me for a few minutes too. Actually, I called Gary about that. It seems when they were done and moved out, he had everything installed that you see now. I think the construction crew had rock walls and concrete floors."

Mark looked at the individual bathrooms each room had and then toured the service rooms at the side of the facility. There was a full scale Laundromat and an emergency medical facility that could handle anything except full surgery.

Jack asked Charlie, "Okay, I like it and I think it will work great for our guests. Tell me; is this "floor five" between our quarters and the computer center?"

Charlie shook his head. "Consider the fortress as a beehive shaped dome in the middle of the mountain. Looking at each floor from a plan view, or above as it were, there are a minimum of four sections like a pie cut twice. Let's label them from the west clock-wise, A, B, C, and D.

There are actually eight levels that Major Danning excavated and used. The top level, Level 8 as I call it is the helicopter hangers, three hundred feet above Level 6. The next six levels are what you know as the fortress. The seventh level is separated by thirteen hundred feet vertical distance and is the home to the nuclear power plant near the bottom of the mountain."

Charlie pulled a piece of paper out of his shirt pocket and sketched the seven levels separated by distance so that they could understand what was going on.

Charlie pointed at the disk labeled "Level One". He used his pencil to color in the occupied areas. "The garden takes up all of quadrant A on this level. The swimming pool, rifle range, and the gym take up quadrant B. Most of quadrant D is storage, water and food preservation. The entrances and garages as well as the elevators are outside this section on this level. This level is thirty feet high to accommodate the water silos and the trees."

Moving up to the second level labeled "Level Two" he indicated that the entire living areas, dining room, kitchen area, War Room, and Mark's offices were all in quadrant C. The other quadrants on this level were for expansion.

On "Level Three", the twelve bedroom suites were also located in quadrant C leaving the other three for expansion at a later date.

On "Level Four" the computer center takes up quadrants B and D.

On "Level Five" the crew quarters took up all of quadrant A. "Level Six" was still empty at this time.

Charlie picked up his drawing and put it away. "As you can see there are no occupied areas one above each other except for the bedroom suites and the living spaces. This keeps security at a maximum and vibration and noise to a minimum."

Jack nodded, "Okay Charlie, get this galley stocked with perishables and we'll assign Aaron and Judah rooms. Since there's room for sixty plus people here and they are the only ones needing rooms, I think we can offer them one room each, if they want that."

Charlie agreed and they got back on the elevator to go back to the living quarters. Charlie picked up a box he'd left on the elevator and gave it to Jack. "Here's the translation of Aaron's data, one copy for each of you."

Mark grinned, "This should give Aaron something to think about." Mark didn't let it be widely known, but he had learned to speak and write Hebrew while in the Navy.

CHAPTER SIX

As the three men walked into the dining area off of the living room, Mark handed the box to Aaron with the comment, "Check this over and see if it's what you wanted to say." Mark then went over and took the seat next to Sarah to eat.

Aaron looked puzzled for a minute and asked, "What is this?" Then he started to read it and understood that his complex notes had been translated, edited, parsed, and printed out in less than thirty minutes. "Oy Vey. That was fast!"

Charlie looked up from his plate and smiled. His wife Linda told Aaron, "Actually, that only took six minutes. The rest of the time it was with Charlie while he was giving Jack and Mark the tour of the crew's quarters."

Aaron's eyes widened and he forgot his lunch as he scanned through the English version of his information. Finishing the last page he looked up with something akin to awe on his face. "Charlie, I am more than impressed! If the Mossad had this capability it would expedite their operations a great deal."

David chuckled, "Yes, but they don't have it and neither does anyone else at this time, do they?"

Charlie smiled, "Not yet and I think we can cut that time down by over eighty percent when we get our new optical scanners. If I had gotten Aaron's data on DVD I could have finished it in about three minutes. The rest of the time was scanning the pages."

Aaron looked impressed again. "Actually, I did have it on DVD; I just never knew you could handle the input."

Jack thought of something he'd forgotten. He got up and went to the control center behind the War Room. Several minutes later he returned with ID medallions for Aaron and Judah. "Here, keep these on you at all times while you're in the fortress. It's our way of tracking your position but more important, it's the NOVASTAR2's way for determining if you are a friend or a foe." Jack showed them a grin that chilled the hearts of the two young men. "You don't want to be a foe!"

Sarah's cell phone chirped and she answered it in Hebrew. She listened for a minute and then spoke again and hung it up. She looked concerned and shook her head. Looking up at David she told the group. "That was Lev Steinmetz. Lev is one of my acquaintances at the Mossad Headquarters. It seems that there was a raid on the facility that managed to gain entrance and penetrated far enough to grab Mr. Beta from the interrogation floor. The consensus is that they had to have inside help or information to gain access and know where they needed to go. One idea being kicked around is the suspicious timing between David's departure and the raid. They are also looking at Aaron and Judah as possible leaks. They're going through the grinder right now over there." She looked at her old boss for direction.

David frowned but didn't seem unduly concerned. "It is standard procedure to focus on any recently departed agent or member in such occurrences. And believe me there were a lot more occurrences than any of the three of you every heard about." He indicated Sarah, Aaron, and Judah with a wave of his hand. They need to remember the spy that we captured that was sending information to the Omicron Cartel from his workstation. That was probably their source of the information. Obviously the OC decided to get their man back and determine what he's told the Mossad."

David pulled out his cell phone and made a call to a highly-classified number that took twenty-three number punches. He then talked in Hebrew for about thirty seconds and hung up. Looking at the others he said, "I just called my old boss and gave him my concepts concerning the raid." He then forgot about the problem. Mr. Beta was beyond saving at this point and David had a cold assurance that his old company would find the guilty party or parties.

A powerful but muted dual chime rang out in the workroom. Actually this sound was heard everywhere throughout the fortress. The voice of Robin Templeton, one of Charlie's computer wizards, followed the chime.

"Attention team members, there is an on-going threat against the fortress at the present time. Be aware that the

NOVASTAR defense system alert level has been elevated to yellow. There is a two man team outside the main entrance attempting to infiltrate an autonomous spy craft into the driveway shaft. Response authorization requested."

Laura selected the proper switches on the panel at her position and the big view screen on the wall of the control center lit up with a somewhat elevated view of two men in camouflage fatigues with a control box and binoculars. There was a small aerial unit just moving away from their position. One part of the screen zeroed in on the spybot as it flew toward the main gate.

Mark asked Jack, "Should we shoot it down?"

Jack had been praying and said quickly, "No, let it get into the drive tunnel and then blind it and freeze it so we can examine it. Get one of the Marine units training on the mountain to grab those two men. I think we need to talk to them."

Robin Templeton in ComSec (computer/security) brought up three programs to handle the spybot while Mark contacted the military command that used the mountain for war games and got a flying squad to take the attacking team.

Robin announced that she had broken the encrypted signal of the spybot and a second window on the screen appeared and showed the information being sent back to the invaders. It was a good shot of the main gate approaching.

Mark got a message that the Marines were in position and ready to capture the two man team of invaders. Mark told them to wait for his signal.

The small aerial unit carefully worked its way through the massive metal beams that made up the moat gate/ramp and flew into the tunnel. It had only gone about ten feet when its screen went blank. The team watched as Mark gave the Marines the "go" signal. The two men were attempting to re-contact the spybot when six; fully armed Marines surrounded them and demanded their surrender. It was over in less than twenty seconds and the men were in custody, manacled, and with a black bag over each of their heads.

Mark told the Marines to take the captives back to the war game camp on the top of the mountain and that he and some of the team would join them there. Mark pointed at Sarah, David, Jack, and Alexis. They got up and headed for the elevator and the helicopter bay.

Getting on one of the helicopter lifts the five person team was raised to the top as the massive blast shield opened to the sky above.

It was a brisk day at the top of the mountain with a biting wind and the sun diminished by a high cloud cover. Alexis was happy she had the fortress coveralls on to dull the chill and wind.

They walked over to the base area past the triple surface-to-air missile emplacements. Directed to the tent used for detaining the suspects they found the two men on their knees with the bags still in place. Mark congratulated the team and their leader on a smooth operation. He dismissed the Marines except for a two man guard outside the tent as insurance.

Jack and David lifted the two men, one at a time and placed them on steel folding chairs in front of a table. Taking the hoods off of the two men Mark stood in front of them while the other four stood behind them out of their sight.

At first the two men tried to bluster their way out of the situation. Mark calmly informed them that they had trespassed onto U.S. Government restricted property and were considered terrorists and war time combatants and would be handled as such. They had very limited rights and no access to attorneys or other outside support. They could openly discuss their intentions or the information would be extracted from them by any means necessary, short of torture.

The taller of the two men tried to ask questions as to how they had located them but Mark was silent. When the man ran down Mark looked at his watch. "You have exactly five minutes to tell me who you are, who you represent, and why you were attempting to penetrate this base, If you don't do this, then I will consider you hostile combatants and use other means to secure that information. Do you understand?"

The two men looked at each other in consternation. The taller one turned back to Mark and said, "You can't do this. We demand our rights. We will not tell you anything."

Mark nodded, "I thought that would be your answer." He walked to the door flap of the tent and spoke to the security detail outside. Then he came back and quietly watched the two men. Five minutes later, Charlie and Linda Wu entered the tent with a small bag.

Mark indicated the taller of the two men. "Start with him."

Linda walked over to the man and produced an extremely short knife from somewhere under her clothing. The man paled and got big-eyed. In one swipe that was blur to everybody else Linda expertly slit the sleeve of the man's fatigues over his right arm. Charlie moved in and swabbed the man's arm with alcohol, tied up his arm and selected a vein. He injected the man and bandaged a cotton swab over the injection site. Stepping back the Asian couple found a pair of chairs and Linda sat down near the heavily sweating man.

Charlie set up recording gear for video and audio. You could tell the man was attempting to fight the serum by the labored breathing and tight muscles in his neck. That he lost the battle was also obvious by the way he quietly relaxed and his head hung down over his chest. While this was going on, Aaron came into the tent and stood next to Mark in front of the men.

Aaron gave the serum several minutes and then nodded to the second man. Charlie got up and walked behind the hostages. He then used a cloth to gag the second man so that he wouldn't interfere with the questioning.

Ten minutes later they had all the information they wanted. The men were employees of the Omicron Cartel and really just low level operatives with little knowledge beyond their instructions to attempt to penetrate the fortress and spy on the Crossfire Team. Their instructions had come to them over the phone and their base of operations was a small office in a strip mall in the predominately Spanish section of Denver's near north side.

To insure their results, they repeated the operation with the second man and asked different questions about the same subjects. The answers were not exactly the same but gave the same information.

While this was going on, Jack talked quietly to Mark, "What do we do with these two? They aren't important enough to use as hostages against OC and I doubt that they would get any real time for trespassing and attempted sabotage considering the civilian courts."

Mark had been considering the same thing. "I think we should let them go. It will discourage other attempts and send a message back to OC that we are aware of their activities concerning us. What worries me is figuring out whatever else they have planned for us.

Jack agreed and the Marines took the two men back to their vehicle and placed them inside, still unconscious. ComSec watched them until they woke up and quickly drove away in a real hurry.

CHAPTER SEVEN

The next two days went by quietly without incident as the team planned their initial efforts for the Chicago assault. Mark walked in and dropped heavily into his seat by the War Room table.

Jack looked up from the Intel he was reviewing from Crayton's search on Howard Vortmer. It was amazing the amount of information the computers had unearthed on the man. Everything from People Magazine to Top Secret CIA files. Seeing the less than happy condition of his friend he asked, "What's wrong?"

Mark gestured at the files in front of him. "No matter how I figure it, we just don't have the trained personnel to properly research Vortmer without giving ourselves away to a trained observer. We need more bodies, different bodies than our own." He thought for a minute, "Do you think we could get our friend in the FBI, Gary Rhodes, to loan us some people?"

Jack shook his head. "I already tried that. Gary is under direct orders to have nothing to do with us in any official capacity. Privately he wants to join us and do what he can. But, I can't let him do that because it would cost him his career if it became known that he was working with us even undercover."

Laura had listened to the conversation and suggested that they pray that Yahveh would give them the help they needed. Since they were the only ones in the War Room at the moment they prayed together. Laura was asking Yahveh for the help they needed again, like the time they prayed in the elevator in Tel Aviv and were given Craig and Kevin Steele to aid their efforts to rescue Christi Steele from the terrorists.

When they finished praying, Laura went back to her map work on Vortmer's Chicago locations and the two men discussed how many more people they'd need. Mark decided that if they could get fifteen additional team members then they could pull off what he had in mind.

The military phone line from the camp at the summit of the mountain chirped twice and Laura answered it. After hanging up she told Mark and Jack to go with her.

Looking at each other they got up and went to the elevator with her. The long ride to the top was silent and when they had exited through the helicopter hanger to the mountain top they met with the Colonel in charge of the training base. Colonel Franklin was a solid soldier with a no-nonsense attitude. He looked at the three of them and said, "General Sirs, and Ma'am, I've got some civilians that want to talk to you. He gestured behind him at a bunch of civilians standing between the tents of the headquarters section of the training base.

Jack grinned as he spotted Craig and Kevin Steele and two dozen other members of the SOG group. He walked over and shook a lot of hands. Then he asked Craig what was going on and why they were there.

Craig made a little smile and waved his hand to indicate his brother and the others. "We all decided to take a leave of absence for the duration and since we each heard from God that we were supposed to come and help the team, here we are. Got any bunk space for us?"

Jack thought about God's timing and the crew quarters they'd just found out about. "Yes, yes we do in fact. Grab your gear and come on down." As they were walking towards the helicopter lift Kevin said, "It seems that General Miles hears from Yahveh too. He "encouraged" us to take this leave and let the rest of the SOG tend to other matters."

Mark counted heads and realized they had all the intelligence operatives that had come to the SOG in the first place especially the Air Force PsyOps women. This was good.

Jack and Laura assigned the troops to the rooms in the crew quarters, gave them medallions to protect them from the internal defense systems, and gave them the grand tour of the fortress. Jack indicated where they could hone their weapons skills on the rifle range and their bodies in the gym and pool. Laura showed them the War Room and the control center and how to operate the elevator. Charlie wanted to hold off on the ComSec tour until they got used to everything else first.

Mark had been gleefully reworking his plans to integrate the twenty six new troops. He called everyone together in the living room area and arranged seats so that they could all see the new 100-inch LCD screen.

He showed pictures of the target, the areas involved and the probable defenses. Then he explained how he wanted a continual sliding surveillance of the man until they could pinpoint a weakness that would allow them to do a sleight-of-hand operation and get the information they needed to destroy the Omicron Group. Looking at the intent faces before him he added, "Understand that Omicron hires the best mercenaries available. These men are very talented, smart and many of them came from the same type of units you did. They will probably know a lot of the things we do. We will have to be on top of our game to stay invisible to them while we case our target. If you think you have been, or could be compromised, break off the surveillance and become an uninterested civilian. We don't want to alert them to our presence."

Laura was shaking her head and Jack whispered to her, "What's the matter?"

Laura smiled at her sometimes dense husband. "I am just amazed at the way the Father provides for our need when we are doing his will. Again, we needed additional team members and they show up while we're asking for them. It is just uplifting to see God directing our path and widening it for us as we walk in faith."

Jack agreed and snorted slightly, "Sort of like the meteorites that destroyed the Trident missiles Severon launched at Israel? That only took several millennia to set up."

Jack was referring to the battle with a billionaire with a grudge against the Jewish nation that the Crossfire Team had been involved in recently.

The next morning the assigned crews left the fortress in a Chinook helicopter for a quick trip to DIA and a fast trip to the Chicago area. Mark had assigned himself, Jack, and David as team leaders and put five personnel under each leader for the first surveillance. The second watch would be headed by Sarah, Laura, and Alexis. They would each have four new people working for each of them and one for continuity. This would prevent the same faces from showing up too often and raising suspicions.

Each watch would take five days and the first team established their base headquarters at a hotel off of Chicago's Lakeshore Drive, just south of the city center proper. While this wasn't the best part of town, it was a part where there would be no questions about their business or their frequent comings and goings.

CHAPTER EIGHT

After three days of planning for their turn of surveillance of the Omicron Cartel executive Vortmer, the second watch was becoming a bit bored. Su Li and Alexis decided that they would go out and do some shopping and have dinner. Alexis checked with Sarah who thought the idea a bit risky but decided it would be a good break. Alexis invited Sarah to go along and before long the group included Laura, Linda Wu, and two of the women from the SOG, Katy Summers and Ashley Freeman.

Even though the women had been more or less at war for the last two years, they easily reverted to eager shoppers and looked forward to just having some girl time. Charlie wanted to tag along but it was too late. This was a girls-only trip. The seven women squeezed into one of the Cadillac Escalade SUVs and made the trip to the Cherry Creek Shopping Mall in short time.

Everyone piled out of the SUV and headed through the parking lot toward the nearest mall entrance. The day was sunny and bright and the girls were enjoying their break from the rigors of combating terror, terrorists, and idiots. Walking into the brightly lit interior of the mall they started visiting different stores and trying on clothes, shoes and accessories. Amid a great deal of laughter and some taunting about fashions they managed to go through three hours and a great deal of purchases.

Breaking for lunch they had a delightful meal in one of the bistros in the mall. Relaxing after their meal they discussed everything under the sun and drank a lot of coffee and tea. While most of them didn't want a drink because that wasn't their life style, Katy Summers had two glasses of wine to take the edge off of her emotions. She had been hearing what she thought was Yahveh calling her in her dreams for the last two nights and she wasn't sure of that call quite yet. Still it disturbed her and she decided after being with this group that she would talk to Laura about her dreams when they got a free moment back at the fortress.

Sarah got everyone's attention by rapping on the table. "Gals, this has been more fun than I've had in years. But, I think we need to get back home and get ready for our trip east in two days."

There were some good-natured complaints but only for a few seconds. Everyone got up and headed for the car. Their purchases would be delivered the next day.

Dusk was settling in as the sun was dropping in the west behind the mountains and the parking lot lights had started to come on. It was still a beautiful early evening and the weather was mild in the Mile High City.

As a group, the women headed back for the SUV discussing their shopping trip and what they'd found.

The first torrent of gunfire came without warning. In front of the group, Laura was knocked backwards off of her feet. Su Li and Katy took multiple hits and went down together in sprays of blood. Sarah was hit but was able to drop to the ground and roll behind the nearest car. She left blood on the ground from two bullet wounds, one in her right thigh and one to her left arm.

Alexis had also dropped and rolled left behind an old pickup truck that had been waiting for the women to pass so it could pull out. Alexis ducked as the gunfire tracked her and hammered the other side of the truck. The glass in the small foreign truck blew out under the impact of the bullets and the elderly man and his wife beside him were killed instantly. Alexis slid backwards behind another car as the driverless pickup rolled forward and continued to shield her retreat. She ducked behind another car and worked her way around more vehicles as she headed for the source of the gunfire.

Linda Wu had grabbed Ashley's arm and pulled her behind a parked SUV without either of them getting hit although bullets had whispered by on both sides of them.

The shooting tapered off as the targets disappeared.

Despite the pain in her arm, Sarah pulled her cell phone out of her pocket with her left hand. Sarah pressed the Emergency Wide Area Notification system known as a EWANS alarm button and pushed the phone back into her pocket. The horrific scene and the noise involved crashed into her consciousness as she heard screams, sobs, and falling glass from the bullet impacts. Reaching around behind her she pulled out the small .45 caliber automatic and forced her hurting body to move. She first glanced under the car she was behind looking for feet or tires approaching her position. She noted the still bodies of Laura lying on her back and Su Li and Katy lying crumpled face down on the ground. She breathed a quick prayer for their safety and began to move back and to her right to bracket the shooters before they bracketed them.

Alexis had pulled a .40 caliber Glock automatic out of her purse and waited for what was sure to follow the first fire.

Five men in full body armor and carrying M-16s got out of a minibus and headed for the three bodies in the driving lane. Alexis waited until they were ten paces away from Su Li and she smoothly rose up and targeted the first man on the right of their group. At the same time Sarah was doing the same thing on the other flank. Joining their actions, Linda Wu and Ashley Freeman stepped out from behind an SUV and fired at the middle men. Not one of the women missed the head shots they had decided on. Ashley and Sarah then took out the remaining man.

That last man died with his finger on the trigger and his selector switch on automatic. The M-16 unloaded the entire magazine as he fell. The bullets stitched the pavement right through the area where Laura and Katy were laying.

One of the other men also triggered off a dozen rounds as he died but these went up and to his left and smashed several windows in the Mall entrance. The huge sheets of glass shattered and fell to the sidewalk where they smashed into thousands of shards. People who had taken refuge behind the entrance screamed and ran back further into the stores.

A second minibus roared up to the area and slid to a halt with smoking tires. Six more men piled out of the vehicle and started moving towards the firefight area with their M-16s up and looking for targets.

A Denver Police car roared up to the location of the firefight and slid to a halt. The driver of the minibus stepped out of the driver's door and fired an RPG at the police car striking it directly on the grill. The car exploded but not before the officer on the passenger side had shot and killed the minibus driver.

Alexis had moved even more to the side of the first strike team. She started shooting at the new men to draw them away from the downed women. Sarah stepped out behind the men as they turned to target Alexis. Sarah shot two of them in the legs and a third one, who wasn't wearing a helmet, in the back of the head. All three went down, one of them forever. The remaining shooters went back to back to defend themselves from Alexis and Sarah and were kicked off their feet by a flurry of rounds to their heads from the side by Linda and Ashley.

The two wounded mercenaries on the ground were trying regain their weapons to shoot back when Alexis's ice cold voice froze them in position. Alexis was angry and yelled at the two men. "Put your hands on top of your heads, NOW! Or die." Both men did as they were told and Alexis approached them with her pistol at arm's length in a two hand grip.

If they moved they would die.

Sarah heard her cell phone chime and carefully pulled it from her pocket. Charlie's voice announced that they were orbiting the Mall parking lot but didn't want to interfere with the Police helicopter and ground troops since it looked like they had things in control. Sarah told him to call her back in a few minutes. Charlie had the chopper they were in standoff a ways from the action.

The sounds of multiple sirens were drawing close and suddenly the parking lot lit up from a police helicopter's bright light. Alexis didn't put her gun down but stood her ground as the speaker on the chopper told her to drop her weapon. She pointed at the M-16s near the two living mercenaries and then bent down and put her pistol on the ground.

As soon as she straightened up, one of the mercs grabbed his rifle to cut her down. She stared at him with pity. There was a sound of a single rifle shot and the man's head snapped to one side as the sniper's bullet from the helicopter hammered the life out of him. The other mercenary had already passed out from the pain in his legs.

A dozen police cars came to sliding halts outside the battle area and police came in pairs with their handguns or shotguns out and up. The women put down their weapons and hurried to the still bodies of their friends on the ground. Sarah left a trail of blood droplets as she limped to where Laura lay face down. Sarah's tears were falling as she carefully lifted the upper part of her best friend off the ground. She hugged Laura and gently rocked her as she called her name. Laura slowly opened her eyes and groggily said, "Sarah, how are the others?"

Sarah grinned a crooked grin. "I don't know yet. Where were you hit?"

Laura coughed a little, "It feels like three rounds to the chest. And it hurts like hell."

Not seeing any blood, Sarah lifted Laura's blouse and saw the body armor with the three impacted slugs still there. Looking up at Laura she smiled and said, "Smart girl! You'll get over the bruises and trauma. But, Oy! It's going to be sore for a while." Sarah prayed for Laura's healing and covered her in the blood of Yahshua.

Linda went to where Su Li was crumpled to the ground face down and turned her over. There was fresh blood coming from a wound at her waist and pooled from a nasty gash to the top of her head. She was unconscious but breathing. Linda pulled Su Li's waistband on the side of her skirt down and examined the wound to her side. It was a through-and-through that was bleeding but not copiously which meant that nothing major had been hit. Linda pulled out a clean linen handkerchief from her purse and tore it in two pieces to cover both the entrance and exit wounds. She tied them in place with a strip she tore off of Su Li's skirt. Then she elevated her feet and put a new sweater she had just bought under the young woman's head.

Alexis walked over as Ashley Freeman used her jacket to cover up Katy's head. Alexis looked with sorrow at the young woman kneeling by her friend's body. Squatting down she put her arm around Ashley's shoulders as the young warrior sobbed and shook.

Ashley looked up at Sarah as she limped over. "Katy was going to get her hair done tomorrow. Instead, she took a round to the forehead, probably never knew what hit her." Then she started to cry and shake again. Alexis held her.

There were dozens of police and medical personnel flooding the area. Two of the EMTs took Sarah over to a Paramedic van and started treating her wounds while a second team did the same with Su Li. A third team worked on Laura to determine how badly she was hurt. The police had disarmed the dead mercenaries and accompanied the living one while his wounds were treated. After pictures were taken, Katy's body was placed in a body bag for transport to the morgue.

The officer in charge of the scene cornered Alexis to grill her as to the events. Alexis opened her purse and handed the man a badge and an ID card. The man looked at it and then back at her. Handing the badge and card back to Alexis he keyed his radio. "Millner here, this scene is now under the NCS jurisdiction and is a federal crime scene. Give them back their weapons." Alexis called her boss and explained the firefight.

Twenty minutes later three cars of federal agents showed up and started working the scene. Alexis dictated her statement to the agent in charge and then walked over to the medical units to see how the girls were faring.

Laura had two cracked ribs and massive bruising but the trauma plates in the body armor had saved her life. The EMTs couldn't give her anything for the pain and she wouldn't allow them to transport her to a hospital. Laura was adamant that other than Katy, the group stayed together. The look on her face as she reloaded and charged the Paraordinance 10-45 was enough to convince the EMTs not to cross swords with her on this issue.

Another team of EMTs convinced Laura that Su Li's head wound was serious enough that they had to get her to a hospital immediately.

So Laura and Sarah went with Su Li in the paramedic van to the closest hospital with a trauma ward. Alexis brought the others in the Cadillac SUV.

Sarah had given her cell phone to Linda. Linda was a professional first and a caring women somewhere after that. She got in touch with Charlie, brought him up to date on the event and their destination. He said that he and some of the others were nearby but would meet them at the hospital.

Later, as they sat at the hospital waiting room Laura was praying in sorrow and grief that Katy had been killed and she and the others wounded. She knew that Yahveh had known what was going to happen and had allowed it to happen. She didn't blame Him, she only pleaded with Him to show her if there had been any sin on her part that put them all in peril. As she prayed, the pain in her body lessened and eventually faded softly away as she felt the nearness of Yahshua. In her mind she cried out to him and asked why. She heard, "Laura, be at peace. Katy was with me before the bullet took her life. It was her time, I needed her here. You have shown your love for me and I am with you. It is through no sin of yours that this happened. It had to happen and I will walk through it with you and each of the others. Be strong because I am strong for you. I love you and always will. As Rose told you before, you will have sons and daughters who will be warriors for me. See, I am telling you now so that later you will remember that I told you."

Laura relaxed and smiled. Praying her thankfulness to a loving Messiah she opened her eyes to see Alexis watching her. Alexis came over and sat next to her. "Are you all right? You looked very sad and then started to smile. Normally I would think that you've gone a little batty since I'm pretty sure you're fairly well balanced normally."

Laura laughed quietly. "Alexis, I think you know we are followers of Jesus as you know Him or Yahshua, Messiah as we know Him. He just told me that He took Katy to be with Him before the bullet hit her. He's with each of us right now, even you. You have to know He loves you more than life itself." This came with such conviction and honesty there was no denying it.

Alexis's mind flashed an image of Laura in flaming golden armor swinging a sword gleaming as bright as the sun, wading her way through demons uglier than sin. "Okay, I believe you." This then led to a large dichotomy in Alexis's mind between what she thought she knew and what she now knew.

The doctor treating Su Li walked into the waiting room and Laura stood up to meet him. He nodded to her. "It's a good thing your friend wasn't two inches taller. She got a concussion and a cracked skull but I haven't found any edema of the brain. She will have a nasty gash on her forehead that will need reconstructive surgery. The wound to her side was cleaned and will heal fine. She's not going to be talking until tomorrow as I have her sedated so that her body can rest and rebuild."

Laura thanked him and turned to tell the others when Charlie and three of the SOG warriors walked into the room. After kissing and hugging Linda, Charlie came over to Laura and listened to the information on Su Li. He assigned two of the SOG personnel to stand watch over Su Li that night. He'd get some replacements there at four a.m. From their looks nobody had better try anything around Su Li on their watch!

Sarah came out of the treatment room with bandages on her arm and leg and leaning on a crutch. Matching that was a scowl and a bad attitude. Looking at the others she said, "I am tired of having my jeans cut off of me so that I can walk with a crutch! Next time I'm going to kill anyone in the area that even gives me a dirty look! Laura wasn't sure that she didn't really mean it.

On the trip back to the fortress, Both Laura and Sarah had a chance to talk to their husbands and brought them up to speed on the firefight and the loss of Katy.

CHAPTER NINE

As Mark listened to his wife tell him about the ambush by Omicron mercenaries and the death of Katy Summers his expression grew grim.

Sarah related how the remaining four of them had taken out both combat teams with a final bit of help from the Denver Police. Then she described Su Li's injuries and their time at the hospital waiting to hear about her.

She played down her injuries but Mark could tell she was in pain from her gunshot wounds. She asked Mark to forgive her for giving the okay to the outing and then not being sharp enough to spot the setup before they got hit. Her voice had a tremor in it and he could tell she was desperate for his understanding. Mark could almost see the tears running down her face as she talked to him. He felt her pain and inside he cried with her.

Hearing a crack and crunching noise he realized he was squeezing his cell phone too tightly. Taking a big breath he forced himself to relax. He told her that it wasn't her fault that the attack happened and that he would have okayed the time off if he had been there. Thinking quickly he said, "Listen; with the injuries you guys took I'm scrubbing the second watch on this character. We'll clean things up here and head back tomorrow."

After he assured her that he loved her and would see her soon he closed the flip phone cover only to have it fall off and dangle from the flexible circuit board holding it to the main piece of the phone. He dropped the broken phone on the table and stared at it while his mind spun up to speed concerning this change in tactics. He prayed for guidance and wisdom about the dark thoughts he was having. A plan developed in his mind and he liked it. He then prayed for his wife and that Yahveh would heal her wounds and those of Laura and Su Li. He thanked Yahshua for His loving care of Katy and His assurance that it was her time to go home.

Mark called all eighteen of the team together. "You have all heard about the attack in Denver and the death of

Katy Summers. We will miss her and even if it was her time it was still on our watch." Military personnel knew that it is unacceptable for successful enemy action to happen while they were on duty which was known as "their watch".

Mark looked at the elite men and women of this group and knew what he was going to propose would give them purpose and an acceptable response to the attack in Denver. He hoped he wasn't stepping out of the will of the Father but he knew they had to do this. Their surveillance of Howard Vortmer had revealed that he personally met with the commanders of the mercenaries once a week. He gave them their marching orders for operations across the western half of America. Therefore, Vortmer was the one who ordered the attack on Sarah's group. The men attending the meeting were the upper echelon of the mercenaries that ran the troops so they had complicity in the attack. That meeting was scheduled for four o'clock this afternoon at Vortmer's luxury penthouse apartment on the Gold Coast just north of the end of Lake Shore Drive on Lake Michigan. Normally he would hold the meeting at their headquarters plant southwest of the city but an alcoholic slip on the part of one of the security team told them of the change in plans. The merc was hitting on Melissa Edwards, one of the PsyOps members of the SOG in a bar near the headquarters. She had been playing up to his pride and he wanted to show her he was "in the know". After that admission she offered to get the next round of drinks. After he drank his and was attempting to kiss her, he passed out. She left him sleeping on the table and quietly left the bar.

There was a cold fury in Mark's soul right then and he wasn't going take this type of assault anymore. Looking at the group he slapped his hand on the table before him. "We are going to truncate this operation as of today. I want everything ready to go back to Denver this afternoon."

Mark could see the thoughts run through their heads reflected by their expressions. They didn't want to cut and run.

"But," he continued, "First, we're going to pay OC back for their attack on our people in Denver and get the information we came for."

That lightened up their expressions a lot.

Mark put the drawing of the penthouse up on the big board behind him along with a dozen photos of the building, the penthouse interior, and one of Vortmer himself. "This is our target for four-fifteen this afternoon. Since we can't take the law in our own hands, as much as I want to, we will make this as bloodless as possible and consider these people suspects instead of war time enemy. Rules of engagement are fire back if fired on. We will approach with invisibility; we will strike like lightning, and withdraw with our target in hand. May Yahveh be with anyone who gets in our way!"

That last was shouted and the whole group came to their feet and cheered. Mark started handing out assignments and weapons lists. They reviewed who they thought would be attending, who would be standing guard, and how to pull this off without coming up against the Chicago Police in the process. Thanks to their extensive surveillance of Vortmer and his operations the team knew where he placed his guards and the amount of guns arrayed against them.

Six hours later Mark started his personal pre-attack focus exercises and checked his weapons for the last time. Reviewing their plan in his mind he realized that there could be lots of variations that could throw them curves and turn this thing into a bloodbath, but he really didn't think that would stop this group of experts.

The vans stopped in the alley behind the high-rise and the heavily-armed group got out. Their uniforms said SWAT and POLICE and they had the entire normal SWAT gear including the face shields and helmets. If anyone saw them it would look like a legitimate operation. That is, if the person who saw them wasn't a police officer or one of Omicron's goons.

The electronics specialist had already put a video loop on the camera watching the dock. The high-rise security had a good view of an empty dock even though there were eighteen people crossing the dock and entering the service doors and elevator.

Careful examination had revealed that the windows on the high-rise penthouse were very thick, bullet-resistant glass so no entry would be available that way. But then Mark had never been a big fan of Hollywood versions of

SWAT assaults. He had his own ideas how to breach a room.

After the team members were in position and the meeting had been confirmed by direct visual inspection, Mark took a deep breath and spoke into his combat microphone, "GO!"

CHAPTER TEN

On Mark's command an RF damping field was activated that prevented any cell-phone or radio traffic from warning the men in the meeting. Nine well placed darts put the elite guards out of the fight. Simultaneously, four three-inch hoses started silently filling the meeting room with a powerful knock-out gas. The odorless, invisible mist quickly filled the room and three visual monitors recorded the collapse and inertness of the inhabitants.

In full combat gear and wearing gas masks, the Crossfire raiders burned three large holes through two interior walls and entered the room. They didn't bother with any of the non-coms or other mercenaries but quickly grabbed Vortmer and the four highest ranking mercenary officers who were easy to identify by their place in the meeting. The closer they were to Vortmer and farther to the front, the higher the rank.

Frisking their unconscious hostages they bound their hands and feet, gagged them and covered their heads with a soft cloth hood. Ten of the troops carried the five men to the elevator. As Jack, David, and Mark got on the elevator and closed the door exactly four minutes had elapsed since the action began.

While Vortmer and the other officers were being secured, the specialists of the SOG were busy taking pictures of the other mercenary officers and getting quick DNA samples for later evaluation as evidence.

Reaching the dock floor the door opened and two janitorial staff were standing there waiting for the elevator. They eyed the dozen and a half men in combat uniforms and armed to the teeth and decided to take a break, anywhere else. Kevin Steele and Bill Owen stepped out of the elevator and used Tazers to drop the janitors.

Quickly making their way to the vans, the team loaded up with the prisoners and left the area. Ten minutes had elapsed since the attack began and there were sounds of two sirens coming in their direction. The vans both pulled over to the curb beside a warehouse and waited until one of the Police cars rushed by them and turned down the alley toward the high-rise.

Mark had planned on the rapid response by the city police and had prepared for it. The vans split up and took different paths to the southwest suburbs. Pulling into a large shopping center parking lot the vans came to a halt next to a large Interstate-sized bus.

The men had changed into civilian clothing and stored the weapons in large rip-stop nylon bags. The men and equipment were quickly stored on the bus and six men were transferred to the bus in wheelchairs. Their heads were covered by jackets with a hood and they obviously weren't well as their heads hung down and they let the men handling the chairs do all the work.

David carefully scanned the area and didn't see any pursuit or even any interest in the exchange from the vans to the bus. One of the SOG troopers had a Class-A driver's license and drove the bus carefully out of the area to a west-bound interstate.

Relaxing in the plush seats Jack looked over at Mark and said, "I guess that wasn't sleight-of-hand, it was more like sight-of-fist."

Mark grinned, "Oh, there will be a lot of consternation when OC finds their number two man and the leaders of their vaulted mercenaries gone. But then we wanted to send them a message in regard to their attack in Denver." Mark then got out of his seat and went back to the back section of the bus where David and Aaron were working on Vortmer. They had a lot of time before they got to Denver and they were sure they could get a lot of information out of the frightened man. Mark hoped it hurt, a lot. The other four men could wait until they got to Colorado so they had been sedated to keep them quiet.

As the bus turned west past Lincoln, Nebraska seven hours later, David called Jack and Mark to the small office space behind the seats on the right side of the bus. Aaron joined them wiping his hands on a towel. David looked at the notes he'd made during the interrogation of Vortmer.

He looked tired but determined. Sitting back he smiled and shook his head. "We struck the mother lode with this guy. He not only controlled the security muscle, but he was in charge of all OC operations in the western U.S."

Jack asked, "Are you sure of your information? Could this just be fake personae like the others?"

Aaron shook his head. "Naw, this guy was sure he was invincible with his troops around him."

David looked at Mark. "We had the help of Yahveh on this one. Vortmer had over two hundred troops defending his Chicago operation. He felt sure that if we were to attack him it would be at his headquarters plant in the southwest suburbs. If we hadn't spent that week observing his actions we would have been fooled and walked into a major trap. That's why he only had nine guards outside the meeting. He didn't want to draw attention to the penthouse".

Aaron continued, "He also was in charge of the Chinese shrinks that put the layers of false identities on people like Ms. TA and Mr. Beta. He wasn't about to let his own employees work on his mind. He was quite simply, just a high-powered executive who believed he was above any possible assault or interrogation. He cracked like an egg and clandestine information poured out of him like water out of a hose. We've got detailed information on all seven levels of OC and their operational orders."

David picked up the narrative. "Vortmer also gave us a puzzle of epic proportions. He has no idea who it is that runs OC at level one. He thinks it is a very powerful and charismatic man. But under sedation with the most effective truth agents he admits he really has no idea who is in charge. He's never met the person, never heard his voice, and doesn't have a clue as to the primary goals of the organization. This is mind-boggling as it turns out that Vortmer and his New York partner on Level two actually run everything concerning the U.S. at OC. The other two men on Level two divide up the rest of the world. That's how important control of America is to OC.

Jack furrowed his brow, "How do Vortmer and his cohorts get their orders if they don't know who the leader is?"

Aaron shook his head. "Apparently, each morning when they get to their offices, their marching orders are on their computers. Usually down to the requirement level. Number one leaves it to the four stooges to fill in the details and make it happen. There have been two others at this level but they were "dismissed" when they didn't perform to the expected level.

No one ever saw them again after their dismissals."

Jack looked introspective for a minute. "If Charlie can get on this input of the mysterious number one who puts their orders on their computers, couldn't he and Crayton back track the transmissions?"

Something echoed in Jack's mind, something about Denver, but he couldn't grasp it. He realized it would come back to him at the right time.

Mark chuckled, "I'll get it to Charlie as soon as Aaron gives me the data from Vortmer on his system and passwords.

Aaron handed a sheet to Mark and said, "Already done." Jack scanned it and sent it to Charlie in the ComSec Center. While he was transmitting it he described what he wanted done on a scrambled and encrypted VoIP line to the fortress from his cell phone.

David looked serious, "Didn't Yahveh say He was counting on us to stop this thing?"

Jack slowly nodded. "Yes, He did. Now, how do we do His bidding?"

David mused, "I wish Laura and Sarah were here. They would have some good insight on this problem."

Jack smiled, "Laura would suggest we pray, so let's pray."

Mark stood up, "In a minute". He looked at Aaron. "Is Vortmer awake right now?"

Aaron nodded. Mark went into the small interrogation room. Vortmer was sitting in a straight-backed chair with the soft hood still over his head. Mark leaned down and whispered in the man's ear through the bag. Mark's voice was ice cold and conveyed complete conviction to the hooded man. "You will keep cooperating with us without hesitation. Any lying or resistance will result in the loss of body parts. You ordered my wife killed yesterday and I will take great delight in hurting you if you are stupid. Are we clear on this?" The bag nodded.

CHAPTER ELEVEN

Laura was sitting in the Whirlpool spa letting the warm water soothe the aches and pains when Jack came into the pool area. Spotting his wife he walked over and kneeled down near her. He bent over and kissed her tenderly and said, "Why is it every time I leave you alone somebody tries to kill you?" He was smiling as he said it.

Laura grinned at him. "I don't know. It just seems to happen." She was very happy inside to see Jack. She reached out and caressed the side of his face. Jack held her hand there for a moment. "I'm sorry about Katy and your wounds as well as Sarah's and Su Li's. I know it happened but I don't want it to happen again if I can stop it. I know you have the Savior's word about our kids being warriors for Him. But I keep remembering that He might be talking about spiritual children rather than flesh and blood ones."

Laura smiled, "I know, but I have come to peace knowing that all of us are in His hands and that He loves us with a love that is beyond our understanding."

Jack nodded, "How are your ribs and bruises coming along?"

Laura looked introspective for a minute. "I'm okay, the aches and pains are less each day and I've started working out again. Sore, but good sore, you know?"

Jack laughed, "Sore, but good sore. That's one I'll have to remember."

Laura turned off the whirlpool and stepped out of the tub. She dried herself off and patted dry the large bruised area. Putting on a bathrobe she gently hugged Jack and walked slowly back to the elevator with his arm around her shoulders and her head on his shoulder.

Jack arranged for heavy police security so that the entire team could attend the funeral service for Katy. He also made sure that her family was generously taken care of by the Crossfire Team in addition to her government benefits.

The service had been upbeat and a tribute to the short life of the girl that wanted to make a difference in the world.

Once they were back at work in the fortress they started sifting through the information that Vortmer had given them. There were several points of weakness to the Omicron Cartel that could be exploited. One decision was to start directly below Level one and the head of OC and work their way down, eliminating his operations and base of power while isolating him.

That led them to James Bostown, Vortmer's equal for the remainder of the U.S. operations. They also knew that Vortmer's replacement would probably be Bill Amherst who Vortmer had been grooming as his number two. Jack was sure they would have to take both of these people out of the game before they solidified their hold after Vortmer's capture and were able to rebuild the organization.

Jack had received a call from the U.S. Attorney General's office that they were investigating the abduction of Vortmer and some of his staff as terrorist activity. The AG wanted to know if they were involved and if so, why. The raid violated Vortmer's civil rights and it was obvious that OC was pushing for an investigation of the Crossfire Team as the culprits.

After a conference with the rest of the team, Jack and David took Vortmer and the evidence they had that OC was undermining the government to Washington. They met with Justice Department agents and turned the information over to them along with Vortmer who willingly testified to everything in return for his safety.

Justice met with the AG and squelched the pending investigation of the Crossfire Team and instituted a sweeping investigation of the Omicron Cartel and their tactics and efforts at subversion.

After Vortmer's testimony, the Justice Department sent agents to the fortress and collected the four mercenary leaders on charges of subversion, acts against citizens, and terrorist activities. While they were in the nation's capital, Jack and David met with President Bollen secretly and outlined what they had been through and done with OC. The President knew about the attack in Denver and offered his condolences on the death of Katy and the injuries sustained by the others. He was still restrained from openly assisting the team but reminded them that even though they had to work at an arm's length, the authorization for the Crossfire Team to combat OC had not been rescinded in the U.S. and many other countries. That is why Justice permitted their raid on Vortmer's penthouse and prevented the investigation by the Attorney General.

On the way back to Denver, Jack and David agreed that it was in the government's interest to keep the Crossfire Team after OC. It kept a subversive organization focused on the team rather than creating troubles for the administration.

When they had originally returned from Chicago, Mark had taken Sarah back to Israeli quietly. Sarah's mother had developed cancer and Sarah wanted to be with her for a while. A staunch Jew, her mother would not let Sarah and Mark pray for her to Yahshua because it went against her beliefs. But then, Sarah was just as stubborn as her mother and they prayed for her by themselves for healing. Sarah was aware that sometimes Yahveh heals a person by bringing them home and she worried about her mother's place in the afterlife.

Still the trip had been good for both Sarah and her mother as it gave them an opportunity to mend old wounds and to have a little time together. Sarah was very wealthy in material goods and made sure her mother had the best medical care available and people to stay with her and to care for her. This her mother could appreciate and thanked her for many times.

The time also gave Sarah's wounds time to heal and kept her out of OC's gun sights while in Israel.

Back at the fortress, Jack was correlating the information they had gotten about OC operations when the echo of a previous encounter slid through his mind again. This time he just relaxed and cleared his mind and did a martial arts training process that let him focus his unconscious mind and bring the elusive memory to the forefront of his mind.

As he rested he realized the connection between the memory and the present action. He decided he needed to pray about the similarities. He prayed for understanding and wisdom. Jack no longer doubted that the Father through the Son would grant him wisdom and waited while his mental processes worked through the ideas.

At last he decided it was valid and needed to be discussed with the team. He got out of his chair in the den attached to their bedroom and went downstairs to the living room. Turning right brought him to the War Room. As he entered he found Mark, Alexis, David, and Laura discussing some of the possibilities for uncovering the leader of Omicron.

Jack sat down and waited for an opening. "I have a thought about this whole OC thing." Everyone turned and looked at him. "I think we have a situation that is similar to the one with the Believer's Church that we ran into last year here in Denver."

Jack waited until everyone had re-examined their memories of that skirmish with the enemy of mankind. Then he elaborated on his concept. "With the Believer's church they ran the operation but used the Satanists as their outer defenses and to do their dirty work. An expendable outer layer so to speak." He noticed the connection being made by the rest of the team members Jack nodded, "That's right, if I am correct in my presumption, then OC is just an outer ring and a very efficient one. I think they are used to infiltrate governments, prevent anyone from determining what the real aims of the central core are, and be expendable. We've been battling with the attached army but not even seeing the real villains or their objectives. If we were to disassemble OC from Level two downward we would be deceived and misled that we were accomplishing something worthwhile. Actually we would be distracted from the actual problem and they would be able to spend their time achieving the real goal without interference. You guys agree?"

Mark slapped his forehead. "No wonder Vortmer had no clue as to the top man. It's not a man, it's another organization. Dear God! We have been spinning our wheels and lost Katy in the process."

Jack shook his head, "Not true. We have made great strides in messing up OC's operation and have reached the point that we now have more understanding which we couldn't have gotten any other way.

Now we have to concentrate on the real objective but not let them know we've figured out what's going on. We need to mount an effort against other Level two personnel just as efficiently as we did Vortmer. We have to still take out OC's capabilities because they are a major problem in themselves. This will also make the inner organization think we're still deceived and not a problem. I suggest we make a small inner group to discover the real enemy while the majority of our team keeps OC busy. Who should be on which team? Each effort is going to require a lot of smarts and focus to keep our people alive.

CHAPTER TWELVE

In the end it was decided that Mark, Sarah, and Su Li would take the majority of the Crossfire Team/SOG force against the Omicron Cartel while Jack, Laura, David, and Alexis would seek out the hidden enemy running the whole show.

Their only, slim lead was the internet orders being sent to the Level 2 heads of the OC. So Jack and David visited Charlie in the ComSec Center of the fortress. David admired the quiet intensity of the center where everything was on platform floors and a lot of sound deadening material had been used to soak up machine as well as human noises.

Charlie had noticed that they were coming into the center and was waiting for them at a conference table in the open area behind his bank of consoles and monitors. He nodded his welcome and indicated the seats around the table.

Jack saw a small smile on Charlie's face. "So, how is the hunt for the inner enemy going?"

Charlie looked at the two men as he marshaled his thoughts. "Not bad, not good, so far." Seeing the curious look on Jack's face he explained. I haven't had a great deal of advancement on tracking the incoming orders because of three reasons." Charlie ticked off the reasons on the fingers of one hand. "One, they only happen between four a.m. and six a.m. on Monday morning. Two, they use an incredible number of bounces and cut-outs. Three, the frequency shift, phase shift, and encryption is very advanced and hard to identify as it poses as regular email. That's the not-so-good news. The good news is that Crayton will identify the sender's location the next time they send the orders on Monday, which is six days from now."

Charlie looked speculative for a few seconds. "However, there is progress on another identification path that has revealed something that is pivotal to your investigation." Charlie's Asian features could be hard to read but this time he was almost laughing. "I saw the time constraints on the orders tracking and decided to use the old investigative technique of "follow the money". They are very devious on how they fund OC's operation but Crayton was able to unravel it in fifteen minutes. You can't beat cubic processor chips for trying every possible alternative and then picking the most likely, several thousand times per minute. The bulk of OC's operating budget does not come from their enterprises but is supplied by middle-east oil revenues from Turkey, Ethiopia, Libya, Iran, and is funneled through the sub-Saharan state of Zyngola. The billions of dollars are being packaged to build military might in those nations as well as Russia."

David sat back and thought for a few seconds. "You are describing Gog." David said this in a quiet voice that was awed by the implications that he saw by this news.

Jack looked at the Israeli, "You mean as in Revelation 20? The Gog and Magog that marshal all the evil forces of the world to attack Israel?"

David shook his head, "No, that will occur after the Millennium, the thousand year reign of Yahshua on the Earth. This refers to the prophesy by Ezekiel in chapters 38 and 39."

Charlie crinkled his brow. "I'm not sure I understand that. Wasn't Ezekiel a prophet around 575 BC.? How does his prophesy apply to this effort of Omicron Cartel today?"

David thought back to the scriptures he had studied over the last two years since Yahshua brought him back from the dead. "In chapter 37, Ezekiel revealed how Israel, which are Yahveh's people, would be restored to their land from many parts of the world. Once Israel became strong, a confederacy of nations from the north would attack, led by Gog. Their purpose would be to destroy Yahveh's people. Gog's allies would come from the mountainous area southeast of the Black Sea and southwest of the Caspian Sea, that's central Turkey today. These allies would also come from the area that is present day Iran, Ethiopia, Libya, and possibly the new Russia. Gog represents the aggregate military might of all the forces opposed to Yahveh. But, no matter when this battle occurs, the message of Ezekiel is clear; Yahveh will deliver his people - no enemy can stand before his mighty power."

"Yahveh will directly intervene in the defense of Israel, unleashing severe natural disasters on the invaders from the north. In the end, the stricken pagan nations will turn on themselves in confusion and panic. All those who set themselves against Yahveh will be destroyed."

David looked ashen. "If these money transfers are for military arms then the possibility exists that preparations are being made for this battle. The hidden company inside the OC shell is preparing troops for the penultimate battle for the existence of Israel and we are Yahveh's point of the spear for . . . what? What are we to do?"

Jack thought about what David had said, "Perhaps we are to interrupt the flow of money and cripple the attack."

Charlie shook his head, "If I read this right, the payments ceased almost a month ago. All the investment is done."

Jack shook his head. "Let's get together with the others and see if we can pray for an answer."

CHAPTER THIRTEEN

Laura listened to the summation of the information and theories and nodded. "Yes, I think prayer would be best right about now. You realize that this is world-changing events we're talking about. Not like some we've been involved in where the world could have ended but almost no one ever heard about it. I doubt that this one will escape the world news. We absolutely must be completely in submission to Yahveh on this action. Anything else would be counter-productive to say the least."

Alexis watched as the other three began to pray to a deity that she wasn't sure really existed. As they prayed she felt denseness close in on the room. The lights seemed to dim and noises faded away. As they continued to worship the energy level in the room suddenly jumped right off of any scale she knew of. She felt an overwhelming need to get on her knees and bow her head to the floor. Alexis slid out of her seat onto her knees and bent at the waist with her face to the floor. She didn't know why she was doing it, only that it was right and it was mandatory. A beautiful sweetness filled the denseness in the room and there was a stirring in her soul that yearned for that sweetness. She raised her head up from the floor and saw a magnificent sight. A beautiful angel floated about a foot off the floor and the glow from the iridescent white and gold colors swirled around like a gown blown by unseen winds. The angel spoke and the truth and honesty of the words struck Alexis's heart with longing.

Rose looked at the four warriors before her. She let a small smile play across her lips. "Laura, I am here. Yahveh has heard your prayers and wants to give all four of you your answers. Laura, your abilities as a spiritual warrior will be sorely tested soon. Stand in the whole armor of Yahveh. Keep your faith solidly based on Yahshua. Listen to your husband as he is tasked with the leadership of this team."

Rose rotated slightly, "Jack, It is commendable that you seek to walk the straight and narrow path the Lord has commanded you to follow. You have asked for wisdom and you shall have it. You are to eliminate the Voltron. They are the hidden group that has arranged for this war on Yahveh. They have read the word and are attempting to bring an end to Yahveh's chosen people through a human creation of scriptural prophesy. You and your team are to see that they never do this again. They are human and demons are assisting them to raise an army like the one Ezekiel prophesied to attack Israel. That time is not yet. The people who make up the Voltron are intelligent but not spiritually smart. Do not let your guard down at any time, pray in the spirit, and let your honor burn brightly in service to Yahveh."

Rose's eyes locked onto those of David Zahavy. "David, this will be a supreme test of your character. You also must cling tightly to Yahshua because the enemy will attack you in your pride and your love for your homeland. You believe that you've surrendered everything to Yahveh, but that assumption will be greatly tested on this quest. Listen to Laura, she knows the way."

Rose then looked at Alexis. "Alexis, you are at the crossroads of your life at this time. You can learn and believe, or you can doubt and fall away. It is your free will to decide to live the rest of your life for yourself or for the Savior." The colors of gold and white swirled out from Rose and flowed gently around and through Alexis. "Yes, He loves you with a love that is eternal. He is asking you to love Him in return. But you need to know that loving Yahshua requires repentance and turning away from all things the flesh desires ahead of Him. It is not easy but it is eternal and worthwhile. You are a warrior and very intelligent. But, you need to know the truth and follow your heart, not your head. Your intelligence is full of man's concepts and falsehoods. Lean not on your own understanding, but lean instead on the one who died for you so that you could live."

Rose swirled in pulsating gold and white and faded out of sight. The thickness to the atmosphere in the room lifted and the lights seemed to brighten. Alexis's heartbeat slowed down and she sat down on the floor of the War Room. Nothing in her experience prepared her for Rose. Nor prepared her for the choice now before her. She was twenty-seven years of age and had never been in a church or even told anything remotely religious. But in her heart she knew every word the angel had said was true. The concepts and changes in her paradigm were battling back and forth in her mind when she felt a soft touch on her shoulder. She looked up and saw Laura kneeling next to her. Laura looked into her eyes and Alexis felt a shock at the authority she saw there. Laura smiled, "Alexis, stop thinking about anything. Let your heart and your spirit speak to you. Don't evaluate it; don't analyze it, just listen."

Laura said quietly, "The creator of the universe made a man in the beginning, his name was Adam. Adam sinned and lost the Earth to Satan and the world became evil. The creator, Yahveh, decided to destroy His creation but saved Noah from the flood to restart the population. Still Satan had caused sin to come into the bloodline of Adam and Noah and all men and women were born into a sinful condition that isolated them from knowing Yahveh, The Father had attempted to find a sinless man but could not find one on the Earth. Therefore, to combat this blindness and isolation, Yahveh created another Adam to right the wrong committed by the first one. Because the sin was man's, Yahveh needed a human man, born of woman to break the bond on men. The Son he created in Mary was Yahshua the Messiah. Yahveh's son heard his true Father from the day he was created in Mary's womb. He walked in truth and His Father's way every day of his life. He never sinned. The darkness in men couldn't stand him and killed him as was foretold by the prophets. He died and shed His blood for you Alexis. He died so you could have access to the Father and restore the connection that Adam broke in the Garden of Eden. After the Son was crucified and buried, on the third day Yahveh's spirit brought Him back to life. And that is what Yahveh offers you today, eternal life through belief and love in His Son."

Laura let Alexis absorb her words and waited a few seconds. Then she said, "Alexis, He's right beside you and he has his arms out welcoming you. It's now up to you."

Alexis's spirit testified to the truth of what Laura had told her. She realized that she wanted that love more than she wanted to live. The huge ache in her heart made the tears run down her face. She nodded her head and softly said, "I want to give my life to Him."

Laura led her in the sinner's prayer, "Dear Yahshua, I know I am a sinner. I repent of my sins right now and I ask you to cleanse me of my sins and to come and live in my heart. I acknowledge you as my master, my savior, and my very best friend. I totally want to follow You and your ways for the rest of time. I unconditionally give you my heart and all that I am forever more. Amen."

The peace and love that flooded Alexis brought a lightness and joy she had never known in her life. Every burden and worry she had ever had was completely gone. She felt fantastic! She jumped up and pulled Laura up off the floor and hugged her. Alexis wanted to sing but instead held her hands up and said with heartfelt emotion, "Thank you, thank you, thank you."

Jack and then David hugged her and helped her to celebrate what she later remembered as the most wonderful day of her life.

CHAPTER FOURTEEN

Jack made two phone calls that afternoon.

The next morning, Jack, Laura, and David took Alexis to Pastor Tim Carson's church in southeast Denver overlooking the spread of the valley. She was baptized and had her session with Gary Eisenthal helping to pray against any existing demonic influences in her life. She was grinning when she walked out of the church that afternoon.

During their time in Denver, Charlie had been digging into Voltron and finding connections with the data he had been intercepting from the OC internet communications. It seemed that Voltron wanted to keep an invisible profile as far as the world was concerned. They weren't on any corporate lists, any foundations lists, or even on the Mossad's lists. They were like a black hole. Since light couldn't escape the gravitational well of the black hole you couldn't observe anything about it directly. You could only notice its effects on things around it and deduce what you couldn't see. Voltron was an organizational black hole. It existed, but you couldn't find anything out about it directly. This made it an extremely interesting puzzle, just the type that intrigued Charlie. He called his wife in to help him. They always saw things differently and one would often discovered truths that the other hadn't seen.

Linda studied what Charlie had unearthed and pointed out an important fact. To have the ability to funnel all the middle-eastern oil money into military arms Voltron had to have a known face or personae

in the arms business and with the military units they supplied. Charlie liked that idea. He could work backwards from the sales to the supplier.

While the Wus were working so diligently on the Voltron puzzle, Jack, Laura, David, and Alexis returned to the fortress and began focusing on the satellite imagery of the various Gog state's arsenals. Some were kept undercover or underground, but some were not. David was comparing similar sat scans from a year ago with the current ones.

The buildup was impressive in the three countries he could get a match on. Alexis came over and leaned over his shoulder and pointed at the Iranian scans. "There are at least five hundred more tanks than before. Where did they come from? If we can find the suppliers we can find the buyers."

David was nodding but his attention was on Alexis's perfume rather than tanks. It was a subtle scent that snagged his imagination. David was a seasoned agent and knew how to redirect his attention so that feminine wiles didn't blind him to his job. This time he didn't want to ignore the closeness.

Alexis moved over to her seat and started pulling up a list of known arms dealers and the quantity of tanks they handled. There was only a few that could handle the size and the price of a tank, let alone several hundred of them within one year's time.

David saw what she was tracking and suggested she use the sequential spy satellite images to see what port shipped the tanks that arrived in Iran. Alexis liked the way that man thought. She smiled at him and he nodded in return.

Three hours later they had a fix on the shipper and that led quickly to the supplier. Russia. She nodded and told David, "Of course! Russia is in desperate need for hard currency. I'll bet they are the suppliers for the other Gog states too."

David came over and checked her data. It was good research. This woman had some excellent Intel talents. He put his hand on her shoulder and congratulated her on her work. Alexis noticed that he didn't take his hand off her shoulder right away. She looked up at him and saw decent interest in his eyes. That would have shaken her up a week ago. Today she just smiled and recognized the Savior's hand in bringing her a friend.

It wasn't too much later when they discovered the buyer's identity for the tank purchases. After all, that volume of money transfers would be hard to hide. The banks involved were the usual culprits in dealings with clandestine funding and Alexis knew all of them. A call to her headquarters, the National Clandestine Service, resulted in a listing of the people at the other end of the petro financial pipeline. Pseudonyms or aliases of course but fake names for people who were known were easy to decipher. Alexis and David went for the power behind the transfers, not the money handlers. After four more hours of intense work they had a single name, Maximillian Hoffnar. His trade name was Maxnar and he had been known as a money man for several shady, quasi-terroristic groups until five years ago. Now it was time to use Maxnar to locate the Voltron operation.

David called in some favors from friends at the Mossad and Interpol and was able to track Maxnar's movements for the last eighteen months. They had a base of operation for him in less than an hour. Sitting back and relaxing David noticed that it was almost nine o'clock at night. He looked at the lady next to him and asked her if she were hungry since they had been hard at it since noon. She admitted she was ravenous. So they adjourned to the kitchen to see what they could scare up in the way of food.

Putting together a meal of leftovers from yesterday's meals they sat down at one of the dining room tables. As they ate they discussed their past lives and the things that led them to that dining table deep inside of a mountain in Colorado.

While David was describing some of his past with the Mossad Alexis quietly appraised her attraction to the man. She had male friends before and she was a good judge of character and intent. But there was something special about David and she looked inside herself to determine what drew her to this darkly handsome older Israeli. It was obvious that he was a very competent intelligence operative. She could tell from his demeanor and in his eyes that he had taken life before and that he would do it again if needed. He dressed better than most men and wore expensive clothes that fit his personality. But none of these things was the basis of the attraction she felt. Then the thought burst into her mind that it had nothing to do with his physical being or his history, it was the gentle spirit he had.

"Now, how did I know that?" she thought to herself. Then she realized that her spirit was alive and she had become a temple of Yahveh's spirit. That was what was attracting her to David. Two days ago she wouldn't have recognized this. As she listened to his voice she tried to do something that Laura had taught her yesterday. She prayed that the Father in Heaven would bless this attraction if that was what he wanted or to take it away if it wasn't in His will. She was pleased when she still felt at ease and comfortable in David's presence. This could be the start of something good.

CHAPTER FIFTEEN

Kevin Steele crouched next to Mark Connelly with sweat running down his face in the heat of the loading dock. As the incoming fire increased in intensity all around them, he looked up at Mark with a question on his face. It seemed to say, "Okay General Strategy expert, we're getting hammered here and you arranged it that way. Now what?"

Mark smiled at the young Marine and glanced at the tell-tales on his action board again. All but one was green. The amount of firepower being directed at the sixteen Crossfire Team members was probably equal to that targeted by a platoon of riflemen. The incoming rounds were being absorbed by a large number of wooden crates at the back of the depressed dock area. Still, the OC mercenaries had a huge advantage in numbers and were pressing that advantage even though six of the mercenaries had fallen to the team's return fire.

Mark's mind ran back over the recent activities that had led to this major ambush.

------------------------******------------------------

The team had determined the patterns of movements by the other Level 2 manager, James Bostown. They then planned a snatch and grab at the obvious place of vulnerability. When Sarah questioned his walking into an obvious trap he replied, "That's the idea. Trust me sweetheart, I've done this type of thing so many times before it's like classroom time."

Then he explained the entire operation to her and she saw the ingenuity of Mark's plan. They scouted the position and set up to take him when he arrived at his New York office building. Mark and a four man team scouted the building the night before and prepared the conflict area. The plan was to take him in the lobby. Mark had deliberately ignored the video cameras hidden in the alcoves in the lobby and set all eighteen of his men to one side of the lobby.

When the time for Mr. Bostown to appear expired without the man being present Mark knew his plan was working. He took his troops, double-time, down a long hall and out into a loading dock area. Instead of running on out of the dock area he had the men take positions behind the last of the docks with the steel doors shut behind them. He had two of the troops spike the doors so that they couldn't be raised. When the first shots came they were expected and everyone took cover behind the concrete dock and returned the fire. The volume of fire continued to increase as more and more mercenary troops joined in the apparent slaughter.

The mercenaries were attempting to surround the dock on the three sides they could get to so that they could fire from all directions. They were throwing so many rounds at the Crossfire Team that only occasional shots could be fired in return. This emboldened the mercenaries to press their attack, move in, and finish off the invaders.

Just as the ricochets were becoming dangerous the last tell-tale indicator on Mark's board turned green. Mark put on a field gas mask and the rest of the team followed suit. Then Mark pushed the red button on the board.

Something like a huge sigh sounded and the visibility in the dock area dropped by half. The swirling mist that filled the area was somewhat greenish in color. Thirty seconds later the team cautiously moved out of the truck dock and examined the sleeping mercenaries. They would be unconscious for the next hour.

The team unspiked the doors and opened them carefully, wary of any mercenaries that had been outside the gas area. The mercs out there had retreated when the majority of their comrades had been knocked out. They knew they had lost the advantage and wasted no time in saving their hides.

Mark took off his mask and led the troops to a nondescript white bus sitting behind the office building. They loaded onto the bus and Su Li drove the bus away quietly.

Su Li had been recovering from her wounds but Mark hadn't felt she was up to possible hand-to-hand combat yet and he was sure she wouldn't have wanted to put on a gas mask at this point. So she got her usual job as she had told

Mark, "Okay, I'm driving the bus again." She smiled as she said it because she was just glad to be alive and still useful. The wound on her forehead was healing quickly but she still had some cosmetic surgery ahead to repair the damage. Right now she was grateful to be useful at all.

As the bus blended into the New York traffic and disappeared, Kevin cocked his head and looked at Mark. "Okay, you were right, you said it would be a trap but you led us in there anyway."

Mark sat there quietly and let the Marine figure it out. Kevin saw the reverse trap that Mark had set and guessed why it happened. "Pretty darn sure of yourself weren't you? We could have all been killed."

Mark shook his head. "Not today. Remember we took the top mercenary leaders captive in Chicago. These were being commanded by the emergency replacement team leaders. I knew their numbers and their capabilities. I wanted them to believe they had us and engage all their troops so we could knock them all out at once."

Kevin thought of the scene they'd left in the dock area. "I'd say you did a good job of that."

CHAPTER SIXTEEN

Sarah and two of the PsyOps SOG women, Carol Jennings and Renee Brazilton, had been standing on the sidewalk for twenty minutes talking when the big, black limousine pulled to the curb thirty feet away.

Four mercenary guards got out of the car and studied the area including the three good-looking chicks along with the other foot traffic on the sidewalk.

Sensing no danger they opened the back door of the limo and James Bostown stepped out of the vehicle. The guards formed a square around the large-bellied man and as a group they started for the entrance to the building behind the women.

A siren announced the approach of an ambulance that stopped and double parked two cars ahead of the limo. The EMTs jumped out and pulled a wheeled stretcher out of the back. They hurried towards the same door as the OC team.

Two of the guards stepped in front of the EMTs to stop them as James Bostown swept by in insolent disregard for whatever medical emergency was taking place. Sarah, Carol, and Renee pulled dart guns out from their skirts and calmly shot the four guards and James Bostown. The mixture in the darts was potent and all five men collapsed to the sidewalk immediately. The EMTs quickly loaded James Bostown onto the gurney and rushed him back to the ambulance. Loading him in the back one of the EMTs got in with him while the other got in front and drove the ambulance away.

All of the people who had stopped to watch the action looked back at the four sleeping guards on the ground. The three women had disappeared without a trace.

In the back of the ambulance Bill Anderson, a Navy SEAL, quickly stripped the fat man of all of his clothes down to his underwear.

Checking the clothing he found at least one tracking transmitter. He quickly bagged the clothes, minus the personal items into a signals safe, metallic-lined bag. He then turned on the GPS jammer and strapped Mr. Bostown to the gurney. He applied a second injection to the man's arm and covered him in a blanket.

The other EMT was Mark Egan, an Army explosives expert. He drove the ambulance under a large bridge and stopped with the flashers on. Immediately, a large van pulled up behind the ambulance and the three women helped to transfer the detainee to the van. Everyone got in the van and Mark Egan drove it away from the bridge covering by executing a U-turn and going back the direction they had come from originally.

Sarah pulled out her cell phone and sent a precoded message. That turned the last tell-tale on Mark's console green so he could neutralize the mercenary troops at the trap in Bostown's office building.

Carol and Renee closed the sound proof door to the specially prepared section of the van and started questioning James Bostown as they drove south out of New York.

Five hours later they turned Mr. Bostown and his "confessions" over to the Justice Department in Washington, D.C. and headed for the airport. The man had been a clone of Vortmer in actions and knowledge of OC's plans to subvert the U.S. Government.

The entire team met up at the private hanger area and loaded onto a Gulfstream private jet for the flight back to Colorado. As the private jet lifted off, Mark leaned over and kissed Sarah. "Good job spylady. The Justice Department is preparing a truck load of subpoenas for everyone concerned with the Omicron Group. Bostown's information pretty much completed the investigation they started four years ago. They said to tell everyone on the team "thanks". Our restraint in using deadly force has gone a long way in taking the wind out of the sails of the OC backers. Even when their mercs are trying to kill us any way they can, if we can keep from responding in kind it gets the Justice Department big points in the court battles."

Sarah appreciated the congratulations, especially since it came from Mark. But the snatch operation had been a snap compared to what he had to go through to make it work. "Do you think OC is going to be hurt over this little bump in their plans?"

Mark shook his head, "No, remember they get their marching orders from Voltron. Some heads may roll and new people promoted but they are a resilient bunch and will regroup. Hopefully this action has taken the spotlight off of Jack's operation and Voltron will think we're still beating the wind with OC while they stay hidden."

Sarah looked over at Su Li who was already asleep in one set of the seats. "Do you think she will be alright?"

Mark looked at his wife with a non-committal expression. "I'd think so, but why don't we ask the man upstairs? He's probably got a better idea about it than we do."

CHAPTER SEVENTEEN

Tired and ready for rest, the team from New York returned to the fortress at one a.m., everyone headed to bed and sleep. At ten the next morning Jack held a meeting in the spacious living area for the entire team. Laura, David, Alexis, and Jack had prepared a hearty breakfast of eggs, waffles, cereal, potatoes, and sweetbreads. Coffee, tea, milk, and several juices were iced down and ready for consumption.

After the breakfast dishes had been cleared away the various progress reports were given to bring everyone up to date. The shocker to most of the team that had gone to New York was the Biblical relationship to Voltron's efforts. Everyone in the fortress was a born-again Christian and had good knowledge of Ezekiel's Chapters 37 and 38 prophesy and it's similarity to Revelation 20.

Sarah raised the point of this human-generated version of the prophesy affecting the actual event. "Will this arming up of the Gog states before the real prophesy prevent the actual event from happening?"

David had been praying about that exact question. "I don't think anything man does to preempt Yahveh's plan for mankind will divert the course of history. This attack, attempting to create the battle in Ezekiel isn't a surprise to our Elohim. He will probably not respond with the same Earth-shattering answer that he will in the real event. But, He will stop them as we've been told by His messengers."

Darren Holtz, one of the Navy SEALs from the SOG stood up. "Mr. Zahavy, what do you think Israel's military reaction will be when these huge forces start massing on their northern border? Do you think they will use their nuclear weapons to stop them?"

David grinned, "You mean the nuclear weapons that Israel denies having? I don't know, but hopefully Yahveh will convince them to restrain their efforts while He does His thing. Then again, that may be the response Yahveh wants to happen. I personally hope not. The corporate angst among my people would be a very heavy burden to carry if they wiped out all life in the area to repel such an attack. Publicly it would be hailed as intelligent self-defense of the home land. Privately, I feel it would be a guilt trip that would last for two generations or more."

"So, what is our job here?" Alexis's question was what everyone was wondering at that point.

Jack had been praying earnestly for several hours that morning on that very subject. "This operation has been on-going for over four years and is just about at its culmination. We couldn't make a dent in the massive military force that is going to be sent against Israel if we had the mandate to do that, which we don't."

Jack got up and walked over to a large view screen and used a remote to key it into life. The vivid colors showed the northern border of Israel and the surrounding territories. Crayton's best guess is that the massed armies will join up as they move down from Turkey with Ethiopian and Iranian forces joining any coming from Russia and the northern tier of states. They will mass just off of the mountains on the northern border in the expanse of desert and open land in preparation for the assault on Israel."

Jack pushed the buttons on the remote and a large picture of a darkly handsome man in his forties filled the screen. "This is Maximillian Hoffnar or Maxnar as he is known in the shady financial world that finances terrorists and other anti-life causes. David and Alexis have tracked the major purchases of war material increases in the Gog countries to him as the man behind the scenes." Another button push showed an elaborate office building in Zurich, Switzerland. Jack pointed out the machine-gun equipped guards at the entrance to a parking square inside the building complex.

"This is the base that Maxnar has been working out of for the last two years that we know for sure. It is obviously more than a normal business even for that part of the world." He clicked off the screen and faced the team.

"Our mission, as far as I can determine, is to locate the top echelon of Voltron and make sure it doesn't have the opportunity to commit future crimes against humanity. I believe that means "termination with prejudice" as the CIA would label it. This nest of snakes, whether they are housed in this office complex or elsewhere has as its agenda, and what the enemy of mankind has been attempting to do since the days of Abram. Eliminate Yahveh's chosen people. Okay, I want ideas people."

David started the session. "First and foremost we need to know the players. I suggest we ask Maxnar to tell us who is involved in Voltron."

Jack agreed to that. "How do you suggest we arrange our discussion with him?"

David waved a hand expansively. "By appealing to his basic greed. Make him an offer he won't pass up. While he is negotiating the deal we'll get him to tell us what we need to know."

Sarah pointed out a possible flaw. "Maxnar is probably very wealthy right now and with the end of his part of this major Voltron effort he might not be interested in any other deals. Also, Voltron could be developed like Communist cells and his knowledge will be limited to one or two other people in the group."

Jack shrugged, "Then we'll do what we've done before. We'll squeeze him and then follow the leads until we've accomplished our mission. Since this thing is in its final stages Voltron will be pulling in all the strings and be connected tightly right now. After the invasion is launched I would guess that the rats will scurry off to their respective plush hide outs to weather the storm of governmental and public protest from the west about their part in the effort. We need to truncate the organization before it does that."

Laura looked at Jack and David. "But that doesn't answer Sarah's concern about Maxnar being interested in a deal so that we can get our hands on him. How do we make sure he will be interested?"

Mark spoke up for the first time. "We make something available on the black market that he can't resist bidding on. Like an advanced jet fighter," He looked at David. "How about offering him a SandSnake."

David thought about the Israeli secret craft for penetration of enemy lands that the team had taken a trip on earlier. "That would definitely bring out the worst of the rats to do the bidding. I'll see if we can secure Israel's cooperation on this in the interest of eliminating their enemies."

Charlie had walked into the meeting five minutes earlier and now he spoke up. "I think I can save us a lot of effort. Maxnar doesn't know any more about the people controlling Voltron than the last two guys you snagged from OC did."

Mark cocked his head to one side, "You know this, how?"

Charlie smiled, "Crayton finally figured out their scheme of sending the instructions to OC. They use the same technique to direct the activities of Maximillian Hoffnar. The good news is that Crayton also pinpointed the real source of the orders. I can assure you that they think they are invisible because Crayton was able to work through all their cutouts and relays, and satellite relays, and dead drops, and finally a three-level firewall without tripping any of their traps. You can't beat multiple Cray computers if you use computers."

Charlie walked up to the front of the group and took the remote from Jack. Punching in a different set of commands resulted in a satellite photo of a piece of desert.

Charlie looked at the group. "See anything unusual?"

Everyone studied the picture but couldn't see anything until Alexis said, "I see two sat dishes and a Yaggi antenna."

Charlie was very impressed. He threw her a red laser pointer. "Show everyone where they are at."

Alexis highlighted an area to the top right of the picture. It was like looking at an optical illusion. First you couldn't see it and then you could. If you knew what you were looking for and where to look.

Charlie pointed at the picture. "Looks innocuous doesn't it?" He punched another button on the remote. A green lined ghostly image materialized under the sand. "There are three levels to this structure and they are full of computers, War Rooms, and support facilities. This is Voltron's headquarters and it's located in the desert one hundred miles southeast of Cairo, Egypt."

Mark was awed. "How in Heaven's name did you find that?"

Charlie shrugged, "Crayton triangulated the final stage signals using three U.S. military satellites and, Presto! There it was. I was able to get a LandSat pass by overriding the commands from Miami and got the underground images."

Jack asked, "Do you think they're operating with the Egyptian government's approval?"

David laughed, "Doubtful that the government is going to admit that. But, my guess is that some levels of the administration had to be in on the building and operation of the facility. It may be a splinter group within the administration or the whole group could be involved."

Mark asked Charlie, "Have the tank groups started to advance on Israel as yet?"

Charlie nodded, "Yeah, they have. It's being done under the guise of a Pan-Arabic war game, but Crayton predicts they will join up just north of the border of Israel in six nights."

Mark stood up. "Then ladies and gentlemen, our deadline is five nights. I want full workups on the area, potential resistance, methods of approach, and scenarios as to how we take the place. It would also be nice if we have an exit strategy." He looked at David. Think Israel would loan us a SandSnake?"

David thought about it. "It would mean we would have to coordinate our activities with the IDF and I don't know that there aren't any OC ears in that group."

Jack looked at Mark and David, "Then I suggest we steal a SandSnake for our use."

David frowned, "How will you get it to work? The spy satellites that determine the path and timing have to be ordered by the IDF and. . . "He looked at Charlie and nodded, "Oh, I see, Crayton can take care of that."

David thought for a minute, "I think it would be wise to allow me to coordinate this raid and our use with the Mossad. I really don't think we want to have half of the IDF chasing us all the way to Egypt."

The meeting covered a dozen other contingencies and then broke up into teams to achieve the decided upon goals.

CHAPTER EIGHTEEN

Jack, Laura, Mark, Sarah, David, and Alexis sat together in the War Room communications section of the fortress. They faced a large video display unit which was dark for the moment.

Laura was, as usual, praying for the understanding of everyone they were going to talk to today. Everyone else sat at ease waiting for the connection to be completed. Crayton was creating a new level of Ultra-Secure electronic communication link and it took several minutes to establish an adequate connection on the other end. This communications link would be completely controlled by Crayton on both ends. The other end of the link had to comply with Crayton's commands and that took some electronic persuasion.

The screen lit up with a view of the subterranean White House War Room. Seated at a table were; President Bollen, Joint Chiefs of Staff Chairman, General Miles, Ron Peetree, Secretary of Defense, and Bill Williams, Director of the National Clandestine Service who was Alexis's boss.

Jack opened up the discussion. "President Bollen, General Miles, Secretary Peetree, Director Williams, good afternoon and thank you for making time in your hectic schedules to speak with us. I think you're all familiar with the people here with the possible exception of our newest team member, David Zahavy, recently a Director of Operations with the Israeli Mossad."

After the hellos were done, the President brought the meeting to order. "Jack, from your brief I understand the severity of this communication and we" The president waved his hand to indicate all four men. "We are in your debt for finding the culprit behind this misguided attempt to attack our ally, Israel. As you said, our schedules are hectic so let's get down to business. Please repeat what you told me this morning for the benefit of these men."

Jack nodded, "In a nutshell, the enemy is a two-layer organization, Omicron Cartel is their visible section which is controlled by Voltron, the hidden part. Omicron Cartel, or

OC for short, is the group tasked with infiltrating and subverting national governments, including ours. They have been at this for the last five years and have been very successful as you all know by their ability to force the Crossfire Team into being isolated by all levels of the government under penalty of political chaos.

They have also been tasked with attempting to control any attempts at interference with Voltron's plan to attack Israel. This has included the murder of many people in over twenty countries and wholesale control of entire industries and companies. Their financial backing is from middle-eastern oil revenues from five Arab states. They have sufficient resources to conduct operations such as the theft of three secret stealth fighters from Russia. Their mercenary army numbers nearly a thousand soldiers. The two, Level 2 directors and the four mercenary leaders we have turned over to the Justice Department have confirmed all of this and much more. These groups have had a major, albeit background role in much of the middle-east violence and unrest."

Jack paused for a second to see how his information was being received. "We, the Crossfire Team, will have to leave damage control to the governmental agencies tasked to prevent the subversion of the government. We have been tasked by Yahveh to eliminate the heart of this enemy which is Voltron."

Jack keyed in a command on his keyboard and the screen showed the two views of the desert compound of Voltron. Jack continued to describe the facility and other aspects of the problem. "This is the headquarters compound of Voltron. It has existed in the desert, unnoticed, one hundred miles southeast of Cairo, Egypt for almost five years. The orders for the OC and the development of the new military units in five nations are controlled from this facility." The picture returned to the meeting room scenes.

Mark took over at this point. "The best possibility we can foresee is that this group is using the Pan-Arab War Games as a cover to move the massive military forces to the position from which they expect to launch their attack, just to the north of the mountains on the border of Israel."

Laura interrupted Mark momentarily, "Mr. President, gentlemen, I want to remind you that this is the same group that engineered the almost successful massive bombing of the United States and Britain slightly over a month ago. If Yahveh hadn't been on our side it would have been successful. We now believe that arrangement by Voltron and the Omicron Cartel was a deliberate effort to reduce our ability to react to this attack. Considering the amount of time and money spent on that effort alone we should not take this effort lightly. Yahveh will stop this imitation attack of the Ezekiel prophesy but has tasked the Crossfire Team with removing Voltron so that they no longer threaten anyone."

Ron Peetree was a thoroughly astute Secretary of Defense. He had seen the results of the actions of the Crossfire Team in nine different actions and had no doubt about their capabilities but he was not a believer. "Excuse me, Mrs. Malone, but I have a problem with leaving the prevention of this assault on Israel in the hands of God. I feel that we need to be ready to assist Israel militarily as well as by prayer."

The President held up his hand preventing any reply from the team.

"I assure you Secretary Peetree that we will be fully prepared, with Israel's permission of course, to help stop this invading army by military means."

The Secretary looked at the President, "But Sir, with only five days left. We can't possibly get sufficient men and material there in time to confront an army of, of. I don't know how big this army is, do you Mr. Connelly?"

"Mr. Secretary, we estimate they can field over four thousand armored vehicles of which over two thousand are tanks and by an accepted ratio of forty troops and twenty support personnel per vehicle that would indicate a standing army of roughly a quarter million men."

The President preempted the Secretary's next complaint about time.

"Ron, we don't have the time to get men there. This would be strictly an air delivery of field-grade tactical nuclear weapons. That would be the only quick answer to such an army."

The Secretary sat there stunned. "Sir? You'd use nuclear weapons on Saudi or Syrian soil? That would be an act of war!"

The President sat back in his chair. "I know what it would mean Ron, but remember, these five countries are permitting the first act of war by allowing the invading army to use their land to attack Israel. We are only abiding by our treaties with the combatants as required."

David broke into the conversation. "Mr. President, I assure you that Israel will welcome your backing but if that option has to be used, they will do it, not the United States."

The President looked at David's image for a few seconds. "I agree with your summation David but the decision to use nuclear weapons will probably be decided by the Knesset and right now they're pretty liberal, don't you think?" David wiggle-waggled his right hand in the air. "Yes Sir, it could go either way."

Mark added, "It pays to be prudent and prepared to act Mr. President but I personally heard Rose say that Yahveh will take care of the armed forces arrayed against Israel."

The Secretary shook his head. President Bollen said, "Okay Mark, I understand. We'll have assets in the area ready to lend a hand if Israel asks us to. But we won't intervene unless the invading army crosses Israel's border. Will that be prudent?"

Mark looked at the others on the team, "Yes Sir!"

Sarah spoke up. "Mr. President, our analysis of this attack indicates that they will probably need to precede the attack with some sort of distraction inside Israel itself. This could be setting off bombs in a major way, a bio attack, or even a sea assault to draw the attention and efforts of the IDF away from the northern border. Our computer analysis indicates it will be some sort of seaborne attack. Can you assist the IDF in defeating something like that before it happens?"

The President looked thoughtful for a few minutes and then nodded.

"I'll get with the Israeli cabinet and the head of the Mossad and see if we can provide them with backup and equipment. Do you have any specifics on this attack or feint?"

Mark answered, "No sir, we have been focused on Voltron and the OC problem. I'd be willing to look into it if you need us to do that."

The President shook his head. "Thanks anyway Mark. We've got a lot of good people that can work on that. You guys stay focused on the Voltron complex. Do you need any assistance or equipment that we could provide?"

Mark shook his head, "Not that I could identify presently Sir, but I'd like to reserve the chance if the need arises."

General Miles spoke up for the first time. "Just give me a call."

CHAPTER NINETEEN

Mark and the rest of the group in the War Room turned to discussing how they were going to attack the Voltron Complex. Charlie Wu had joined the group and showed them what they were up against. He used the big screen to show a graphical detail of the complex.

He continued with the general description of the complex. "As you can see we can determine that there are five levels to the main building. They have a single vehicle entrance that is hidden by some form of moving cover that blends into the sand when closed. The two comm dishes are sand colored and level with the dune they are buried in. As far as we can tell there are no sensor systems or weapons emplacements on the surface. This is obviously to make the entire complex invisible to spy satellites, aircraft, or even wandering nomads on camelback. They have installed a rather ingenious monitoring method. They continually operate a small, unpiloted airborne vehicle or UAV. By its movements I don't think it is autonomous but actually remote controlled from the complex. This UAV hovers over the complex at an altitude of approximately five hundred feet. It is only two feet long and with a wingspan of about four feet. Colored light blue on the bottom it is essentially invisible from the ground. It probably has cameras that feed directly to the complex. With this coverage they can observe a two mile area around the complex and zoom in on specific targets. Crayton found it by the communications between it and the complex. They bring it down every six hours and refuel it. There is a twenty minute window when they are not able to observe the area during refueling."

"The only other vulnerability is the fresh air inlet which is hidden in a Wadi just north of the complex. It is located inside a riff in the side of the Wadi wall. I can't tell what type of sensors they may have embedded around the inlet to detect intruders or vermin."

"On the five levels of the complex we have been doing some more LandSat geophysical scans and I believe that the top level is a garage and defensive arena. Obviously the inhabitants feel that anyone attempting to penetrate the complex will have to go through the top level so they prepared it to repel any attempts to get to the lower levels."

"They have buried a nuclear power source below the complex for power generation. Being below the complex would keep its signature normally covered but with the LandSat information we were able to detect it."

"Lastly we feel that the second and third levels are the labs and working areas including the communications center. The bottom two levels seem to have a large body of people in them at all times so we think that is a barracks for troops and supply or storage spaces."

Charlie put down his notes. "I see this complex as an extremely well designed and fortified facility. You could easily bomb it out of existence but that would obliterate any positive identification of the people and purposes of the place. I look forward to your strategy for taking it."

Mark had been studying the graphics and the layout of the complex. He had a new method of developing strategy and it had paid off. He prayed for guidance and wisdom for such an attack. Yahveh didn't let him down this time either. He stood up and used his laser pointer to indicate points on the diagrams. "We are going to use the SandSnake to get within the area. We will then time out the down time of the UAV and get to the air inlet. It obviously supplies the entire structure.

We won't engage any sensors or defenses but simply flood the air source with Xegene-13 gas. It is odorless, colorless, detectable only by sophisticated analysis, and only affects humans. They will simply go to sleep for the next six to eight hours. We can tell that it is working when the UAV wanders off or crashes."

Mark then indicated the complex structure. "Then we will approach the complex from above. We will use a twenty foot JPL-designed, vertical blast ring set to penetrate to the second level and enter there."

"Our first objective is to secure anyone we find on the second and third levels and to sap the elevators and stairways from the fourth level to the third in the event the troops avoid the gas or have been able to don gas masks quickly enough."

Mark looked at Charlie, "As to our exit strategy I think a couple heavy lift choppers could do it."

Charlie thought for a few seconds. "What I didn't mention is that there is an Egyptian army base less than six miles away from the complex. They could be a problem. They have heavy armor and troops."

Mark shook his head. "If we do this right, we should be able to get the entire group of Voltron personnel and evac before the army is aware of anything happening."

David said, "That's only true if the army base isn't there to protect the complex. That base was established about four years ago, right about the same time that the complex was established. Also, I find it hard to believe they could bring in enough supplies and equipment to build such a complex without the tacit approval of the Egyptian government. In that case we could be facing their army trying to protect that secret arrangement."

Mark thought about that for a few minutes. "Okay, I'll plan on either possibility. The SandSnake isn't big enough to get us and our detainees out of there so we need to come up with additional transportation somehow."

The meeting broke up with each small group developing detailed plans and ordering equipment and supplies they would need for the assault. They had only one hundred hours until the military assault on Israel.

CHAPTER TWENTY

Laura sat on the console next to Mark and had a puzzled look on her face. Mark looked up from his call list and said, "What?"

Laura looked at him for a second, "Okay, what's a "twenty foot JPL-designed, vertical blast ring set"?"

Mark sat back and flipped his pen up onto the work surface. "Jet Propulsion Laboratories suggested a self-opening hole in the lunar soil. Their concept was taken by an aggressive corporation called "California Battle Supplies" and converted into a quick entrance device. Essentially you start with a big ring with an inside diameter of ten feet, two feet tall, and eight inches thick. You place the ring where you want your entrance.Once you fire it off, the lowest part of the ring pulverizes all matter inside the ring for about eight inches of depth and blows the pulverized dirt up and out of the hole. The ring drops the eight inches and repeats the pulverization. This action is repeated as many times as necessary for the depth you select before you start. Each explosion blows the pulverized soil up and out of the hole. The interesting thing is the speed at which it works. The twenty feet we want will be a series of twenty five explosions in less than ten seconds, bang! bang! and you have a ten-foot hole twenty feet deep."

Laura was impressed, "How much does our ring weigh?"

Mark sat up and looked at the spec sheet. "Eighty-two pounds. Two man carry."

Jack walked over to them, "I just got off the phone with General Miles. I inquired about the possibility of Egyptian army interference with the operation. He told me that we would need iron-clad proof that the people in the complex are behind the attack on Israel before the U.S. could confront the Egyptians."

Mark thought about that, "Then let's get in and out before the army comes calling."

Jack agreed. "It's the exit strategy I'm concerned about. If we have twenty "detainees" that will make nearly fifty people in the middle of a hostile state with which we want to avoid any entanglements."

Mark nodded. "Okay then how about two night-camo Ospreys and we'll do it at night?"

Jack thought about that. "That could work. Let's get down to details. Like how are we going to come up with two black Ospreys and get them there in the next eighty hours?"

Mark laughed, "That's the easy part. They are already there. We just have to "borrow" them from the Israelis."

David had been listening to their conversation. He smiled and then sighed. "Let me make another call."

Jack looked at David as he punched in a number on his cell phone.

In an aside to Mark he said, "I wonder when the Mossad will begin to wonder if they made a good decision letting David go."

Mark was about to answer when he was interrupted by the alert phone from the military base on top of the mountain. "Go ahead" Mark said after pushing the button.

The voice that came back was obviously nervous but controlled. "General Connelly, there is a three chopper invasion force attempting to land on our base. They literally came out of nowhere. They are strafing the base. I think our commander was killed along with most of the officers. What are your orders, Sir?"

Mark stared at Jack, "Use your Stingers before they can land. We will reinforce you as quick as we can get there!" He broke the connection, hit the "INVASION" button that sent the alert throughout the fortress and armed the NOVASTAR2 system. Hitting the intercom general call button he said. "Invaders at the mountaintop base, three helicopters, arm up and move out." Punching in Charlie's number he got him on the first ring. "Charlie, can you distract those choppers above the top of the mountain?"

Charlie came back with, "Right away, Mark."

The idea of a possible helicopter assault on the fortress had been foreseen by Major Danning during the design phase of the fortress. He had planned on the troops being able to hold their own but had created some backups if they weren't able to hold back the invading force.

86

Charlie brought up the video of the military base and IDed the three Chinook helicopters attempting to destroy the base so they could land. Bringing up the defense screen he zeroed in on the first chopper and pushed the FIRE button. A concentrated laser beam flared into brilliant light on the front of the first chopper. The concept was to blind pilots during daylight. Since this was a night operation it was even more effective. Both the pilot and copilot were wearing NVGs but the laser overloaded the pilot's optical nerves before the automatic "bloom" circuitry in the NVGs could operate. Both pilots lost all their references and the chopper slid off to its left and dropped nose first. It hit the edge of the flat surface of the mountaintop and flipped over the edge going upside down. There was a major explosion when the chopper hit the side of the mountain.

Charlie targeted the second chopper and fired a steel cable out of a hidden alcove. The cable arced over the second chopper and dropped down. The cable was designed to foul the single rotor of a chopper like a Huey. The cable was caught by the front rotor of the Chinook but the back rotor wasn't affected and the effect was dramatic. The front of the chopper stopped in place but the back spun around in a clockwise arc to the left. Men and equipment spilled out of the open back ramp/door of the Chinook to be scattered over the mesa on the top of the mountain. The distance was only eighty feet but the implied momentum of the spinning helicopter threw them harshly to the ground.

Todd Shuman, the U.S. Army Spec-4 that had called Mark had finally gotten past the gunfire of the helicopters and reached the Stingers. Opening up the first one he stared in amazement as the first helicopter crashed into the mesa and fell over the side. Then the second began to gyrate in a circle and he aimed at it and pulled the firing lever on the Stinger. It was only two hundred yards and the Stinger didn't need to home in at all. It blew the rear end of the spinning chopper to pieces and the whole thing came crashing down. Todd threw himself behind a large boulder next to the weapons tent as a wave of fire and shrapnel came his way.

At that point, Mark exited the elevator to find all twenty-five members of the SOG armed and waiting.

Behind Mark were Jack, Laura, Sarah, David, Su Li, Alexis, and Linda Wu. Mark ducked along with everyone else as the second chopper crashed into the plain and exploded. One of the rotor blades smashed into the top of the elevator building but bounced off because the building was built to withstand a nuclear strike.

Mark saw the third Chopper landing beyond the camp and detailed his troops to the left and right on the double. Moving toward the helicopter from cover to cover they encountered the invaders quickly. Rifle fire in both directions began to home in and everyone was involved. From the left side of the skirmish Mark estimated that the last chopper held about twenty troops that looked to be armed with M-16s and M-429 SAWs. Keying his combat microphone he focused the fire on the two men with the SAWs to eliminate the most severe threat first.

On the right side, the invaders had isolated four of the SOG personnel and were surrounding them when an explosion threw all four of the men dead into the air. Todd Shuman had fired a LAW he'd found in the weapons cache at the attacking troops to lessen the odds against the SOG warriors. The other six men turned their fire on Todd. Hit low in the chest Todd went down and crawled into a slight depression. His body armor had stopped the round but it had knocked the wind out of him.

While the mercenaries were concentrating their fire on Todd the SOG troops broke cover and closed on the invaders. Their combined firepower eliminated that pocket of attack.

The firefight became a stalemate between the two groups as they each had secured cover and were sniping at the other.

The stalemate was broken when a fourth Chinook showed up and started strafing the area where the Crossfire Team members were hunkered down. Mark called Charlie, "Charlie we got to stop this bird!"

Before Charlie could answer the Chinook exploded in a huge ball of flame and crashed to the ground behind the invaders. Mark said, "Nice work Charlie!"

Charlie came back, "Thanks, but I didn't do that."

The warzone lit up suddenly as a triple flare went off above the plain. Starkly revealed were four Cobra gunships with Marine markings hovering behind the mercenaries. Mark now knew why the Chinook blew up. A speaker blared, "Throw down your weapons and stand to your feet with your hands on top of your head, NOW!"

One pocket of mercenaries turned to fire on the Cobras and were obliterated by 20 MM. cannon fire. The rest did as they were told. There were only eleven of them left. Mark was put in contact with the lead chopper by Charlie. "Marine Cobras, glad you could make the party. This is General Mark Connelly and I have thirty-six troops in the engagement area. I will have them stand down and sling their arms." He ordered the Crossfire personnel to comply.

The Marine Commander came back with, "You're welcome General. Would you have your troops secure the enemy so we can land?"

Mark replied, "Gladly."

Forty minutes later the bodies had been tagged and bagged, the fires put out and the surviving officer of the mercenaries stood in front of the Marine Major and Mark Connelly. Mark asked him who ordered the raid. The man wouldn't answer. Mark shrugged and told the two SOG warriors behind the man to handcuff him and turn him over to the Arapahoe County Sheriff's deputies on the charge of murder. The man stared at Mark, "You can't do that! I am a prisoner of war."

The officer in charge of the Cobra force, Marine Major William Barkley laughed, "And what war would that be?"

The mercenary realized his position and shut up again. The SOG men took him out of the tent. Major Barkley looked at the holes in the tent and the blood on the floor and shook his head in anger. "Twelve good marines, including four officers, died here tonight, and for what?"

Mark studied the man for a few seconds. He could understand his anger and even agree with his position, but there was more at stake here than just a fly-by shooting. He righted a chair and sat down. He indicated that he wanted the major to do the same. After the man was seated he was still angry.

Mark said, "Major, what you don't know is that these men, under the guise of training were guarding our base. We are known as the Crossfire Team and we have been in almost constant combat with forces dedicated to destroying

America and its way of life for the last three years."
"Standing Presidential policy keeping our activities secret means that you probably haven't been informed about our activities or the real purpose for troops to be stationed here and that you maintain this level of secrecy. The men who died here tonight were killed by a hostile mercenary force tasked with stopping our team. Within the next week we are going to invade a hostile middle-east nation and decapitate the snake that commanded these troops to make this attack.

At the moment they are massing a large army to invade the nation of Israel. If they aren't stopped, thousands of good men including American Marines will die in the war that ensues. This is, of course, top secret. I will report your excellent efforts to General Miles and I commend your rapid response. We will need to rebuild this base and obviously improve the shield against helicopter assault. But, it will go on doing a very vital service."

The major had calmed down as Mark talked and nodded. "Yes Sir, I'm sorry to have been so flippant, I didn't understand the stakes involved."

Mark stood up and shook the man's hand. "I still want to thank you for your timely intervention."

Mark left and the major walked outside to observe the clean-up. Now he understood the urgency his commanding officer had shown when he was ordered to defend the mountain. He had heard of the Crossfire Team and especially their actions at the Arctic Circle and in Zyngola. But, he didn't know they based in his operational arena. He was now glad they were there.

CHAPTER TWENTY-ONE

Everyone gathered together in the living room of the fortress at five in the morning. They prayed their thanks for the successful outcome of the battle and for the families and loved ones of the men and women killed.

They also were going through debrief and unwinding from the sudden action on the mountaintop. Six had been wounded, none seriously in the firefight thanks in a big part to the excellent body armor they had been wearing. They were being treated in the dispensary in the SOG quarters. Mark looked over the troops and was glad these were seasoned military personnel. They didn't need any handholding or explanations. They knew what was going on and they responded professionally and as a team.

Laura noticed that Su Li was quiet and sitting alone in one of the plush recliners to the side of the group. Laura walked over and sat in the next seat and looked at the Asian beauty with the bandage on her forehead. "How are you doing?" she asked.

Su Li looked up at Laura and tipped her head to one side. "Okay, I guess. I just shot two men to death and I really don't care. They were attacking us and they asked for it. But, to be honest, those are the first two that I've killed close up, one-on-one. I expected a reaction, but there is none. I'm like hollow inside. I don't have any guilt about doing it. I feel the Father agreed it was them or me and He isn't blaming me. It's just that I thought it would mean more to destroy two other living people."

Laura prayed for the right words to say to her friend. A thought formed in her mind and she trusted it was from Yahshua. "Su Li, I know what you mean. I had the same type of reaction the first time I had to take a life. I prayed and worried about it for two days. The feelings you don't sense right now are still there. Your mind has put them away for a while. The Father built in defense mechanisms into His children to allow them to process a shocking event slowly, so that we can come to terms with it in His timing, not all at once. Try to relax and let Him work it out in you.

He will, I guarantee it. As to your destroying two other living people, don't you think Yahveh knew what was going to happen to you tonight? It was your choice to join us and serve Him. Those men made the choice to defy Elohim and destroy us. Yahveh is simply cushioning the emotional effects on you and letting you handle them slowly rather than all at once which might traumatize you." Laura thought about the future. "You know, as a part of the Crossfire team this will probably not be the last time you have to take a life to accomplish your calling."

Su Li absorbed Laura's words and let them sink into her. The unresolved burden she had been trying to shoulder fell away from her and she realized that her friend and mentor was right. She would assimilate her actions into her psyche and trust Yahveh to resolve the emotional issues. She smiled and looked at Laura. "Thank you. I do believe what you said is right. I'm starved; I'm going to get some food."

She got up and headed for the kitchen.

Laura sent a quick prayer of thanks heavenward and was about to get up when Alexis sat down in the seat Su Li had just vacated. She looked at Laura for a few seconds with an intensity that made Laura feel naked under her gaze. Alexis spoke quietly. "You know that what you just told her was so exactly right concerning combat fatigue that I would expect you to have had many years of military service. I know for a fact that you don't. How do you do that?"

Laura again prayed for wisdom to respond to Alexis. "You are looking at this with worldly eyes. Look at what just occurred in the spirit not the world. My words were those of Yahveh, not mine. He's had more combat experience than anyone. He knew what she needed. I simply became a vessel and let him lead me."

Alexis digested that and realized she still had a lot to learn about this aspect of the new life she had embraced. "Okay, I'll take that as a valid answer. You know I watched you during the combat up there and you performed as a professional soldier. In fact you reminded me of me. I will tell you that years of training and experience have made me capable in combat situations but I'm impressed by what I see in you. Later, can we make some time to pray together to help me see things from Yahshua's perspective rather than my own?"

Laura nodded, "But it won't be until after Egypt. We don't have any time left."

Alexis smiled, "That's all right. I don't think Voltron has much of a chance after watching this team tonight."

Laura thought back to some of the actions they had been through and she chuckled. "You ain't seen nothing yet." She got up and went over to her husband to discuss their remaining arrangements before they left for Egypt.

Alexis sat in the comfortable chair and remembered a time of combat earlier in her life when things were a lot less comfortable.

-----------------------******-----------------------

Alexis remembered her job description as her training officer had explained it to her. As an agent for the NCS she reported up through the DO. The Directorate of Operations housed special groups for conducting counterterrorism and counter narcotics, tracking nuclear proliferation, and other tasks. Alexis was an agent of the Special Operations group's elite cadre called the Special Activities Division. Each agent was highly skilled in combat, weaponry; covert transport of personnel and material by air, sea, and land; guerrilla warfare; the use of explosives; and escape and evasion techniques. Her training had been intense and she had been prepared to respond quickly to a myriad of possible needs, from parachute drops and communications support to assistance with counter narcotics operations and enemy infiltration.

Special Activities had a symbiotic relationship with the Special Forces, and was run largely by ex-Special Forces soldiers. Alexis had started out her assignment to the NCS directly out of a covert group of female U.S. Army Rangers. She always thought the reason she was picked for the NCS was her special acting abilities which they sometimes called sneakiness.

Special Operations staff recruited assets with specialized skills such as her ability to speak German, Dutch, and several Arabic dialects. Alexis Taggert knew that she had become one of NCS' finely tuned assets.

Considering all of that she had to chuckle at her present disguise. She was dressed as a street walker in a tight blouse, short skirt, fishnet nylons, and way too much makeup.

The organization her team was to penetrate was protected by a large cadre of street thugs all familiar with the local area and people. They knew everyone who should be in the vicinity except for patrons of the "girls" who trolled the streets looking for quick sex and quicker cash. The girls weren't a static group but changed constantly due to those dying from abuse or psychotic patrons, those that were able to get out of the business and live to tell it, and those that went looking for greener pastures to sell their bodies. Alexis had walked the streets in this area twice this week so that her face, if anyone ever looked at it, was familiar to the lookouts. She had gone with enough "Johns" to convince the thugs that she was a working girl all right. Actually, each time she got "picked up" it was with one of her group or the police undercover officers assisting the operation.

The area directly in front of the target "office" was off bounds to her "kind" and she worked her area fifty feet away. Her biggest problem was that she was a tall, good-looking blonde and dressed the way she was she attracted a lot of attention that she really didn't want but had to seem to be trying to get.

One of the thugs that stood in front of the target doorway walked over to her after she had turned down the offer from a guy in an expensive car and asked why she didn't want to go with the guy who obviously had money to burn. She smacked her gum and grinned at the hoodlum. "He was a cop."

That satisfied the goon but, he liked what he saw and that evening he told his boss about her.

Alexis was aware that the strike was scheduled for that night and her job was to make sure no additional forces had been added to the mix and to distract the watchers just before the team arrived. She had a bone-conduction microphone and speaker as part of a choker she was wearing which allowed her to stay in contact with the team. She was about to declare an all clear when the door to the target opened and a well-dressed man came out and spoke to the inquisitive guard from the other night. The guard pointed Alexis out to his boss and the man walked over to Alexis. Seeing the action Alexis worried that her cover might have been blown and this guy was their answer to that.

The guy was obviously a fitness junky. His upper arms and chest were massive and under the two-hundred dollar shirt he was wearing his abs were rock solid. He walked like a boxer or wrestler, sort of a bouncy step rather than a full stride. He came up to her and looked her over.

"How would you like to make a thousand dollars tonight?"

Staying in character Alexis smiled at the thought of all that money.

"What did you have in mind?"

The man didn't beat around the bush. "Two guys, all night, money up front."

Knowing the team could hear this conversation she decided the chance to get inside would be worth the risk since the raid was scheduled in the next ten minutes anyway. "Okay, but I want the cash first."

He man took her by the arm with a grip that was firm but not cruel and led her to the door. The guard opened the door for them and they went inside. The man led her through a darkened and empty store front to the expansive back room that was probably a store room in an earlier life. Instead of the drug and money laundering operation they had been told of she saw crates and boxes of guns, ammo, and LAWs. Realizing the team could be compromised by this unexpected firepower she said,

"Wow! I never seen so many guns and rockets before, you must be some kind of government bunch." She stopped, forcing the man to stop also. "I don't want to get in trouble with the law." Alexis said, apparently worried about the implication that all the guns would only be connected to the police.

The man smirked and told her, "Don't worry your pretty little head about this. These are just our stock in trade, like groceries, you know?"

Alexis got wide-eyed in her portrayal of a simple street walker. "Oh, okay, yeah." She dropped her voice into a conspiratorial whisper. "It's just that I never seen so many boxes of guns before."

The guy laughed, "Come on, I'll show you an even bigger gun."

Alexis looked at him with a coy grin, "I've heard that before."

They walked through the stacks of guns into a living quarter's area and the guy pointed at a door to one side. "Why don't you go in there while I get your money?"

Alexis traipsed over to the door in her three-inch spike high heels and opened it. Of course, it was a bedroom and there was only one guy in there, sitting on the bed. He got a leer on his face when he saw her.

Alexis closed the door and dropped her small clutch purse on the table by the door. She smiled at the overweight man and played with the top button on her blouse.

The man gestured for her to come over to him and she walked over with the clock on her head counting down the time until the raid.

Now in the movies she would pull out a gun and try to take control of the situation. This was real life, not the movies. The man put his hands on her hips and she rotated her upper torso to the left. Using body torque she slammed her right elbow into the man's right temple hard enough to knock him out and slam him onto the bed. She stepped back and said,

"Okay guys, I've started the festivities, any time would be good. I saw six men here in the room behind the storeroom with the guns. Move quickly."

She heard, "We're pulling up front right now and have just eliminated the guards."

The door to the room opened and the muscular man that had picked her up on the street walked in with money in his hand and a smile on his face. The smile disappeared when he saw the other man lying on the bed. His face clouded over and he said, "What happened to Saul?"

She feigned innocence. "I don't know. He was that way when I came in."

Rushing over to the recumbent man he checked him for life signs. He stood up and stared at her, "He's dead!"

Throwing the money down he came at Alexis like a storm. "What did you do to him?"

Suddenly an alarm started going off somewhere outside the room. The man looked at her and told her to stay put. He reached around to pull a large automatic out of a holster behind his back as he headed for the door. Alexis timed it out and side kicked him in the ribs with her right foot while his arm was still behind him. Normally this is not a good thing to do when the other person has a gun but Alexis knew she had an advantage. The three-inch spike heel punctured his flesh and punched a hole in his right lung. That, plus the fact that the kick had sufficient force to knock the guy over and slam him to the floor made him drop the gun and grab his side.

Alexis scooped up the gun and used the toe of her left foot to turn out the man's lights with a kick to the head. Gunfire sounded in the room next to her and the door opened suddenly with two guys trying to get through it at the same time. Both of them were armed with pistols.

Alexis dropped into a Weaver shooting stance and yelled at them. "Federal Officer, Drop your weapons, NOW!"

The first man tried to aim at her so she shot him through the throat. He flew backwards into the other room and the other man dropped his gun and put his hands on his head.

Two of the NCS team came up behind him and took control of him.

Alexis's boss came into the room and surveyed the damage. Looking up at her he asked, "Did you really need our help?"

Alexis laughed with him. "Sure, the more the merrier."

------------------------*****------------------------

The memory faded away and she stared at the other people in the living room of the fortress. A decision was forming in her mind but she'd give it more time to gel. After they got back from Egypt, if they got back.

CHAPTER TWENTY-TWO

David finished reviewing his lists and ticked off the last item. He walked over to Mark's position and squatted down next to his chair. "I've got everything prepared and ready for shipment to Israel. I've convinced the Mossad of the vital necessity for our strike and they've given me the use of two SandSnakes to penetrate and two helicopters for exit. They've stipulated that they want two of their soldiers to accompany us for the raid. Is that all right with you?"

Mark considered the request and nodded. "Yeah, it's okay. We're going in to destroy an operation not do an Intel strike. They just want to see everything and get what Intel they can about both Voltron and the Crossfire Team, right?"

David nodded. "That pretty well sums it up. They will be Mossad spy-soldiers and their allegiance will be to Israel."

Mark smiled at his Israeli friend. "As long as they obey my orders during the raid things will go right." Mark thought for a few seconds. "Do you think we can depend on them to follow through with their end of the deal concerning the Vertical Take Off and Landing (VTOL) exit and that the detainees are ours and not theirs?"

David had been wrestling with that question in his mind most of the morning. "I think the Mossad and Israel owe this team a lot of gratitude and respect for the many times we've saved the nation from terroristic attacks. But, remember that their mindset is on Israeli survival first and foremost. We will have to watch their actions closely. I do think they'll get us out because of their people, the Intel they may get, and because they've given me their word."

Jack signaled Mark, "Okay Commander, everything is set and we need to move if we're going to make this schedule."

The team and the SOG members took four vans to the Denver International Airport and disembarked inside a huge hanger. Alexis was impressed that they had an Air Force C-5 Galaxy sitting in there. Everyone loaded the gear and the unique equipment for the raid and took seats. The vans left by the vehicle door under the watchful eyes of several Special Forces types that were armed with M-16s with M-79 grenade launchers attached under the barrels.

The C-5 was sealed up and the big hanger doors were opened. A tow cart pulled the giant aircraft out of the hanger and onto the tarmac.

Mark made his way to the cockpit to check their flight times and refueling schedule. He was glad to see Major Mike White at the controls. Mark squatted down next to him as the aircraft began to taxi towards the runways. "Hey, Mike, I thought we were on the out-list as far as any military support."

The Major turned control of the aircraft over to the co-pilot and smiled at Mark. "Well, it seems that Washington is starting to frown on the people that forced that concept on us. But, anyway, this is just a training flight ordered by General Miles. The forty-five of you guys are travelling as observers on this flight."

They coordinated the schedules and Mark went back to find his seat before the bird went airborne. As he buckled in Jack asked him the same question. Mark grinned, "Apparently we are besmirching OC so badly the government is starting to abhor their base of power. The tide is turning buddy."

Eighteen hours later the team loaded everything they were taking to the target onto a covered truck for the three hour trip to the base in southern Israel. The two Israeli commandos that were to accompany them had joined up at the airport. The whole group drove to the isolated base and used the time before they could move out to rest and prepare for the raid. They went over the plan several times and the contingency plans twice.

Jack and Laura settled down in a corner of the hanger and rested on two mats on the concrete floor. They had spent several hours of the flight in prayer and continued during the down time. Laura rolled over onto her right side and smiled at Jack who was watching her. "I think Yahveh is going to give us a break after this so that we can stand down for a while. That would be good. We need to spend some time together without the combat."

Jack agreed with her. The last three years had been exciting, dangerous, frightening, scary, exhilarating, and ninety-miles-per-hour. But it was hard on their personal relationship. Holding your wife in your arms would be more romantic if you both didn't have on body armor and combat gear.

Laura reached out and took hold of Jack's hand. "Get some rest honey," she said, "I think the next few hours will be challenging."

Jack smiled and lay back on his mat. He was glad Laura had decided to wear the new light-weight trauma plates in her body armor. She didn't want to get more bullet damage to her almost healed chest and abdomen where she had been hit in the parking lot raid in Denver.

As he settled down he asked her. "I don't understand it honey. You are our spiritual leader because of your close walk with the Father. Yet, you pray for me and the others and we get healed. Why didn't the Father heal you?"

She smiled a small smile. "Because he didn't heal me. I don't know why not, I just know I spend more time praying while I'm healing and have more time with Him. When I find out why, I'll let you know."

Mark sat at a table with Sarah and studied the latest LandSat details of the hidden compound. Sarah had been considering the attack and asked, "Mark, what if they are the fundamentalist type and rig the nuclear power source to explode when we attack?"

Jack and Mark had thought about that and the consensus was that it wouldn't happen. "That is a small nuclear generator that heats water to power a steam turbine and thereby generate electrical power and heat. It probably doesn't have any weapons grade material and the worse that could happen is an overheat and meltdown situation. That would be bad but we would be gone long before a radiation leak could affect us. To make it a bomb isn't realistic. Now that's not to say they don't have some other doomsday device or plan. That's why I want them all asleep when we come calling."

Alexis and David were sitting on their mats. Alexis was reassembling the .40 Glock autoloader she normally carried. She had taken it apart and carefully inspected the parts and the mechanism. She cleaned the assembly and carefully dried it and put a light coat of gun oil on it. When she had it back together she tried the operation and reloaded a full magazine and put a round in the chamber. Putting the weapon back into her holster she looked up to find David watching her. Smiling at him she patted her gun and said, "I like to keep things ready to work."

David smiled back at the lovely blonde woman. "I suspected that about you. Your training was very intense and detailed. I spent a few years training new agents and I can see that you were probably a good student."

Alexis stretched and lay back on her mat. Rolling over to her right side she stared at David for a minute. "Tell me what it was like when you were in training."

David thought back to his first days at the training camp for the Mossad. It had been a completely different time and his training covered a lot of things that the new students today didn't get because of the visibility required after several Mossad reorganizations and shakeups. "I would liken my training to yours in that I was a soldier that became a spy, like you. We didn't have all the technology and computers we have today. I was trained to use my mind and understand the hidden clues and signs during an operation. I frequently had to complete a mission alone and with no support of any kind. If I was caught there was plausible deniability and I was still on my own. The training had a flavor of "be the best or leave". You really didn't have a choice in the matter."

David laid back on his mat and looked at Alexis. "We were expected to eliminate any of the enemy that could compromise us or were in the way of our mission. I learned many forms of hand-to-hand combat, usually the quickest and nastiest techniques. I was expected to master any situation I got into and to keep the needs of the country ahead of my needs. The training was sixteen hours a day and that included physical trials and class work. I remember one time when my lighter weight and, at that time, skinniness, had my trainers worried that I couldn't have enough stamina to do the job. So they had me run an obstacle course against some of the strongest students. They stipulated that we had to continue until there was only one of us still going."

David smiled in remembrance. "There were six different courses that took about thirty minutes each to negotiate. They cleared them all and had us run one after another. They were betting I wouldn't complete all six one time. Nine hours later I was the last one moving through the courses."

He looked intensely at her. "Other than the other students we hadn't seen anyone for nine hours. When they realized I had beaten the best they had they sent one of the trainers out to tell me to stop. He came out of the woods almost right on top of me and I didn't realize it wasn't part of the training game. I saw the man moving into my path and even though I was pretty well spent I mustered up enough energy to do a decent flying side kick. He wasn't expecting it and it caught him completely unaware. He flew backwards and hit his head on a tree. He was in a coma for four days and we thought we'd lost him several times. They had to restart his heart once."

"On our graduation day, he was the one that congratulated me and gave me my Mossad ID. I'll never forget what he said. "Zahavy, if I am in the field, I want you on my team." David looked inward and speculative. "He was killed in a border skirmish with the Hezbollah six years later."

Alexis was moved by David's words. She continued to talk as her mind flew back to that time.

-----------------------*****-----------------------

"It must have been tough at that time. After my Ranger duties my spy school for the NCS was mostly class work and maintaining my edge. I was able to hold my own with all their instructors in martial arts, street combat, and gunplay. My trainers also thought I might be too fragile for the work but that was resolved when four men, mercenaries I think, were sent to my home during a break. Their job was to eliminate me because they thought I had information about a crime spree they had been on earlier. I didn't know anything about that but when they busted into my father's house with drawn guns they got more than they could handle."

Alexis sat up on the mat. "My dad's dog, Furry, had apparently heard them when they broke open the garage door and he went on guard growling at the door that connected the garage to the house. My parents had gone to bed and I was in pajamas, raiding the refrigerator. I have always had excellent night vision and wasn't using any lights. That's why they thought they could break-in before we knew it. I heard them trying the inside door and realized my gun was upstairs in my room. So, I tiptoed over to the door and unlocked it quietly. I yanked the door open and caught them flatfooted."

She made a sour face. "As soon as I saw the guns I knew it was a kill or be killed situation. I did a full force knuckle strike to the throat of the first man and then kicked the second one back into the garage into the other two men. The first guy let go of his gun as he tried to get air into his lungs through a crushed throat. I took the gun away from him and shot the other three men. The last two were firing back at me but I had pulled the first one over in front of me as a bullet sponge. My dad came downstairs with a loaded shotgun and surveyed the bodies. He nodded at my handiwork but asked me if I had to make such a mess in the process."

------------------------------******------------------------------

"I had to stay one extra day to complete the paperwork for the police and the inspectors so I took a copy of the report back to my trainers so that I would be excused for missing a day. After they read the report they decided I was more than durable enough to be an agent."

David grinned, but he wasn't sure it was because he could see Alexis in her pajamas taking out four assailants or because he could see Alexis in her pajamas.

CHAPTER TWENTY-THREE

The team assembled at a small hanger just after dark. The doors were opened and they walked into the space and towards the two SandSnakes.

Alexis was intrigued by the machine. She nudged Mark, "What type of aircraft is this?"

Mark shook his head. "First time I saw it I didn't know what it was. At that time I thought I was up on all the varieties of combat aircraft in the world but I'd never seen anything quite like this."

The craft was painted in sandy camouflage and had stubby wings with large humps in the center of the wings. It was about fifty feet long and only about ten high. It wasn't sitting on wheels but on feet and had another large, sandy-colored hump towards the rear of the chassis. The back of the craft sported two stubby wings with short tails on them. The whole thing was obviously designed as stealthy with only front windows which were raked back at an extreme angle. There were angles around the upper surfaces to mis-direct radar. The team broke into two groups with each group headed for one of the machines.

David waved everyone in the first group up the short set of steps into the fuselage of the SandSnake. There were fifteen jump seats on each side of the fuselage and a storage area for gear in the rear. After everyone racked their gear and strapped into the seats the crew of two locked the door and went up front. There was a much muted whine from accelerating turbofan jet engines and then the craft lifted off of its feet and hovered in the hanger.

Alexis raised her eyebrows looking at David. He said, "I didn't think you would know about this aircraft. Very, very few people do. The operating altitude for the SandSnake is eight feet. It is primarily an air-cushion vehicle pushed by jet engines and travels very quickly and very quietly across the desert."

Alexis asked, "How can you zip across the desert without being detected by anyone?"

"Because we don't go near any observers, have an extremely low radar image, and blend into the ground in case any enemy satellite is staring in our direction." came the reply.

At the questioning look he got in reply to that, David continued to describe their means of transportation. "This vehicle is computer controlled and guided by a combination of satellite and AWACs inputs. It is very quiet, doesn't raise a great deal of a sand track and is highly maneuverable. The satellite data shows any possible contacts and then they determine the best path to avoid those contacts. The camouflage paint and the low altitude prevent anyone that is outside of a mile of the path from seeing anything. There are times when we have to lie doggo on the sand for a time to clear complicated contacts but that is rare because the desert is a large place and is primarily uninhabited."

Su Li asked David, "How long does it take to get a good satellite position that will cover our entire trip?"

No more than had she said the words and the Sand Snakes began to glide out of the hanger in the dark. As the two craft exited the base and left the vicinity they began to pick up a very high forward velocity.

The trip to Egypt was complicated and took the rest of the night and the majority of the second day. The teams passed the time resting, going over the plans again and watching the news that had begun to notice the large gathering of military units just north of Israel. The countdown clock was running out of time.

Under the cover of darkness the two SandSnakes moved within a mile of the target and quietly buried themselves in the sand. Sarah set up a small camouflaged observation post on a sand dune near the lead SandSnake and covered the operations of the hidden base. Her concentration was on the small UAV hovering over or flying in slow circles around the base. The rest of the teams prepared for the attack.

The second SandSnake would move within one hundred yards of the perimeter of the buried air intake carrying a team of ten. The first SandSnake would move to a position almost on top of the complex itself.

The entry team consisted of nine Crossfire team members and twenty-five SOG personnel. This crowded the interior of the SandSnake but it was only for a short time.

Just before the estimated time for the refueling of the UAV Sarah saw a luxury car drive toward the base and disappear down the entry tunnel. Ten minutes later the UAV descended and also disappeared.

Sarah ran back to the SandSnake and both vehicles extracted themselves from the dune they had buried themselves in and quickly moved to the predetermined strike points.

Su Li led the knockout team and quickly steered the group into the ravine or Wadi and to the cleft in the wall where the air intake was hidden. Approaching quietly in the dark they could feel and hear the wind as the intake unit pulled in enough fresh air to supply the complex.

Being careful not to set off any hidden alarms she had the team set up the Xegene-13 dispensers. She had everyone don their gas masks in case there were any errant wind currents. Checking her watch she saw that they had three minutes left before they started the gas.

The other team quickly dug in and covered themselves up to prevent detection from the UAV as the SandSnake quietly slid away into the darkness on its perilous trip back to Israel.

The equipment and personnel were hidden as the small UAV flew back into the air to resume its observation duties.

Mark watched the time and pushed the button to start the counter when it hit the time for the gas to be released.

Su Li signaled the three-man teams and they began to disperse the gas into the cleft in the Wadi wall. Since Xegene-13 was odorless and colorless they could only watch their instrumentation as it told them the gas was been emitted. When both tanks were empty Su Li sent a comm signal to Mark to let him know it had been done.

Mark got the signal and told Sarah who was watching the UAV. It continued to hover five minutes later. Mark shook his head. "It's probably preprogrammed for the duration of the flight unless the operator sees something unusual and takes command of the flight. We can't use it as an indication that the gas worked. So, knock it down and we will go in anyway."

Sarah had a silenced .50 caliber sniper rifle and she fired one shot. The fifteen-hundred grain slug smashed through the UAV and knocked the motor out of it. The little craft went into a nosedive and crashed into the sand a thousand yards north of their position.

Everyone was up and running at once. As Mark ran he remembered doing this before in the deserts of the middle-east. The sun-heated sand here had a unique odor and texture. He remembered the smells and the coolness of the evening hour as they reached their position and placed the explosive ring. Jack triggered the ring and the evening silence was fractured by the ten-second string of explosions that went farther down each time. The last two rings were timed to drop to the floor of the first level and open the hole to the second. Mark was the first one into the hole as the anchored drop lines fell into the darkness.

Mark sensed more than saw the dark first level as he slid down the rope with his M-8 at the ready. As he dropped to the floor of the second level he noted the damage done by the exploding rings as they made the hole in the concrete ceiling. There were several bodies in the area of the hole. He let the rope go and moved away a small distance to cover the others as they descended. Most of the lights in this area were knocked out but the rest of the large room they were entering into was still illuminated by several lights at the far end of the room. Mark could see a number of people lying on the floor or crumpled on desks. His gas mask limited his ability to see but it was obvious that the gas had worked, at least in this room. By now the damaged area was filling up with people as the remainder of the team rappelled down from the desert floor.

Following their plan they split up into smaller teams and started advancing through the second level of the complex. Each team had photographs and ID kits and they checked the unconscious people as they moved through the area. The ones they identified as probable leaders of Voltron or scientists they handcuffed, searched, gagged, and moved back to the room with the hole in it. David was with Alexis and Jack when he stopped and looked at three men in tailored uniforms in a room that looked like a conference room or control center. He checked the three twice and shook his head.

Jack came up next to him and asked, "What have you found?"

"These are the three missing leaders of the ASF." Jack was stunned. "I thought that we had hunted the Arab Strike Force out of existence."

The Arab Strike Force had perpetrated the mass poisoning of Israel and the U.S. two years earlier with a variation of mad-cow disease. Yahveh had responded to a world-wide prayer and fasting led by Sarah in Israel and cured the millions infected in the two countries. The U.S. and Israel led a global man-hunt for the members of the ASF with the assistance of the entire Arab world who didn't want to be associated with the ASF because the U.S. President had promised to wage all-out war on any country that harbored any member of the sect. There were only three high-ranking members that had never been found and were supposed dead. Now here they were.

Jack's anger flared up and he signaled two of the team from the SOG. "Crate these after you very carefully search them." David took pictures of each man with a digital camera. He contacted Linda Wu back in the fortress and up-loaded the photos to her. Mark sent out the word that the gas had dissipated and they could remove their gas masks. There was an explosion and a flurry of gun fire from the main hall.

Jack and Mark ran to the door as Mark asked what was going on over the combat comm gear. Craig Steele came back with a situation report. "Apparently the gas didn't knock out the two lower levels and they are coming at us from both ends of the hall where the stairwells are. They were using the elevator but Kevin blew that away with a forty-mike, mike grenade. We've got them bottled up at the doorways but there must be a lot of them because they keep trying to jump over the dead ones and charge our positions."

Mark and Jack hugged the walls of the hall and used whatever cover they could get as they moved to Craig's position behind an upturned desk. Joining him Mark commented, "It won't be long before they start using explosives too. Let's close the doors." He spoke into his combat microphone. "Kevin, get four of your team to use their rifle grenades to destroy the door to the stairs. Warn everybody that the enemy is probably going up to the first level and could come at us through our own entry hole or some other access. Move it now. Everyone get the detainees we've identified and head back to the hole."

CHAPTER TWENTY-FOUR

Twelve of the SOG troopers followed Sarah to the hole and pulled themselves back up to the first level. Fanning out they approached the two stairwell entrances and immediately came under heavy fire from the east stairwell. Two of the SOG troops went down and were pulled behind cover by the others.

This floor had been set up as a defensive floor assuming that the enemy would be coming in the traffic entrance. That mistaken assumption now worked to the Crossfire Team's advantage as the heavy weapons were fixed to fire in that direction.

Sarah directed the team's rifle fire towards the men spilling out of the stairwell on the east. It became a skirmish with as much danger from the ricochets as from the initial rounds because almost everything was concrete. Bill Sanders slid off to the right side and caught the defenders with their guard down. One 40mm grenade and twenty rounds later the garage floor to the east stairwell was theirs. The sapper or explosives man on the team primed a C4 charge. Bill opened the stairwell door and fired a whole magazine into the opening. He knocked down two men headed up the stairs their way. Chuck Noctal threw the charge into the stairwell and Bill slammed the door. Both men ran to the sides yelling, "Fire in the hole!"

The C4 exploded and the entire door and its metal frame flew down the garage and destroyed a new Rolls Royce car. The explosion knocked almost everyone down and destroyed the stairwell down to the third level. The explosion also brought down the roof of the garage for twenty feet and tons of desert sand spilled in and filled up the new hole that had once been a stairway.

Sarah headed back to the west end to repeat the performance. She wondered why they hadn't been attacked from that end. When they opened the door she saw why. The grenades on the second level had collapsed the stairwell into a huge pile of scrap metal blocking the stairwell. A rifle round slammed into the ceiling of the stairwell from the third level and Sarah jerked back and slammed the door. She radioed Mark to bring the detainees up from the second level to the garage and they would then extract everyone to the desert above.

Sarah checked on the wounded troops and found that both of them had died of the gunshots. She'd have to mourn later because they had created a situation that trapped the hundred to two hundred defensive troops in the bottom two levels but had not incapacitated them. They had to move quickly. She had the two men placed in body bags for the trip home. She said a quick prayer for both of them. Then she called Mark and asked what the delay was.

Mark's answer chilled her. "Charlie tells me that we have company upstairs. There is at least a company of soldiers and six battle tanks. The Ospreys have had to stand off. They've got us trapped."

Sarah frowned, "The guards downstairs must have had some communications line to that military base and called them as soon as we attacked. If they can make a way up to the second level we will have a firefight from both sides. We've already lost two men and I don't have an answer to this one."

Laura who had been busy identifying the detainees came up to Jack and spoke quietly to him. He looked at her and smiled, because her idea was brilliant. He walked over to where Alexis, Mark, and David were conferring. "Mark, I think Laura has the answer to our problem. He explained it to the three of them. Mark and David grinned and Alexis nodded in agreement even though she hadn't been involved in the action in Israel before.

Mark made a phone call and got the answer he wanted. He looked around with his flashlight in the darkness of the garage. He went over and took a piece of white material that was hanging haphazardly off of the destroyed Rolls. Breaking off the old-style wire antenna from the car, he fashioned a white flag. Going to the vehicle entrance he slipped by the damaged gate that had been too close to the stairwell the C4 had destroyed. He walked up the ramp holding the white flag above his head.

Coming up to the surface he couldn't count the number of Egyptian army troops that were surrounding the entrance. He had no problem seeing the tanks with their main guns pointed at him. Ignoring all of them he walked slowly towards what looked to be a command post that had been hastily set up. He had left his weapons in the garage level and was unarmed. Two soldiers came out, frisked him, and escorted him at rifle point to the Colonel in charge.

The Colonel looked at Mark with interest. Assuming him to be American by his face and battle dress he asked, in excellent English, "Have you come seeking terms of surrender?"

Mark studied the man for a few seconds and decided he was a real officer not an "appointee" who got the job because of his money or family. "Yes, I have."

The man smiled, "And you have demands or requests before you surrender?

Mark smiled back. "Most definitely. The terms of surrender are that you take your tanks and your troops and return to your base and allow my team to take the prisoners and exit your country."

The Colonel was taken aback. "You want me to surrender? Look around, we have you outnumbered and outclassed in firepower. There will be additional troops here in the next half hour to back us up. Why do you think you have the advantage to ask me to surrender?" This was asked as a tactical question with no sneering or anger in the man's demeanor.

Mark looked at his watch and said, "In about the next ten minutes you will get a phone call from your superiors telling you to do exactly what I asked."

The Colonel frowned, "Why?"

Mark took the digital camera out of his pocket and placed it in front of the Colonel on his field table. "If you'll sequence through the photos there you will see that nine of the prisoners, three leaders and six scientists, are the missing ASF terrorists that the U.S. and the rest of the civilized world has been looking for over the last two years. They were resident in that compound in your country. Your quick response to our raid proves that Egypt knew the compound existed. Right now our President is calling yours and he is still the same President that promised any country that harbored ASF members was in fact, at war with the United States. Your President will have to make a decision to allow you to stop us and go to war, immediately, with the U.S. forces in the area, or to allow us to remove these people without interdiction. I would guess that his decision will be to allow us to leave. If not, we definitely have the firepower and resources to repel your forces for the thirty minutes it will take for the first wave of U.S. Navy fighter bombers, which as of five minutes ago, are already on their way, to get here from the Med."

The Colonel sat there for a few minutes. He made a quick phone call and his tan face showed signs of concern. He looked at Mark for a few seconds and said, "You were telling the truth about the Navy aircraft, they are on the way here now. Then he handed the camera back to Mark. "How do we know that those people are really here? Those photos could have been taken at any time."

Mark shrugged, "If you or one of your representatives would like to accompany me back to the compound I will show them to you. This is a white flag truce and there will be no harm to your people."

The Colonel smiled faintly. "Very well, I will go." He gave several commands in Arabic and one of his aides followed the Colonel and Mark back down the ramp. Once in the garage the Colonel looked at the troops spread out in the dark garage. He noted that they were professional and ready to fight. He also noted the body bags laid on the concrete to one side. Mark led the two men over to the prisoners and let them examine them. The Colonel stood up and shrugged. "There can be no doubt, it is them all right."

The aide had taken some digital photos of the prisoners and turned the camera towards the Crossfire Team. David, who had been shadowing the man since he came in, reached up and covered the lens. In perfect Arabic he told the man, "To take pictures of our troops would be disrespectful and would necessitate the destruction of the camera and possibly the holder."

The Colonel looked at David noting the pistol in his hand and his obvious capability to do what he'd just said. The Colonel motioned that the aide put the camera away. He walked over and studied David for a few seconds. "You're Mossad, right?"

David smiled at the man and shook his head, "Ex-Mossad, I am part of the Crossfire Team now."

The Colonel looked around at the team and nodded, "I have heard about this team. I am glad we don't have to fight. You fight against evil in our world. Unfortunately", he waved his hand around to indicate the compound, "this evil will result in a political black eye for my country."

Looking back at Mark he made a small frown. "Like you, I believe our President will order us to stand down and let you take this vermin out of our country."

Mark looked at David and then said to the Colonel. "We have trapped a couple hundred of the mercenaries used to protect this place in the bottom two levels and I expect they will be boiling out of there in the near future. You might want to talk to them about their business on your soil."

The Colonel smiled a grim smile. "Oh yes, thank you. But aren't you going to have to bring in specialists to go over this facility?"

Mark shook the man's hand, "No, We don't want to make this an international flap. I'm sure your people can take care of the inspection quite nicely."

The Colonel and his aide shook hands all around and left. One of the Mossad personnel approached Mark. "Don't you think you're being a little hasty in providing this gold mine to the Egyptians? They won't share anything they find with you or us."

Mark slapped him on the shoulder. "Don't worry; we've already drained this place of all their research and projects. Anything we didn't get I think we can get out of the detainees. The SOG computer experts then destroyed the radio communications and research computers as well as any projects. The buried charge I put at the antenna position will destroy any possibility of future data or voice communications. This place is completely out of business."

The man looked doubtful, "How could you get all their information in the short time we've been here with the battle going on?"

Sarah had walked up to them and spoke in Hebrew. "Computers my friend, nobody keeps notes on paper any more. Our three computer experts in the SOG uplinked all of the data on Voltron's computers to our computer center in the U.S. and collected photos and samples of any physical projects. We will be sharing our findings with your people, I assure you."

Both David and Mark noticed the subtle shift in Sarah's statement from her previous way of speaking of the Mossad as "our people" to the new, "your people".

The man nodded and spoke Hebrew back, "I understand, but that had to be terabytes of information. How could you get it that quickly?"

Sensing the coy effort to get more information on them, Sarah smiled and said, "We are way ahead of them in that area. It was no problem." Actually Linda Wu had taken the satellite uplinks from Charlie on only one Cray computer and it really was only a small effort.

Mark got a call from Linda, "The tanks and troops are retreating from the area and the Ospreys have been given permission by the Egyptian government to overfly their territory, land, and take you out of there. The fleet has recalled the fighter bombers."

A workable forklift was located and used the pull the damaged door away from the auto ramp, clearing the way to the outside. The entire crew extracted up the ramp taking their prisoners, eight wounded and two dead with them. They watched the two black VTOL aircraft home in on their GPS signal and quickly settle to the ground.

They rapidly loaded the prisoners, their fallen teammates, their combat gear, and themselves. The two aircraft lifted off of the sand and quickly converted to forward flight, heading toward Israel.

Twenty minutes later a blast reverberated through the compound and the mercenary troops used ladders to climb through the hole they'd blown in the ceiling of Level 3. They then used the ladders to reach the garage level. It took over fifteen minutes for the surviving one-hundred and sixty-eight mercenaries to get assembled on the garage level. Not finding the enemy they formed up to chase them in the desert. Seething with anger they moved out quickly. Reaching the desert they used night vision gear to search for the invaders.

They were about to go searching when two spotlights lit them up like daylight. A voice in Egyptian told them to lay down their arms. When the mercenaries saw a reinforced battalion of Egyptian army troops and a dozen main battle tanks they complied. Not a shot was fired. The troops to the rear that slid back into the compound were quickly captured. No one was stupid enough to attempt to escape over the desert sands.

CHAPTER TWENTY-FIVE

As the team landed back in Israel, the military attack on the Jewish state was about to begin. The war games had ended with the majority of the forces returning to their countries. But a portion of each army turned away, met with additional forces, rearmed and refueled from pre-stocked and hidden reserves, and then assembled at a point just north of Syria's border with Israel. As the assault group formed up there were almost two thousand tanks, two thousand motorized gun and troop carriers, and nearly four hundred thousand troops all precisely controlled by Voltron and arranged in the most effective order to invade and completely destroy the Zionist state.

As they waited impatiently for the signal to go, all communication with Voltron suddenly ceased. All attempts to contact them failed. At this point Yahveh gave the officers and the troops over to their basic desires. He inflamed their pride, hardened their hearts towards cooperation, and elevated their egotism.

The leader of the troops from Syria decided that they didn't need control from Voltron. He would order the attack and lead the assault. He used the overall communications channel to command the troops. The Turkish contingent's leader told him to assume his correct place and do as he was told. The four other country groups chimed in with their demands to lead the attack. Each commander felt it was his right and demanded the others obey them.

The Syrian leader was livid with indignation that any of these mongrels would challenge his leadership. He told his front two tank groups to take out the command vehicle of the Turkish group. In every leader and most of the troops passions were high since the entire group was on the brink of attacking Israel. The other four countries saw the perfidy of the Syrians and attacked them more to protect themselves from the Syrians than to avenge the Turkish attack. The entire army fell on itself in a concerted effort to determine who would lead. There were hundreds of tanks shelling each other and the troops associated with each group.

To the Israeli and American observers it looked like the entire attacking army had gone mad. The strife escalated as one group annihilated the other or died trying to erase their fellow warriors in an insane battle to dominate.

During the battle the wind began to increase from the mountains. It started to blow sand so hard it was difficult to see who one was shooting at. The larger parts of the army began to attack themselves due to no communications and now, no vision.

As the tanks and troops decimated themselves they fought ever harder to be the sole survivor. Because that was what the battle had become. It wasn't pride or greed anymore, it was sheer survival.

In the end, the remnants of the huge army gave into the sand storm that began to blow too hard to stand up against. All through the night it blew. The next morning there was nothing to see except endless sand dunes. No sign of life existed on the plain. It was as if the attacking army created by Voltron had been erased from the face of the Earth. Out of three hundred and eighty-five thousand men there was not one survivor. Those that hadn't been killed in the battle had died in the sandstorm and were buried forever.

The news reported that a battle was supposed to have been taking place in the area but there was no sign of any combatants and all regular army units had been accounted for in all the countries involved. The press decided it was a lie the Israelis had made up to get sympathy. The intelligence and administrations of the world knew better. They had watched the satellite imagery of the formations, the battle, and the all-consuming sandstorm. It had been an object lesson in why one didn't battle against God.

The Voltron ASF members were interrogated in Israel under a joint group of CIA and Mossad investigators. Linda Wu provided the analysis of all the data that the Voltron computers had coughed up and between the two sources cross-checking each other was simple. The summation was that the ASF had almost succeeded a second time in destroying Israel and its allies. Neither public notice of the raid nor the existence of Voltron was released. Egypt cleaned up the remnants of the Voltron base and it's mercenary soldiers and buried the whole issue so that they could save face with the Americans, Israelis, and the rest of the world.

Jack and Laura, accompanied by Mark and Sarah flew to Washington, D.C. for several days of testifying before a select congressional committee. This bi-partisan committee had been created to root out the OC people in the American government and to neutralize the damage they had done.

After two days of testimony the committee declared a break over the weekend with the final day's testimony on the following Monday.

The four Crossfire Team members suddenly had a weekend to fill in the city of Washington, District of Columbia.

CHAPTER TWENTY-SIX

Seeing an advertisement for a theater five blocks from the hotel they were staying in during the committee hearings the two couples decided to act like normal people and take in a local play.

In their suite at the hotel, Jack looked at Laura and realized that he was more in love with her now than he had been when they were first married. He still felt a burning passion for her and a growing desire to always be with her. But experience had shown him the depth of her mettle and the good values she lived by. Her walk with the Lord was deepening and her obedience and her will to sacrifice was amazing. Her outer qualities matched to her inner ones. He watched as she put the finishing touches on her blonde hair in front of the mirror. He was glad to see that the bruises from the earlier bullet strikes against her body armor had faded away from her chest and abdominal area.

Laura had chosen a beautiful light lavender dress with lace at the throat and the hem. She added a diamond necklace, matching earrings, and a hair pin that matched her necklace. She was wearing matching lavender high heels and a small clutch purse of a darker shade of purple waited on the bed. Her makeup was light but highlighted her beauty. Delicately arched eyebrows above her jade-green eyes which presently seemed to be full of humor, or possibly mischief, Jack couldn't determine which.

She put down her hair brush and stood up. She looked like she had just stepped out of Vogue magazine. Her six foot height gave her a slim image even though she was full figured. She saw him smiling at her and knew, as all women know, that he was pleased with her looks. She smiled back at him.

As she straightened up the dresser she evaluated Jack. He was four inches taller than her and even at twenty-eight he was a very handsome man. His short cropped blonde hair framed a seriously intelligent face with gray-green eyes and a solid jaw line. He filled out his navy blue evening suit nicely looking very contemporary. She knew the suit hid an extremely solid body with very little body fat that moved with deliberate grace and power. He was buff without the bulges and had a precision in the way he moved any woman would have been happy to have him as her escort and Laura thanked Yahveh that she was the one.

Checking to see that he had the tickets he blew a kiss to his wife and opened the door to the hotel room. Laura had picked up a light shawl to ward off the evening's chill if necessary. They were quiet and comfortable as they rode the elevator down to the lobby. They talked about the committee hearings as they waited the ten minutes before they were joined by Mark and Sarah. Sarah was resplendent in a knee-length black satin gown and rubies. Her black hair was unadorned but beautifully styled. Her dark brown eyes looked stunning with a light sprinkling of glitter and dark eyeshadow. Her black high heels matched those of Laura's in height and made her already muscular legs look really good. Sarah weighed about 130 pounds and stood right at five foot ten inches tall and had a healthy athletic glow that attracted men. Some saw the intelligence in her eyes and quickly faded away. Other men who continued to be attracted to Sarah saw Mark and found better things to do.

Jack smiled as he realized that Mark was a good match for him at six foot two inches. At two hundred pounds he was as solid as a steel door. He was buffed up through daily exercise and his "on-the-edge" lifestyle. His build resembled Dwayne "The Rock" Johnson's body. Mark's face was rock-jawed and handsome, framed with thick black hair. His blue eyes spoke of honor and determination. He made a nice compliment for Sarah and as a couple they were as awesome in their evening dress as they were in combat.

The two couples exchanged hugs and left the hotel for the theater five blocks away. They walked slowly knowing that their play wouldn't start for almost an hour and enjoying the pleasant evening air. This break in their recent combat-filled lives almost seemed unreal. The four of them had been in non-stop, direct combat or pursuit of combat for the last three years. Laura realized as she walked carefully in her high heels that she had become accustomed to combat boots and carrying and using a large variety of weapons for so long she felt positively naked tonight.

Jack had continued to teach her both martial arts and sword fighting. Mark taught her weapons every chance they got. It suddenly dawned on her that she knew more about field stripping an M-8 than she did about the latest fashions coming down the runway.

Regardless of their dress or the casual outing tonight they were all still on guard. It had been thoroughly ingrained in their psyches for survival. As they neared the halfway point between the hotel and the theater they started to cross an alley when three young hoodlums stepped out with knives and demanded their money and jewels.

Mark stepped between the thugs and his friends, stifled a laugh and shook his head. "Why don't you boys go away before you get hurt?"

Mark would be a load for any mugger but these young hoods were high on themselves and possibly something else. The one in front said, "Look @%#!@, I said give me your money before I cut you!" He waved the knife back and forth in a menacing manner.

Jack asked Mark, "You want me to handle this so you don't mess up your suit?"

Mark thought about that and said, "I guess you could." He looked at his wife and noticed her grin. "But I think that Sarah is interested in taking care of these idiots."

The punk was getting madder by the second. These fancy-suited old folks were making fun of him in front of his friends and it really made him mad. Smooth shaven with an olive complexion Marice was the leader and the most blooded. It was even rumored that he had killed a rival gang member. He thought to himself, "These gym jocks and their urban housewives will fold like cardboard if I shove this knife in their face. Shouting, he said, "I'm telling you for the last time! Get your wallets out and. . ."Marice stopped talking and took in a deep breath. An ice cold feeling of dread came over the young punk. He started to shake and the whites of his eyes showed around the irises.

An incredible cracking and creaking noise was accompanied by a foul stench that washed over all of them as a large black demon stepped into the human dimension fifteen feet in front of the little tableau. This demon was probably the ugliest one that anyone on the team had seen. His misshapen face had a black lipped mouth full of fangs and sharp teeth. He was heavily muscled with thick gnarled limbs and obviously functional yellow claws on his feet and hands. His breath was a miasma of rotten flesh and dead things. He fixed his three red eyes on the seven people and advanced carrying a huge three-bladed ebony sword that looked incredibly sharp.

The spirit in all three of the punks quailed in such absolute fear they were frozen in place, unable to speak let alone run. One was so frightened he wet himself and didn't even notice.

Jack, Sarah, and Mark spread out facing the oncoming demon as a police car screeched to a stop behind the gruesome figure. The demon stopped in place and spun around quickly to face the two policemen that got out of their car with their handguns out demanding that the creature drop his sword. With great bounding steps, the demon quickly covered the distance to the police car, the two policemen each fired twice at the demon with no effect and then decided that survival was more important than authority and they took off running. Not wanting to lose his original prey the demon stared at the departing officers and decided not to chase them. Instead, the demon vented his anger by bashing the police car into rubble with his massive black sword. The flashing lights and siren died with the rest of the car.

Turning around, the demon bounded back toward the team. Each leap caused everyone to shake from the mass of the outlandish creature as it came down on the pavement. Laura had been praying, "Father, this is truly a monstrous beast and my heart quails at the sight of it. I believe you are with me and I will do your will." She made her choice and with a wry look on her face she handed her handbag to Sarah. As she walked toward the on-coming demon she started praying, "Yea, though I walk through the valley of the shadow of death I shall fear no evil." This time she really felt that she was in the shadow of death.

The demon brought his sword back above his right shoulder to cut the insolent woman down, gloating to himself how the others would scream and run as he destroyed her. They wouldn't get far.

On her third step the darkness of the street was shattered by a bright golden light as Laura's armor appeared along with her shield. That light was eclipsed by the hard white light that sprang from the Sword of the Word she held in her right hand at mid-guard. The esteem of Elohim was flowing from the sword blade in waves that sang praises to Yahveh.

Infuriated, the demon swung his massive blade from his right to his left with all his might at the golden image. Laura knew Yahveh had anointed her to do battle with this kind of creature. She raised her golden shield on her left arm in what looked like a useless effort to block the massive blade. The ebony blade was almost twice the size of the shield and probably weighed eighty pounds. Even though it had smashed the police car into rubble, when it hit the golden shield of faith it stopped as if it had hit a battleship. The three black blades shattered throughout their length and the demon dropped the useless handle in surprise.

Laura then swung her sword in a crosscut motion but the demon quickly stepped back so that the blade missed his midriff. She feinted to the demon's right and he jumped quickly to his left. Considering his massive frame his agility was amazing but his control wasn't anything to brag about. He smashed into the building next to the alley and crushed the brick wall inward. There were three moans from the punks. Mark stepped back and said, "I'd back up a little, you could get hurt here." But paralyzed by fear they were beyond even comprehending what Mark had said.

Laura lunged forward but the demon jumped upward and over her. Landing on its feet it spun around and attempted a viscous side kick to her back. Laura danced away from the kick. Then the demon rushed the smaller woman his feet pounding the ground and shaking everything as he made a hideous cackle-hiss noise. His big black left hand snapped out to grab Laura's hand and the hilt of the sword. She pulled her blade back so that his hand grabbed the blade itself near the hilt. He roared at the top of his lungs while he attempted to immobilize her sword as he raised his mighty right fist to smash her into the ground. Instead, he felt a burning sensation and looked down to see most of his left hand lying on the ground. The sword had sliced through it like it had been soft butter.

Howling in rage and spraying orange-gray blood in an arc, the demon pulled his injured hand away as he swung his right foot in a powerful arc in an attempt to kick the golden woman into next week. The sword flashed again and the demon fell to the ground with only one leg. The ground shook as the demon, screaming his rage and hatred tried to get back up. Laura stepped forward and with a twirl of flashing light she pulled the blade behind her and swung it in an arc over her head and down at the demon's neck. He gave a grunt and a moan as his head left his body. Then his great mass slowly dissolved into red smoke and disappeared completely.

Laura prayed her thanks to a powerful Elohim and turned around. Breathing deeply, she slowly walked back to the others as her armor and sword faded from sight. Getting her purse back from Sarah, Laura blew out a big breath and rearranged her bangs. Then she turned to the three punks still standing frozen with their knives in their shaking hands. She stepped toward them and said, softly, "Shoo!"

All three of them dropped their knives and ran screaming down the alley as fast as their legs would carry them. The demon had scared them witless but the woman with the sword of light frightened the darkness inside of them even more.

Sighing, Mark started to walk out to meet the police. "I think we may be late for the theater" as he watched the two policemen stare at the wreck of their car. Jack took Laura in his arms and hugged her. "You were great!"

As Mark talked to the police, Sarah hugged Laura and thanked her for her efforts. Laura noticed that Sarah was trying to suppress a grin and a giggle. When Laura tipped her head to one side and looked at her with a question on her face Sarah said, "You know what was interesting about this time?" As Laura shook her head Sarah laughed, "This time your golden armor included golden high heels too." Both women and Jack started laughing. It helped to dispel the pent up emotions of the last few minutes.

Mark had talked to the precinct commander on a portable radio one of the policemen had rescued from the wreckage of the cruiser. He explained the supernatural angle of the attack and suggested the commander call Gary Rhodes of the FBI in Denver to verify what he was saying. Gary had previous experience with the Crossfire Team and demons present in our world.

They still had ten minutes to make the play but it had lost its glamour after the street attack. Instead they found an upscale restaurant and had dinner. The girls decided that they would go shopping on Saturday while the guys rested and had some down time.

The next morning Jack held Laura in his arms and asked her if she would be all right going shopping. "Considering what happened the last time I am a little worried about you. The OC is not out of operation yet even though we cut the head off the snake the body is probably still in their "Kill the Crossfire Team" mode."

Laura smiled and kissed Jack on the lips. "Not to worry, we're going to be ultra sneaky and ultra careful this time."

The weekend went without incident and on Monday they finished their testimony to the committee and were congratulated on their work against this enemy of the free world.

Su Li was waiting at Ronald Reagan Airport to take them back to Denver in the Citation X. The cosmetic surgery had gone well and there was only a small bandage to remind everyone and herself that she had been shot.

CHAPTER TWENTY-SEVEN

Returning to the fortress, Laura felt she needed to seek Yahveh's guidance in a major way and began to fast and pray between workouts in the gym, in martial arts, firearms, swordplay, and spy craft. She shook her head about the two courses of her life which were so different in aim and effect yet were so intertwined. She knew the Father was love, yet he used them to stop violent people or violent groups from destroying everything and all of His children. She felt that she was supposed to love everyone but this calling was so strong. She determined it was because of His love for His children that He directed the Crossfire Team to stop His enemies. She had never, ever, felt her place in life was to deal death to anyone. But, Yahveh wanted her to fulfill the destiny He saw for her, not the one she thought she was to play. Therefore, she trained harder and became better at the art of war while praying harder to reach out in greater love.

As most thoughtful husbands would do, Jack noticed her efforts and determined to support her by joining her in her activities. During a prayer time in their bedroom suite Jack decided to get some water for them both. He got some ice and purified water in two mugs. He sat Laura's down next to her seat and turned to go to the couch at which he had been praying.

Laura noticed the water when suddenly the bedroom disappeared and she saw a beautiful landscape that contained colors and hues she liked but couldn't identify. Everything she saw was like visual happiness.

It just felt good to look at the order and the peace of the grass and trees and sky. The sky was a light blue at the horizon and tapered to a light lilac and then to a darker purple as it ascended.

Laura felt the contentment she had known when she had been wounded and healed by Yahshua previously. She analyzed the feeling. It wasn't just a physical peace and ease. It was a spiritual peace and even happiness. She looked around and found she was in a gazebo-like structure with a lacy superstructure and roof above her. She climbed to her feet and stepped out of the gazebo onto the grass. She was still in her dressing gown and barefoot and the grass felt wonderful on her skin. It was soft but supportive, almost caressing her feet.

She looked around and saw a marvelous building at a short distance. She started to walk toward it. Noticing that the light was everywhere but didn't have a source like the sun. Looking down she noticed that she didn't have a shadow in any direction. Still, everything was crystal clear, both near and far. She didn't see any people or animals, just the park-like setting and the building. Looking back she could see the delicate gazebo constructed of the purest white material she'd ever seen.

As she neared the building she noticed that she wasn't in a hurry nor was she taking her time. It was like there was no pressure to stop or go.

She reached the front porch area of the building and noticed that the flagstones were pure white marble and the door ahead of her was something like pewter in color but shiny and smooth. She reached out and pushed against the plate on the left of the two doors. The doors smoothly opened without a sound. Laura stepped into the building and was amazed all over again by the beauty of the interior. The decor was beyond description. Everything blended perfectly into the building and was made of a beautiful dark wood, the pewter-like metal, or glistening stones that could have been gems. The floor was carpeted with a plush deep-blue carpet that felt as good to her feet as the grass had. There was only two chairs to sit in, beautiful furniture, facing each other about four feet apart. They looked very comfortable. Laura walked up to one and felt the material. She couldn't identify it. It was like a mixture of suede leather and satin. She was tempted to sit but decided to explore the house, because that is what it felt like, a house that someone lived in.

After making a slow tour of the room she decided that there were no other doors or passageways out of the room. Obviously she was supposed to stay in the room. She admired the way the construction of the walls formed some form of artwork that was an integral part of the wall, without frames.

She went over to one of the chairs and sat down in it. As she sat back she felt the chair adjust itself to her weight and body shape. It wasn't uncomfortable at all. In fact, even though she was sitting down, there wasn't any pressure on her bottom or legs. The chair supported her mass at every point of contact without stressing any of them. She realized that she could sit in this chair for hours without getting tired.

She suddenly noticed an older man sitting in the other chair, watching her. He spoke in a deep and resonant bass voice that was pleasant to her ears. "Hello Laura, how are you feeling?"

Laura smiled, she felt completely at ease in the man's company. "I am very comfortable and at peace. I am wondering where I am and how I came to be here."

Smiling slightly the man nodded. "That is a normal reaction. My name is Hugo. You are here at the desire of Yahveh so that you can be offered some information concerning your walk with Him."

Laura detected a wry humor in the man's comment indicating that he knew what was going to transpire and he would enjoy the time. Laura nodded, "As His servant I am always willing to learn from my Elohim. I would have expected to see Rose or Caleb in this type of situation."

Hugo's eyes twinkled as he smiled. "They are busy working to keep the enemy off-base and unaware of our meeting. But I want you to be at ease." He tipped his head to the left and Rose appeared next to his chair. She was mainly in her gold phase with the bright white dimmed down. She looked at Laura and smiled at her. Laura thought that it was probably the first time she'd ever seen Rose so happy.

The angel floated closer to Laura. "Hi Laura, I see you've met Hugo. I'm glad that you were given this opportunity. I told you that you and Jack were headed for major increases in your conflicts. Well, those increases are offset by increases in your abilities in Yahveh. Hugo is a good source of help. He taught me millennia ago and I respect him highly. "Rose looked sharply to her left at something Laura couldn't see. "I have to go now. Learn your lessons. I will see you later." The fierce whiteness flared up as she drew her sword and disappeared.

Hugo also looked a something that Laura couldn't see. "Rose is a wonderful messenger and a very competent warrior for the Most High. I enjoyed our time together and am proud to have helped her. You are fortunate that the Lord assigned Rose to you."

Hugo focused on Laura. "I am to instruct you in some basic understanding of the spiritual realm as it relates to your world. You have been given a power by Yahveh to combat demonic forces and have acquitted yourself very well considering you are working from an earthly or human viewpoint about the forces you contend with at those times. Have you ever considered what happens to the demons you dispatch or to angels that are destroyed by the enemy?"

Laura recalled the knowledge that she had on those subjects. "I believe that angels are created beings made by Elohim to serve him. They are spirit and as I understand it, spirits cannot be killed. So, if an angel is "killed" by demonic forces I believe they would return to the Father and if a demon is "killed" then I suppose that Yahveh would consign it to the pit until the Day of Judgment."

Hugo steepled his fingers and stared at her. "From the knowledge you have those are fairly accurate descriptions. Yahveh gathers the spirits of his fallen created ones and keeps them for the Day of Judgment.

To them, just as to the humans who have fallen asleep, no time will pass before they are judged, even though many eons may have passed in your time. He looked thoughtful for a few seconds. "Like the Lord's Word says in your Scriptures, in 2 Kepha 2.4, which you may know as Peter, "For ... Elohim did not spare the messengers who sinned, but sent them to Tartaros (hell), and delivered them into chains of darkness, to be kept for judgment..." and also in Jude 4:6, "And the messengers who did not keep their own principality, but left their own dwelling, He has kept in everlasting shackles under darkness for the judgment of the great day."

"Demonic spirits also go to what you call the pit until the Day of Judgment, but for them there is no relief. That was their master's desire that they suffer every day until the end. There is no good or compassion in Satan, remember that always."

Laura thought about that and asked, "Hugo, do the faithful and unrepentant sinners both sense no passage of time until the end?"

Hugo nodded, "That is true, because they have not yet been judged. Each man and woman has to be judged before they are declared a true believer worthy of heaven or a sinner worthy of damnation. There are special cases such as the ones under the throne crying out to Yahveh for justice. But even they do not sense the passage of time before the end."

Laura asked, "What actually is Sheol, Tartaros, or Hell? Our Scriptures define it as a place of woe, gnashing of teeth, fire and darkness."

Hugo looked through her and said quietly, "The Lake of Fire is a continual, horrifically painful place where the spirits are tormented constantly in front of the angels. While the pain is great and unending, the worse thing is the hopelessness. There is no hope that Yahveh will relieve them or release them from their torment nor that they will ever hear, know, or even sense the Most High and the Kingdom again. Yet they will always remember the love, the gentleness, the sweetness, and the beauty that they can never have again. Yahveh was all of these things unto them before they rejected Him."

Hugo determined her line of thought. "Don't focus on the truly bestial, the murderers, the vile, the haters, liars, and the demonic. They knew the choices they were making and didn't care. They know they deserve what they are getting. It's the good people, the misguided people, the well-meaning, the cheaters, and the sinners in little things that don't understand that a loving relationship has to be returned.

Yahveh doesn't want people in the Kingdom who are "hedging their bets in case He is real, or the ones that are attempting to avoid the fires of Hell. He wants people that show their love for Him and His Son during their lives. Not outwardly so that others can see their great works, but inwardly, with humility, and in thankfulness for their salvation. People who truly give their lives to Him to do as He plans for them. People that understand that the suffering and hardships they have in this life are training

131

and positioning for their life on the Earth and in the future with Him."

Laura listened to Hugo for three days. She understood many things she hadn't known about and concepts which were made crystal clear. She never once felt that she needed to move out of her chair. She also never felt sleepy. Hugo thanked her for her faithfulness and reminded her that even though much of what he revealed to her would remain hidden in her mind until needed, now that she knew more, she was responsible for more.

Laura watched Hugo, the house and everything fade into her bedroom at the fortress. She saw that the ice water was exactly like it was when her vision started. She picked it up and drank some.

Jack finished sitting down on his couch and looked at his wife. "Have you gotten anything yet?"

Laura smiled, "Oh yeah." Then she told him of her vision. She could only give him a summary of the things she'd learned. It would take more than eight years before it was all revealed.

CHAPTER TWENTY-EIGHT

A concern that had been building in the back of Jack's mind was brought out by the prayer times he was sharing with Laura. Technology Alternatives was faring well but needed guidance. Several important sales and deals had been lost because he hadn't been there. He knew what he was doing was Yahveh's will and he wasn't about to go against that. He'd gotten a direction while praying and followed up on the thought.

Sitting at the computer annex in his suite Jack brought up the files on the SOG personnel that had been interviewed for their participation in the group. One of the wounded SOG personnel was intriguing in his capabilities. Alexander Dunhill had been one of the elite SEAL team members whose background was similar to that of Jack's. His college had been in the East, at Harvard University and Stanford University but his majors had been in the fields of finance and business. Graduating Summa Cum Laude he had been offered a premier position with one of America's best financial institutions. Even though the job started as a Vice President Alex had turned it down to go into the Navy after the attack on September 11th, 2001.

He had excelled in his training and had made team leader quickly. He had a good mind and a grasp of the business world some men never understand. He was a solid believer and had been led by the Father to join the SOG. Now, because of that decision, he had a problem. Jack thought the answer to Alex's problem could also be the answer to his own concern. The bullet that had wounded Alex had been a ricochet off of a wall in the garage during the firefight. The problem was that it had hit him in the lower spine and created a problem with his legs. He'd had surgery which would put him back on his feet but the injury ended his combat career.

Jack prayed about his thoughts and then sought out Laura, Mark, and Sarah. He explained the concept he'd been given and sought their advice. After each person had given their view Jack knew it was still his choice. Thanking them he took some paperwork and headed for the garage. Taking one of the new Cadillac CTS-V 556 horsepower coupes they'd purchased and had modified by the CIA, he headed for the rehabilitation center in the Denver Tech Center where he knew Alex would be that morning.

Finding the right building took several laps of the parking lots as the buildings were all the same and the addresses were vague. Punching the arming switch on his key fob he locked the Cadillac and entered the rehab center. Speaking to the lobby receptionist he was able to find Alex working out with weights to maintain his upper body strength that morning.

Jack waited until the solidly-built young man had completed his reps and sat down to wipe off the sweat he'd built up. Alex was surprised to see him and smiled a big grin as he held out his hand. Jack shook the offered hand and sat down on a weight bench next to the one Alex was on. "How is your rehab coming along?"

Alex was obviously not a quitter. "Fine, General Malone, I've got the doctors to let me walk with just two canes now in lieu of the walker. My legs are coming back slowly but surely."

Jack smiled, "That's great Alex, and how's everything else going?"

Alex tipped his head to one side, "You know, it's hard doing a career change on such sudden notice." He brightened up. "But at least I can use my education to find a good position in a civilian job. It'll be tough transitioning but, pardon the pun, I'll land on my feet. Thank you for asking. A bunch of the guys and gals from the SOG have stopped by and as soon as I'm reasonably mobile we're going to have a farewell party in my honor."

Jack nodded, he had been aware of the visits by the team members to their wounded friend. "Have you got any hot prospects as to employment?"

Alex shook his head, "No, I wanted to wait until I was walking normally before I started interviewing. It would make a better impression. Although, I will admit it will be tough trying to match the income I was making with the SOG and your team, especially in the last few weeks."

Jack spent a few minutes determining Alex's stand on a wide variety of things and his training in management. It turned out that Alex had worked as an interim manager for a financial firm for the last three years while he was in college and had done quite well for one so young. Praying again for guidance and words, Jack made the offer he'd been considering. "Alex, I'd like to offer you a career position. It won't be a cake walk but I think you'll handle it well considering your walk with the Father and your background."

Seeing the slight frown on the man's face Jack realized that Alex had a misconception about his offer. "This offer is more for my benefit than yours. I'm not trying to make up for your injury or loss of combat status, far from it. I really need a highly competent and honorable man to help me with my company, Technology Alternatives here in Denver."

That made the soldier curious. "What would the position entail?" Jack thought to himself, "Good, he's more interested in the challenge than the salary or the position itself." Taking a paper out of his folder he handed it to Alex.

Alex sat there and reread the offer letter twice. Then he looked up at Jack with a glint in his eyes that could have been tears or possibly real interest. "I am honored that you would consider me for this position. I don't know how soon I could start, or even if my abilities will return fully. I can sense the requirements for me in this position and I honestly don't have any experience to judge my capability to fulfill it."

Jack nodded, "That's all right, I do have the experience to judge you and how you'll do. The position is one that will wait until you're ready and give you the chance to work into the full operation slowly. There is a lot to learn and I won't be able to guide you most of the time. There is a really good source available in Bob Wexler. His knowledge of processes and plant operation will take a lot of the burden off of you while you're transitioning into the job. The salary will start with your acceptance and automatically take over any insurance requirements that we haven't covered for your treatments, now and in the future."

Alex prayed for a few minutes. Jack knew the drill on this one and waited quietly for the young man to get the guidance he was seeking.

After a short while Alex looked up and smiled. "You've got yourself a Vice President, General."

Jack reached over and shook Alex's hand again. "Welcome aboard. Since this is a civilian position you can call me Jack, okay?"

Alex nodded, "Okay Jack, I figure I'll have to keep retraining my body for another five weeks and I should be fairly mobile by then. I'll let you know how it is going and if there are hitches or breakthroughs. Can you get me any information I could study before I actually start the job?"

Jack laughed, "Don't worry, I have a staff that will familiarize you with the company, our products, and the general lay of the land. I will make time to bring you up to speed on the marketing aspects of the job that I have not had the time to handle and I think has cost the company some significant contracts." Jack thought for a few seconds. "I want you to concentrate more on selling the company's capabilities for technical research and development than day-to-day operations for the first six months or so. That's the area that needs the most attention right now. You will become the most critical link between TA and the military on some of our products. It will bring your experience to the foreground and ease the interfacing with the various military purchasing departments. As you get into the operation you will also get the delightful opportunity to travel to Washington, D.C. to explain our offerings to various congressional and Pentagon groups."

Alex grinned, "Worse than fighting hand-to-hand in Africa, right?"

Jack nodded, "It can be, but it is important that you learn to educate those people as to how their vested interests will be served by working with our company."

Alex sat back and thought for a few seconds. Sitting upright he asked, "Jack, what if I have ideas or concepts I think will help the company? Do I run them by you or implement them?"

Jack had to reign the enthusiasm in somewhat. "At first, you need to present them to me so that I can use my knowledge and experience to see if the idea is sound. As you develop a successful track record I'll be putting more of the responsibility for these concepts on your shoulders.

Eventually I expect you'll be able to pretty well run the show. I know how enthusiastic a person can be to change the world for the better and I like the energy. I want to help you avoid pitfalls that I've seen in the past if possible. That said, don't expect every idea you have to be acceptable. There will be trial and error as you grow. I expect that and look forward to any good ideas you have. You're an intelligent person and if you'll pray about things I think you'll stay on the right path. I do want you to ensure that the other managers and employees are taken care of as they are the lifeblood of the company."

Alex nodded, "Fair enough. I really appreciate the chance and I will make the best of it." He started to stand up and Jack saw the pain lance through his body and reflect on his face.

Jack stood up and offered Alex both of his hands, "Here, lean on me."

Together they got Alex up and moving on his canes. They reached the door to the shower and Alex made a turn towards Jack. He smiled at him. "This could prove to be an exciting challenge. I look forward to working with you. Thank you again."

Jack smiled and shook his head. "Don't worry Alex, you'll earn the big salary if you do the job right. Since the Father already told me you would, it's a given. Take care and I'll get together with you when you're ready. Thank you for accepting the challenge."

Jack realized the effort it would take to bring Alex up to speed on TA while he was running the Crossfire operation. But, it was what Yahveh wanted and therefore the time and effort would be there.

CHAPTER TWENTY-NINE

Rose met Caleb in the air, high over Colorado. "I fear for them this time. There are forces aligned that could cost them everything."

Caleb smiled, "Stand firm Rose, I have a feeling we will see the true faith of these people shine forth. Yahveh needs them now and, I believe they will be obedient and do what is needed."

Rose looked downward at the Fortress. "I know, but the cost is so great. Can human spirits stand the test?"

Caleb nodded, "I believe so."

An interdimensional distance far away from the two angels, the major demon urged his lesser demons to new heights of fervor as they prepared to destroy the entire world of the hated humans. "See that the humans are fully versed in how to perform the ceremony. I don't want any slip-ups. This is an opportunity with more potential than any we've had for centuries."

Later, the major demon visited the pristine lab and gave the project leader a brilliant idea. The concept was so well thought out Gregory Tolovich couldn't believe he'd just thought of it. The demon was subtle in his prompting and leading. Gregory picked up the telephone and called his political backer in Moscow. The demon whispered in the man's ear, describing exactly what he needed and where to get it.

The backer, whose name was Ivan, sensed that Gregory Tolovich had lost his mind, but a quickly planted thought made Ivan think, "it was such a brilliant mind it probably seemed strange to anyone without the mental capacity of Gregory Tolovich. The backer made arrangements and personally travelled to the back-alley book store. Paying an enormous sum of precious American dollars he was able to acquire all three books.

What the demon knew, was that the previous two dozen customers that attempted to purchase the books had been denied, rerouted to various dead ends, and several had lost their lives in the attempt. For this buyer it was very easy, because it served the demon's interest.

Ivan boarded an AeroFlot airliner and eighteen hours later he handed the texts to the project leader at the lobby of the lab. Ivan knew that even though he supported the facility his security clearance wasn't sufficient for him to enter it.

Gregory Tolovich scurried back to his lab, triple-locked the access door and called his two assistants to the floor. He handed a tome to each man and took the primary one himself. This would be a great day for Mother Russia. They would finally have the power to dominate the American forces and all the other so-called Western powers. Russia would rise to its proper supremacy in the world. The time had come. Ivan walked over and turned on the energy field powered by the main nuclear power plant. A stasis field formed in the air over the floor of the lab, directly over the arcane symbol painted on the floor.

Having practiced the requirements several times they were ready. The distortion in the air over the floor was clear as crystal. He opened the ancient text and began to read preselected passages. His two assistants added the information from their texts on cue. The field began to darken as he read and was energized with a wondrous power that filled him with satisfaction and awe. The power emanating from the field grew steadily until he reached the final verse. Reading with a powerful voice the project leader was rewarded with the opening of a twenty foot wide and twelve feet high interdimensional rift firmly supported by the nuclear powered field.

His satisfaction and glory at providing a new and ultimate weapon for Russia turned to ashes in his mouth as demonic forces began to pour out of the rift. Frightened now, he turned to shut off the power to the field when a particularly gruesome demon stepped into his way.

Reaching out with a clawed fist the demon grabbed the scientist by the arm. The scientist knew then that he had birthed a horror on the world that would never end.

He watched helplessly as the other two men died from the claws of a single demon. He thought he would pass out from the sheer horror of what he was seeing. Hundreds of demons continued to fly, crawl, or walk out of the rift into the building. Brushing aside the locked door to the outside, the demons quickly went through the building and killed every human being they found, from the highest director to the lowest maintenance man, with the exception of the scientist.

The demon dragged him along and he watched sadly as the multitude of demons flowed out of the building and into the other three buildings they continued the slaughter until the site was populated only by the demonic forces and him. Then they brought more of their type out of the rift and began to move out from the plant site in all directions.

Compelled to follow along with one of the demon raiding parties the scientist saw that every living thing they touched died, usually horribly. The scarce plant life withered and any animals that were there died also. As they came to little villages and towns they left nothing but bodies in their wake. The demon holding him finally spoke in hissing words.

"Thanks to you we cannot be defeated"

The demon has specific orders to keep the man alive because he was linked to the rift by the spells he had spoken. If he died, so would the interdimensional rift, or more likely, their ability to use it.

Their elimination of the human race had begun.

CHAPTER THIRTY

When the Crossfire Team had captured the leaders and destroyed the control headquarters of Voltron; the Omicron Cartel lost its leadership. Due to the multinational hue and cry over their revealed operations Omicron was being beset on all sides and had lost their ability to function. The financial chaos they were in did not look to have an end. The lawsuits for violations of governmental, corporate, and personal rights were growing by the day as many countries sought reparations for OC's nefarious activities. The witch hunt was on by everyone and Omicron Cartel people and their, once powerful, influence was being eliminated from governments all over the world. OC had been officially labeled a "terroristic organization" and the name became a curse. Groups that previously supported the organization tripped over each other in attempting to be the first to deny any association with OC and to demand their elimination.

As the Crossfire Team's involvement with Voltron and OC wound down, there were no crises or emergencies that needed their attention for the time being.

Laura got her desire for a stand-down. The SOG members returned to their group and the rest of the team tended to personal matters that had piled up during their campaign against Voltron and OC.

David, Alexis, Sarah, and Mark went to Israel to see old friends and make new ones. The Mossad offered David his old job back but he declined the offer. Instead he agreed to act as a consultant to them if they needed his help and his activities for the Crossfire Team didn't prevent it.

Aaron and Judah decided to tour some of the U.S. and get a flavor for the country rather than return with David. Their first destination was New York City and the northeast cities such as Boston. Su Li joined Charlie and Linda Wu for an Asian vacation that excluded China.

Laura oversaw a thorough house cleaning at the fortress while Jack made sure the provisions and necessities were restocked and replaced. His duties also included the stubborn pool filter that would not work part of the time.

After that was done, Jack and Laura took time off for themselves. They flew to Texas to see Laura's older brother and to develop some corporate connections for Jack's company. After three days they rented a motor home and drove down to the Gulf of Mexico and spent two weeks doing nothing but enjoying the beaches, the sun, and mostly, their time with each other.

Sitting on a beautiful beach in the warm early fall days, Jack finished the last novel he'd brought with him. He closed the book and looked at Laura lying on her stomach getting some more sun on her back. He knew the SPF-40 suntan lotion she had on would prevent any burn so he wasn't concerned as he saw the heat waves above her legs. Taking a last sip on his drink he looked out to the horizon over the Gulf of Mexico from a mostly deserted beach. It was after vacation time, school had started and most people had abandoned the beach for the rest of the year. The breeze had lost its warmth and was beginning to chill in the evenings. Jack realized that he had rested about as much as he could. He felt the urge to be doing something but it wasn't urgent yet, just an urge. Still he sighed deeply anyway.

Laura didn't look up but asked him, "Getting tired of relaxing?"

Jack laughed, "Yeah, you too?"

Laura sat up and brushed the sand off of her legs. "Actually, I was ready to get back to work a couple of days ago. But you were still enjoying it, so I went with that. What do you want to do?"

Jack looked around, "Well, there's not enough people here to start a football game so I guess we'd bettered turn in the mobile palace and head back to Denver."

Laura got up and shook out the towel she'd been lying on. "Okay, move it buster." Jack drove the motor home north until they reached the Ft. Worth dealership around nine p.m.

They turned in the motor home and caught a cab to DFW. The next morning they caught an early flight and arrived at the Denver International Airport before noon.

Picking up the Escalade they'd left there they drove back to the fortress.

Jack was looking through the mail that had piled up in the last three weeks. He extracted an envelope from his banker and read the contents.

Laura saw him studying the thick package of paper and asked him what was up.

Jack looked at her. "Well, our personal worth just exceeded two hundred million dollars and I have no idea how to spend that much money."

Laura smiled as she put a set of dishes in the dish washer, "Why don't you ask Yahshua what he wants us to do with it?"

Jack was about to answer when his cell phone chirped. Answering it he heard a familiar voice. "Jack, this is General Miles, I can't get in touch with Mark, do you know where he is?"

Jack thought for a second. "He's in Israel with Alexis, Sarah, and David. I don't know why you can't reach him except that he's on vacation and may not want to answer the phone."

"That's not like Mark. Could you see if you can reach him and have him give me a call immediately?"

Jack heard the seriousness of the General's tone. "Yes Sir, I will. Can you tell me what the problem is?"

As Chairman of the Joint Chiefs of Staff Howard Miles knew that what he had could be explosive if given to the wrong person. But he had come to know Jack and Laura and trusted them. "We've got a situation in Siberia which calls for your team's special capabilities. Let me know when you can get in contact with Mark. I'll make a trip to wherever he is to save you the time coming here. I need to be very specific about the military action on this one. We could start World War Three in less time than it takes to say "I'm sorry". This is extremely urgent and potentially disastrous for a large part of the world's population. Move on this with all speed, okay?"

Jack agreed and hung up. Jack sat down and prayed for guidance. He asked specifically if the mission was one that Yahveh wanted the team to tackle. He heard Caleb's voice clearly. "This is your mission Jack. The Most High wants this abomination wiped from the face of the Earth.

Beware though; there are hidden dangers for all of you. But, whatever happens stand firm in your faith in Yahshua." That caused Jack to frown as he tried to imagine what was going on. Laura looked at his serious expression with expectancy. Jack thought for a few seconds, "Arctic weather gear, and weapons later when we get more detail." Laura nodded, got up, and headed for the armory suite.

Jack tried the numbers for Mark, Sarah, and David without success. Then he tried Alexis's number and she answered in her warm friendly voice. "Hello Jack, how are you and Laura doing?"

Jack smiled, "Hi Alexis, well, we're getting tired of resting and it looks like it's about time. Is Mark around there?"

Alexis said, "Yes, he and Sarah are in the pool right now. Do you need me to get him on his phone?"

Jack agreed and three minutes later he heard his best friend's voice. "Oy! What's up?"

"I think it's time to go back to work buddy. Howard Miles needs you to call him right now."

Mark became much more business-like. "Okay, I'll call you back after I talk to the General."

The phone chirped eight minutes later. "Jack, get Laura and Su Li and get here as quickly as possible. We'll meet with General Miles here tomorrow evening around six p.m. It's a bad situation and I'll fill you in when you're airborne. Oh yeah! Sarah and David say hi."

CHAPTER THIRTY-ONE

Laura got in contact with Su Li while Jack got their gear ready to travel. "Su Li, we need a pilot immediately, how soon can you be available?"

Su Li chuckled, "Hello to you too, Laura. Actually, I'll be at DIA in less than an hour. We're coming in on a flight from New York. I'll just get a ride to our hanger and warm up the Citation X. It should be completely ready after its air worthiness inspection and rebuild. I can preflight it and be ready to take off in a couple of hours. What's the rush?"

Laura laughed, "Sorry for being so blunt. It's urgent and we don't know the details as yet. We need to get to Israel by six p.m. local time there tomorrow. I'll call out to the hanger and have the crew there preflight the jet and get it warmed up for you. We'll bring your gear with us. Tell Charlie to kiss Linda goodbye and go with you. I think we're going to need his talents. We'll need Linda's abilities to run the ComSec operation. Vacation time is over and we're going to have to earn our pay again."

Jack went by pushing a luggage cart stacked high with the cold weather camo gear and weapons, ammo, and high-tech vision and communications gear for all of them. Laura looked around, checked the functions telltale in the kitchen. She turned off the lights and headed for the door right behind Jack.

Two hours later the militarily-modified bizjet lifted off the runway at DIA and headed east. Jack coordinated with General Miles for in-flight refueling on their high-speed dash to Israel. Su Li had been training Jack along with Sarah on flying. He went forward occasionally to spell Su Li and let her stretch her legs and take care of bathroom breaks and personal business.

The Citation X was a sweet plane that almost flew itself. Most of what Jack did was monitor fight instrumentation and radar as the aircraft was on autopilot and really didn't need his attention. But it gave Su Li time off to ease the long flight. One time she got into a conversation with Laura and left Jack alone at the controls for over an hour. Jack used the time to study the manuals and try different settings on communications, radar, stores settings, and other side issues. He let the autopilot fly the plane over the Atlantic Ocean because it was better at fuel conservation than he would be at this point in his flying lessons.

The Citation X landed at Ben Gurion Airport at three-thirty p.m. middle-eastern time the next day. Securing a military guard on the aircraft the four team members took an armored limo from the airport to the hotel the rest of the team was staying at during their vacation.

Arriving on the fifth floor of the hotel it was easy to determine what room they needed by the two U.S. Marine guards at the door. They had on full combat gear and weren't there for show. One of them kept the four team members covered while the other checked their identities.

Once they were cleared by Mark from the suite they were allowed into the room.

General Miles, a Colonel who was an aide, and a young soldier acting as a notes taker and recorder were seated in the living area with Mark, Sarah, David, and Alexis. Nodding to his team mates Jack and the others found seats.

General Miles welcomed them. "I'm glad to see you were able to get here quickly. Let's begin. The Chief of Staff signaled to his aide who was standing by an easel. The aide removed the covering sheet and displayed a thirty-six inch square blow-up of a photograph. The scene portrayed in the picture was of a bleak landscape taken by a spy satellite. There were three buildings of very large size in the middle of the picture. The scale was provided by several cars and trucks parked near one of the buildings. Jack mentally estimated that each building was a quarter of a mile long and half as wide. The buildings seemed to be identical and all were single story, at least above ground. They seemed to be made of concrete, even the roofs.

The ravaged landscape surrounding the buildings showed a grove of trees which had no leaves and the trunks and limbs were gnarled and twisted. The photograph looked like a black-and-white until one saw the color on one of the cars. It looked like a thoroughly uninviting area.

General Miles looked at the photo and shook his head. He indicated that the aide show the next picture. It was an identical shot of the three buildings except that the surrounding area was alive with tundra grasses of a muted green color, the grove of trees were in full bloom, and there were fifty or sixty vehicles in the lot with people caught moving between the buildings and the vehicles. It looked like a research facility anywhere in the north.

Howard Miles addressed the group. "This picture was taken three weeks ago by a K-11 reconnaissance satellite. The buildings are the Karestainy Development Labs for nuclear research for Russia. It was the same when it was the U.S.S.R. We've known about this facility for the last twenty years since it was built to develop advanced nuclear weapons for the Soviets."

The General got up and had the aide replace the normal photo with the ugly one. "This picture was taken at 1400 hours yesterday. As you can see the area has degraded severely. It seems that blight has started spreading out from the plant site in all directions. Everything it touches, dies. The Russians aren't talking about it because the plant was supposed to be a big secret that they never revealed in any of their treaties with us. The CIA had a team in-place to penetrate the labs in an effort to determine what they were working on. This is the message Langley got last Friday." He pushed the button on a voice recorder. The voice speaking was obviously a courageous person who was up against something they couldn't fight or handle. The fear was evident in the overtones of the man's speech. "It's moving at an incredible rate considering that it is moving out like a wave from a stone in a pond. In other words it's going in all directions at once. We're trapped between a large force of Russian military trying to evacuate the area and stay ahead of, whatever this is. We can't run because we would be caught but I don't think we have the capability to defend ourselves from this type of attack. I am watching unearthly creatures, very terrible in visage, that are moving toward us. They are killing anything and everyone in their path. Bullets don't stop them and bombs don't either. But when they reach a person that person dies and drops to the ground. I've lost two of my team to them already and that only leaves the three of us. We're going to lie doggo and see if these demons bypass us. Oh No! They're already here! Bob, look out behind you! Aieee." Then silence until a creepy hollow laughter was heard and the transmission was terminated by a click.

The General turned off the recorder. "That click was the transmitter being shut off. The significance to that is our assumption that the attacking force of demonic creatures are knowledgeable enough to know what the transmitter was and how to shut it off. That makes the enemy even more dangerous. I prayed about this and Yahveh showed me your team. I honestly don't have any other group, other than the SOG, that can battle in this realm. The ring has enlarged since this photo by another two miles in all directions. It doesn't seem to slow down as it enlarges. My best analysis is that it is being fueled by whatever is in those buildings. The Russians won't ask for help until it is far too late. That is their normal modis operandi and I don't expect it will change this time. So, if you go in there it will have to be without their permission and you may have to battle on two fronts."

Mark asked, "Why don't the Russians just bomb the buildings out of existence. That is another of their usual tactics."

The General looked gloomy. "The CIA believes that a nuclear attack on those building would only increase the power that is fueling this blight. My guess is that a conventional bombing attack would be useless and the Russians have indicated they agree with me by not bombing the site. I have a hypothesis that really concerns me. We had a coded message from a "friend" on the inside that the Russians have given birth to something that has gone horribly out of control. From what he told us I believe that they have been dabbling in the black arts in an insane attempt to increase the power of their weapons and the combination has allowed something from the demonic realm, powered by the nuclear power plant of that facility to start a program to rid the entire Earth of mankind. Whether or not that is really what's happening, I don't know."

Laura spoke up. "General, guys, we need to pray, right now, for guidance and I do mean with real heart. Okay?"

To the General's aide and the secretary/recorder soldier it looked like the entire group had lost it as the General and the team got down on their knees and Laura led them in prayer. Everyone on the team knew the stakes here and that if they didn't walk in Elohim's will they would be consumed. As Laura beseeched the Creator of the Universe for his leading, the heartfelt prayer language reached a fervent level. The aide was embarrassed that the General would involve himself in such stupidity.

As the prayer ran deeper the weight of the Almighty pressed down on them and they knew that the Father was with them. There was a sudden gust of wind that increased in volume. A bright light appeared in the room near the door and Caleb appeared in full battle dress. He was more than imposing in his true angelic form. His voice was deep, rich, and full. "I have come from Yahveh with His words for you. *"This abomination exists because of the evil in men's hearts. Seeking power over other men they have unleashed an evil far greater than their own. An ancient, hungry power that seeks the death of all men. The end of this peril lies in its creation and Yahveh's will is that you fight this evil for Him. I will be with you and so will others to defend and protect you. But it is your strength of belief and trust in Yahveh that will let you make the hard choices ahead of you. Go in faith and believe."*

Caleb had no more than stopped speaking when an explosion blew in the door and part of the front wall of the suite. The body of one of the Marines flew through the air and slammed lifelessly into a wall before falling to the carpeted floor. Caleb moved his left hand and said a word. It was a heavenly word of power that was unpronounceable in any language that Jack knew. The force of the explosion blew into the suite but was completely robbed of power after several feet into the room. The explosion simply died and everything being blown into the room at the people there simply fell to the floor.

A dozen men in hoods and armed with machine guns ran into the room through the hole created by the explosion. Firing as they came they sought to destroy the people in the room. Caleb's sword gleamed white hot and he moved, somehow faster than thought. In less time than it takes to describe it he cut down all of the attackers with his sword, before they recognized he was there.

Caleb turned back to the team as the last three men were still falling dead to the floor. "Beware, the enemy obviously knows about you and this meeting. You all need to stay in the faith, pray in the spirit, go with Yahveh's blessing." The angel faded out.

Springing to their feet the team moved out of the room with their handguns out and looking for more targets. Mark and Alexis escorted General Miles and his two attendants out of the room and back to the lobby. David had already called for military support in the event there were more of the terrorists in the area.

As they exited the hotel, Mark yelled, "Incoming!" Everyone ducked or dodged behind something solid. An RPG round slammed into the doors to the hotel scattering flaming debris and glass everywhere and killing three non-combatants. Sarah and David started shooting at a large van parked across the street. There were at least five assault rifles responding and peppering the front of the hotel and the cars parked in front of it. The whole street turned into a battleground with rounds streaking both ways.

The General noted that the blue sky belied the violence surrounding them. There were no more civilians around and the damaged lobby looked deserted. General Miles' mind reminded him of other, less violent encounters he had been in. Like the Gulf War. This time the good guys were out-gunned, out-manned, and pinned down.

CHAPTER THIRTY-TWO

Mark called to Sarah who was huddled behind a mail box that was taking an increasing number of bullet strikes. "Have you got any support in route?"

Sarah nodded and jerked back as a round chipped off a piece of metal which pelted her in the arm.

Alexis had gotten down behind a concrete wall next to the damaged entrance to the hotel and was concerned about more RPG rounds. She saw a shadowy figure in the side door of the van raising the barrel of a grenade launcher. She rested her pistol on the top of the wall and carefully squeezed off a round. Her aim was true and the bullet punched the shooter back into the van. He fired the RPG but almost straight up as he fell backwards. The grenade went over the hotel to do damage beyond.

Jack, Charlie, and Su Li had sought protection in a walled walkway to the north of the lobby when the RPG hit. Staying low enough not to be seen, Jack led them down the walkway and quickly across the street in front of the van. It was a gutsy move considering the amount of firepower coming out of the van. The other team members were returning enough fire Jack felt they could make the move without being noticed.

Once on the van's side of the street they moved to within seventy feet of the front of the van and took refuge behind an alley wall and a car.

Jack's idea was to sneak up on the van and attack the men inside.

Before he could move on the idea a door opened on the sidewalk side of the van and armed men started to deploy. All three of the team members started shooting and knocked down three and wounded one. That one lurched back into the van and slammed the door to stop any more incoming rounds.

David had been talking to the Israeli Defense Forces and was relieved to see two military vehicles bearing down on the van from both ends of the street. Although not tanks, both of these multi-wheeled personnel carriers had

151

surface-to-surface missile capability. David yelled at Jack to seek cover. The three team members scurried into the alley as a missile from the northern unit flashed past them and into the body of the van and penetrated. The entire body of the van exploded from the inside out, spilling bodies and weapons. Flaming parts of the van flew everywhere including at the front of the hotel.

There were some sporadic shots from one of the terrorists that hadn't been killed. That was answered by a burst from a minigun. At that point silence of sorts fell on the scene and the fight was over.

The team reassembled down the street from the battle scene and counted heads. Everyone was there and no one was leaking blood in any major way. They had scratches mostly. It was evident that Yahveh's hand had been on them, protecting them from all the flying projectiles and shrapnel.

David walked back to talk to the authorities while the rest of the team formed a defensive ring around General Miles and his two attendants. The aides seemed to be somewhat in shock. Jack wasn't sure that was from the combat or the appearance of Caleb. General Miles on the other hand had a gleam in his eyes and a smoking pistol in his hand. He had shared in the fighting and had relished the chance to do so. He lived up to his reputation and had obviously earned all the medals that he declined to wear on his everyday uniform.

Before he quit smiling the General asked Mark if there was any more ammunition available. Mark saw that the General had a .40 caliber H&K autoloader. He asked Sarah for an extra magazine. Sarah reached behind her and produced one. Mark passed it to the General. As he reloaded his automatic General Miles realized that he was more than impressed that Sarah was carrying at least six mag pouches on her belt under her jacket.

The amount of security units rolling into the area was almost matched by the amount of press that arrived. Not wanting to be caught in the tabloids or on the evening news, the Crossfire Team and the Washington team walked away from the action and the cameras. David caught up with them accompanied by a Colonel in the IDF who was talking into a radio.

A large black bus turned onto the side street and stopped by the group. The IDF Colonel boarded and was quickly followed by the others. The bus quickly pulled away and headed for the airport. On the bus Colonel Goldman expressed his apologies to General Miles for the attack but suggested next time that the General meet in a more secure area. He also suggested that a person of General Miles standing needed to give the IDF advance warning of his intention to be in Israel.

While this was a half-military and half-political hand-wringing rebuke it showed the Colonel's concern. This happened to be the General's area of expertise. He thanked the Colonel for his concern and the timely intervention of the IDF troops. He then explained that the covert necessity behind his trip to Israel demanded no notification because of an extreme emergency on the world scene. The attacks on himself and the team were an indication of the urgency and importance of the situation.

Even though he never told the Colonel what the emergency was he had indirectly pointed out that he was a personal emissary of the President of the United States and on an urgent covert operation. This necessitated complete cooperation by the IDF due to the working arrangements between their two nations.

The radio in the Colonel's hand gave a tone and he listened to the Hebrew coming out of the earpiece. He spoke back and looked at the General. "Sir, I'm not sure you're out of the woods yet. My men report that there are at least three more vans of the same type that attacked you at the hotel which are looking for us right now. They found this out by questioning one of the surviving terrorists."

Sarah had listened to the comments and used her cell-phone. The answers she got were gratifying. She spoke to the Colonel, "Colonel Goldman, there is a large underpass about two miles ahead. If you will get the bus driver to stop in the middle of the underpass there will be three Mossad vans waiting for us there. I suggest that you go with us and let the bus travel partway to the airport and then stop somewhere to give the driver a chance to escape."

The Colonel was aware of Sarah's background and could guess the answer, but still felt he needed to insure the safety of General Miles. "Who is going to be there?"

Sarah smiled, "The Mossad has agreed that the situation is too dicey with us all on one vehicle. If the terrorists have somehow identified this bus it would be an easy target to get us all at once."

Colonel Goldman spoke to the driver who was an IDF soldier. He nodded. Tension mounted as the seconds ticked by until they entered the underpass. There were three non-descript vans parked by the right side of the road and the bus driver pulled up behind them and opened the doors at the same time. Jack counted out the team members for each van. He wanted Sarah and Mark to go with General Miles and David to be in the second van. He and Laura took the third van. Alexis went with Jack because she spoke fluent Hebrew. The rest of the team and the Colonel split up between vans. The bus had pulled past them as they boarded the vans and was already out of the underpass.

The three vans pulled out and separated themselves from each other by allowing other traffic to get between them. They had to pull over as two IDF armored vehicles raced by with emergency lights flashing.

The Colonel pointed out the armored vehicles as protection for the bus. Jack nodded, "That's good because it will protect the driver and will look like we're still on it."

The three vans regrouped in a military enclave at the airport. David and Sarah thanked the drivers and let them leave. Entering a secure building they were able to sit down and let their guard down for the first time since the attack at the hotel.

Colonel Goldman was speaking with the General's aide. "What I don't understand is why the terrorists are attacking this group. Who are they and why are they important enough to this enemy to engender all-out street warfare in the heart of Tel Aviv?"

General Miles overheard the question and spoke up. "Colonel Goldman, I appreciate your assistance but for the present I would like to keep any information about us and our being here classified." The Colonel nodded and bid goodbye to everyone. He left the room talking on his radio asking for a pick-up.

Alexis shook her head, "Well, if the enemy has any reasonable Humint capabilities they will know where we are now."

Mark thought about that, "Not necessarily. That radio he was using was scrambled and probably working through a base-repeater which would cause its signal to be relayed and broadcast from an entirely different location.

General Miles sat back and addressed the entire team. "I've had the opportunity to research in writing, and video, every action you people have been in lately. I was really impressed. But, I assure you that today's actions, especially the spiritual ones, have brought home to me the real fight that you are involved in on a daily basis. I applaud each and every one of you. I guarantee you that the next political nay-sayer that wants our government to stop working with your team will get a chance to accompany you on assignment. That will keep them from such stupidity again."

Jack smiled, "Thank you General, I think. I'm not sure it would impress some of the officials from Washington because if they survived they would rationalize the whole thing as a put-up on the administration's part. We'll settle for your backing as Chief of Staff and your support with the President."

Mark had been thinking about their assignment. "General Miles, I think I have a contact in the Russian military that could provide us with access to the lab site. It wouldn't be official but it would keep us from fighting on two fronts as you said."

The President looked at Mark, "You are talking about General Serakov if I am correct?"

Mark nodded, "Yes Sir, he was extremely competent in the Ring-of-Fire operation."

The General nodded. "He would be an excellent choice to get you in, but I'm not sure even he could get you out once you've been inside their super-secret labs."

Mark smiled, "That's up to Yahveh."

CHAPTER THIRTY-THREE

The team moved to a Mossad safe house and discussed their new assignment. Sarah asked, "What does the comment Caleb made, "The end of this peril lies in its creation" mean to us?"

Jack answered her, "I think it means that to destroy the source we need to stop the thing that the Russians started. If the General is right then perhaps they've augmented some kind of demonic access with the nuclear power of the reactor on the grounds of the labs. So, if we can put a stop to the interface we can eliminate the peril."

Sarah looked thoughtful as she considered what that meant. Then her eyes widened and she said, "Oh! This could be tough. You do know that every person the demons are coming in contact with is being killed or simply dropping dead, right?"

Jack nodded to show he was aware of that fact. Then Sarah looked at Mark.

The military leader of the group smiled back at his wife. "Don't worry honey, we've got Laura on our side, they don't stand a chance."

Alexis was frowning as she pointed out that the CIA report said that the demons in this case were impervious to bullets and bombs but killed people anyway. Not what she'd seen before.

Laura said, "Yes, but then Caleb said that Yahveh gave us the assignment to stop it."

David sighed, "If we are going to survive this one, I think we'd bettered be one with His will." David wasn't one to be afraid or worry about the enemy but he could tell that this one would be a supreme test of his faith in Yahveh and Yahshua.

Quiet descended on the room as they all thought about what they could face in Russia. Even Laura wasn't as confident as normal.

After much soul-searching and discussion it was agreed that they needed to do as Yahveh directed, regardless of their personal fears, qualms, or concerns.

Mark, Charlie, Jack, and David drew up an outline with as much coverage and backup for an insertion team as possible given the conditions and the fact that the Russians themselves may try to interfere with the assault.

Mark made a call to General Serakov in the Russian heartland. Informed that the General was busy Mark asked his aide to have him call back as quickly as possible. To spike the General's interest he mentioned the subject involved nuclear spirits.

The phone rang within two minutes. Mark answered in Russian, "Da?"

General Serakov came to the point. "Vat do you know about atomic spirits?"

Mark nodded, "I know they're killing your countrymen and you need a solution very soon."

"You have such a solution?"

Mark sat upright in his chair. "With a little help on inserting a team I think we can solve your problem."

The silence held for almost a minute as the General thought through the problems involved in bringing in his country's major enemies into the supposedly, super-secret facility. No matter, they obviously knew about it anyway. "What do you have in mind?"

Mark smiled, "I have eight people, four for backup and four for assault. We need to get as close to the edge of the death zone as possible and then penetrate the largest of the buildings. We will then try to stop this horror before it engulfs the entire world."

Serakov asked, "How do you plan to do that?"

Mark looked across the room at Laura, "We've got a spiritual secret weapon that should do the trick. But we need to do it very soon or it will be too late."

The General mused for a few seconds. "How soon can you get your team to Anadyr on the Beringovo Sea?"

Mark thought of the distances between Israel and the northeastern Russian coast. He had to figure for a military flight to Eareckson Air Force Base on Shemya Island, Alaska, a transfer to a sea craft and time to reach the coast. "Twenty one to twenty three hours."

General Serakov chuckled quietly. "That's pretty good time from Tel Aviv. I will meet you personally when you arrive. Call me on this number when you are one hour out of port so that our forces don't, Ahh, slow you down. You can do this, all right?"

Mark was aware of the costal defenses the Russians had in place in the Siberian wilderness. "Yes, it is good, absolutely!"

Hanging up he thought for a minute. Looking up at the concerned faces he said, "General Serakov is going to facilitate our arrival and intervention in the lab problem. I don't know if he can facilitate our extraction from the site or from the country."

Jack nodded, "You mean he's reliable but his bosses may not be, right?"

Mark nodded back, "Yes, I do."

Sarah said, "Then we need some insurance. I think Charlie and Linda can provide that for us in the form of video reconnaissance while we're in the labs. What we will have should be sufficient to make our presence immaterial to their security."

Charlie smiled, "I think that Crayton will be able to decipher and analyze the operations sufficiently that imprisoning you so that you won't tell won't matter. I think the Mossad can provide us with the cameras and other spy gear to make that possible."

David spoke up. "Yes, they can, but if they do, everything you get, they'll get too and that could prove problematic to the Russians. Can't the American military services get you the gear we need before we get to Alaska?"

Mark agreed, "I'll see if it's possible." He picked up the phone while Jack called General Miles to get the priority they needed to make the trip to Russia.

CHAPTER THIRTY-FOUR

On the flight to Alaska the team worked the phones and spent time in prayer seeking Yahveh's directions and coverage for the mission.

Laura was calm and knew that regardless of the circumstances their Father would not send them unless it would serve His Kingdom. But, she also knew that did not mean that they would necessarily survive the trip in serving those goals. She was also absolutely sure that He would never leave them or abandon them. But she had this unsettling feeling of gloom concerning the situation.

Jack finished his latest phone call to arrange for their delivery to an Italian flagged cargo ship that would be less than an hour out of Anadyr when they got there. Mark and Charlie were working quickly to assemble the equipment they needed and the comm links they would use. The rest of the team was resting, sleeping, or praying in their own way. He looked over at his wife and saw the concern on her face. He got up and went over and sat down in the sling seat next to her. "What's the problem honey?"

Laura looked at Jack and felt the love she'd had with him since they'd met rise up and she broke into tears. He put his arms around her and resisted the male effort to fix the problem. He just kissed her head and held her while she cried. After some sobs and tears she sat back and dabbed her face with a Kleenex. Her eyes and nose were red from the crying and she stared evenly at Jack. "I'm a female who is subject to hormones that take over now and then. I apologize for breaking down like this. I'm just concerned I could lose you this time and I realized just how much you mean to me."

Jack studied her face for a few seconds. "We need to do what we're called to do. I've had to give up worrying about you because Yahveh is handling that for both of us. I don't know what we'll face this time and it does sound like it could be beyond our abilities. But, as you say, we serve a greater Elohim than the enemy. I love you more than my life and would ask you not to go on this one but I know you'd just quote my words back to me and anyway, you're probably our best bet with the demons we could run into. Remember that Caleb said that he and Rose would be with us too."

Heartened by his words Laura pulled him down and kissed his face. "Thank you, I needed to hear that. Let's keep our faith in Yahveh high and visible to the others."

Jack nodded and got up to see where the others had gotten to in their searches.

Mark motioned him over to the desk he was using. "I've got the weapons, comm gear, and optics that we need. A NSA team is going to meet us in Alaska with everything before we get a VTOL ride to the cargo ship.

Jack thought about the preparations and realized that they were gearing up as if it would be a normal mission. But, they had no idea what they faced this time. Their weapons and tactics had been refined against normal human targets, with the notable exception of Laura's capabilities.

This would not be like that. The demonic assault, if it was powered by nuclear power, would be unlike anything they'd faced before and he was worried by the unknown dangers to them all. He nodded at Mark and went back to his seat, swaying as the aircraft began to descend into the airfield at Eareckson Air Force Base on Shemya Island, Alaska. The small island was only four miles long by two wide and was presently being whipped by snowfall being driven by a fierce wind from the west. The pilot was good and they made the landing smoothly even though the plane was crabbing at a twenty-degree angle to offset the wind.

Climbing out of the plane the team was met with the feeling of isolation and a sense of remoteness that is unique to small islands in the cold sea. Hurrying into a hanger they shook off their new coats of snow and met with the team from the National Security Agency. They quickly took the offered weapons and electronics and with gratitude boarded a USMC Osprey VTOL inside the hanger out of the weather.

The hanger doors were opened and the tilt-rotor craft powered its way out into the wind. Using the wind it quickly rose upward off of a taxiway and began the transition to forward flight with ease. The snowstorm had abated for the moment and the team could see the deep blue of the sea which was the color of a swimming pool.

Mark and Charlie assigned the electronics to each person. The plan was for Jack, Laura, Mark, and Sarah to penetrate the perimeter of evil and hopefully the lab buildings while Charlie, David, Su Li, and Alexis manned a backup and support position just outside the area of devastation. The backup team would track the penetration team through the use of GPS tracers and radio links which Linda Wu would track via satellite from the fortress in Colorado.

As they approached the Russian coast they spotted the cargo ship making slow progress in the heavy seas. The Marine pilot of the Osprey was very careful not to hit any of the cranes situated around the ship's deck and was able to hover just above the deck so that the team could jump during the lull between waves. Everyone was ready and the exit only took fifteen seconds including all of their gear. The pilot lifted the Osprey up quickly as the ship began to climb the next wave. For a few seconds it looked like the ship was going to climb faster than the aircraft.

The pilot poured on the power and pulled backward away from the lifting ship, climbed into the cloudy skies and quickly disappeared.

The team were met by some of the crew who helped them stow the crates they had in a secure storage area. The ship was lurching from side to side as well as acting like it was on a roller coaster ride over the waves. Everyone slipped and slid across the icy deck under the gray and snowy skies. Struggling inside a cabin they shook off the weather they had accumulated and were welcomed by the Captain of the ship. He led them to a small dining area where they would wait until the ship docked at Anadyr. Mark made the call to General Serakov and everyone checked their gear and rested.

CHAPTER THIRTY-FIVE

The effects of the weather on their headway lessened as the ship moved into the lee of the Siberian coast and into the dock area of Anadyr. Another hour passed as the small freighter was assigned a dock area and tied up. The gangplank was lowered and secured and the crew struggled through the frigid air and slowly falling snowflakes down to the dock.

Acquiring the two large crates they had brought with them, the team moved to the gangplank. Jack sought out the Captain of the cargo freighter and gave him the package of funds that the NSA had provided him in Alaska. The Captain opened the package and surveyed the contents. Smiling he shook hands with Jack and headed back to his office and the safe under his bunk.

Mark and Sarah walked down the gangplank and looked at the empty dock surrounding them. Mark was about to pull out his phone when two Russian army trucks appeared and drove up to their position.

General Serakov carefully jumped out of the first truck and walked across the icy dock to shake Mark's hand. "You like our weather?"

At Mark's smile the General continued. "Don't worry, there is a lot more of it waiting on us on our trip to the site." Mark noted that the General didn't make reference to what the "site" was or contained. Mark signaled to the rest of the team who struggled down the gangplank with their gear and the crates.

Several Russian soldiers got out of the second truck and helped the team load the gear into the two trucks. The front truck had a solid body and served as a mobile command post. The General and the whole team climbed into the command post and grabbed seats as the truck lurched into motion.

Taking off his foul weather gear, General Serakov displayed a massive chest and powerful arms. Although he was in his early fifties the General was in excellent shape. He smiled at everyone and offered them coffee. Since

Russian coffee can be strong and bitter only David accepted the offer.

The pleasantries completed the Russian officer sat down and stared at the small American team. Looking at Mark he remembered their cooperation at the Arctic Circle in defeating the Master Prophets and their scheme to use stolen Russian nuclear weapons to threaten the entire world. It had been this team that had organized the defense that had defeated the Prophet's plan. The General would not underestimate the capabilities nor the dedication of these people. "Okay Mark, what is your plan to defeat this enemy?"

Mark understood his relationship with the General and didn't waste time trying to sell the Crossfire Team's ability to handle the demonic zone of death. "We want to split into an assault team and a backup team." He pointed out each person as he mentioned their names. "Jack, Laura, Sarah, and I are going to penetrate the site. David, Charlie, Su Li, and Alexis are going to man the backup position providing us with whatever surveillance we can get and stand ready to pull our tails out of the fire if it gets too dicey."

The General nodded his approval of the battle plan. "How do you plan to get to the site through this zone of death that surrounds it?

Mark knew he had to convince the General that they could do exactly that. "We are going to use fire to fight fire. General, I'm not sure of your understanding, either of the situation or of your belief system concerning this "enemy". Could you give me your thoughts and what the official position is at this time?"

The General frowned. It was not a pretty sight and many Russian officers dreaded to see that particular frown. "This situation has most of our people completely dumbfounded. As Atheists we don't believe in God or the devil. Yet, there are observable spiritual entities killing our people and dominating an important military research facility. We can't kill these things with any of the weapons we have and rest assured that we have tried to. I've lost over a hundred troops in the effort. The general opinion is that we'd probably make things worse if we used nuclear weapons against them. We are facing an enemy we don't believe in. We say they can't exist, but they do. We have run out of answers and that is why I am risking my career and my life to bring you into our country, illegally, to combat this scourge."

The General stared intently at Mark. Mark was a military man like himself and would understand what he was about to tell him. "I have used a strategy on my command structure that will keep them too busy to interfere as we tackle this problem. They aren't so dumb that they don't know I'm up to something they would never allow. But this situation is so far off their scale of understanding they will look the other way until we resolve it. I don't know what they'll do if we do end the problem. I hope you've got some miracle escape route planned. I'll probably have to go with you after what I'm doing comes to light."

Mark chuckled inside his own head as he contemplated the General's statements. If the team was able to defeat the demonic enemy the Russian's job would be to dispose of all evidence that such a thing every happened and that might include the Crossfire Team and their own General. At that point, Atheistic Russia could go back to denying that there was a spiritual world.

Mark nodded at the glower on the General's face. "General Serakov, Demetri, if it is all right for me to use your first name, I understand the unfamiliar ground you and your countrymen are on at present. I had to make a transition from the physical-only world to the understanding of the spiritual side of things myself not too long ago. The problem you face is worse than you imagine. The spiritual world is far more powerful than our puny little efforts in the real world we see and move in every day. Our advantage is that we have the creator of the universe on our side and He is against the forces that make up your present headache."

Mark studied the man in front of him for a few seconds. "I'm not going to ask you to become like us. That is a decision that is between each person and the Savior. We have submitted our lives and everything we are and have to His will. Because of that, He will protect us on our foray into the death zone and the labs. God Himself has given us the mission to stop this abomination and we are going to fight the battle without a single thought to the

164

political implications of our cooperation with your country. Our goal here is to stop this empowerment of the demonic enemy and eliminate their ability to attack all of us."

The General sat back and played with a pencil as he thought about what he had just heard. Making up his mind he sat up and stared at the team. "I am a practical soldier. I believe in what I can see. The problem here is not that I can see this "enemy" but with the belief system I've been taught my whole life. As a practicing realist I have to set aside my learned beliefs in the light of an obvious truth that doesn't align with that system. I don't know about my understanding or my believing in "God" but I will keep my mind open during this assault. Now, the one condition I will place on you and your people is that I accompany you as you penetrate the facility. Ostensibly I am doing this to lessen the threat you pose to our research. But, in reality, I am a soldier and this blight is attacking my country. I am required to fight it but don't have the tools. You, apparently do. Also, can I ask that you abstain from any active "spying" during your efforts on our behalf?"

Mark laughed, "General, I sincerely doubt that we are going to have the time or the interest in deciphering your research efforts. I think we are going to have our hands full stopping this spiritual death machine."

The General nodded, "All right then! I think I've come up with a way to expedite our entrance into the facility through the expanding death zone. There is a small-gauge railroad track that runs through the zone directly to the outer fence surrounding the facility and I believe we can utilize it to get us there with as little attention as possible."

The evening turned into night as the trucks rumbled on over the snowy roads of Siberia. At first Mark and Jack went over the plant plans the General had for the research facility. Both team members quickly realized that the LandSat and Keyhole satellite information they had on the buildings was more recent and more informative than the Russian versions. Needless to say they did not mention this fact to the General.

Several pit stops and meals later the two truck convoy came to a halt. The team had been in the command post part of the first truck with only black and white television screens of the outside world during the trip.

They had seen the large numbers of people fleeing the death zone who looked at the men in the trucks like they were walking dead going the way they were headed. The political nicety of the enclosure was that no one could see the Americans.

As they stepped out of the command post into the weather it seemed that things had gotten much worse than when they boarded the truck in Anadyr. The skies were grayer, lower, and seemed more threatening. The temperature was at least twenty degrees colder than at the coast with a blustery wind that seemed to freeze their cold weather gear and the chill seeped through into their bones. The area they were in was usually deserted but now it seemed haunted by a sickly expectation of evil. Laura didn't know how much of what she felt was her mind projecting those feelings and what part of it was real.

General Serakov pointed out a flat area to park the trucks and set up the backup. Looking to his right he pointed at a broken down vehicle about a quarter of a mile away. "That's the present border to the dead zone."

Jack couldn't tell much difference between the land beyond the vehicle and the land on this side of it. "How can you tell where the border is?"

"I can tell because the two men in that car were mine. They drove carefully, alert to any danger. Yet they died without a sound. That's why I can identify the border of the dead zone." The General seemed upset about the soldiers who died less than twelve hours before.

CHAPTER THIRTY-SIX

After setting up the backup/command center with the computer equipment from the crates they had brought with them, the reserve Crossfire Team members made contact with the fortress. Charlie ran the setup with his wife Linda back in Colorado. After they were set up they did a concentrated scan of the area between their present location and the closest building in the secret site. It was not a pretty picture. Even in such a small corridor, only fifty feet wide, there were at least eighty bodies and everything they saw was dead, plants, insects, birds, everything.

Laura looked up from the screens and looked at Jack, only to find him staring back at her. She had a foreboding that chilled her more than the air outside the truck. Shaking her head she smiled at her husband and concentrated on what they would have to do to get to the site. Due to the high probability of air-borne contamination from all the decomposing bodies they had brought combat field oxygen masks that would keep the bugs out and let them breathe. Mark had routinely packed several extra masks in the event of failures so there was one available to the General.

The Russian pointed out the little railroad track they planned to use. "I have had a small, electric tram placed here that fits this track width. It is located less than a hundred meters from this spot. I suggest we use it soon before the zone increases."

Mark had an idea. "I want to examine that car before we start for the plant. Is that all right with you Demetri?"

The General nodded and started up the road with his rifle at the ready. He and Mark moved up the track until they reached the snow-covered car. Mark wiped the snow from the driver's side window and used his combat flash light to illuminate the interior. The two men in the car had obviously been dead for a while. There were frozen blood trails down their faces. That seemed odd to Mark. He was about to open the door to check the bodies when the

General elbowed his arm. Mark looked up to see a frightful demon floating down the road directly at them.

Whispering quietly to the General, Mark told him to stand still and not fire his weapon. Mark moved slightly forward so that he was between the General and the on-coming wraith.

The demon stopped directly in front of the car and seemed confused. It sensed something but couldn't detect what it was. Mark stood still quietly praying for Yahshua's covering and mercy. Mark realized that a year ago this would have scared him half to death. Now it was simply another one of the enemy.

The demon decided that there was nothing to his sensing and faded out of sight. Mark and the General waited a full minute before moving.

The General blew out a big breath. "I really don't like those things."

Mark snorted, "Neither do I, but, it wasn't able to see us because the Father in Heaven is concealing us from it."

Mark carefully opened the door and examined both bodies. Noiselessly closing the door he indicated that they should return to the group.

When they returned the General told the group about the close approach of the demon. He ended the description with, "It isn't right that those things killed my men and didn't give them a chance!"

Mark tacked on his views. "I agree with Demetri, the men in the car died of extreme fright. At least that's my guess not having time to do an autopsy.

The General looked at the sky. "We'd bettered get started if we want to get there while there is any light at all."

No one could come up with an acceptable reason not to get started, so they donned their masks and small portable tanks and carried a large oxygen tank to the little tram. Strapping it in place they each hooked up to the big tank to save their little tanks for extra-vehicular activities. Each of the five people took a position on the flat surface of the tram and the General switched on the motor. The track had a voltage running through it and the tram used the energy to run its motors. The tram had an average speed of approximately five miles per hour and the site was over three miles away. It would take them roughly forty minutes to make it to the fence.

As the little tram moved slowly forward, the four team members were praying for the Savior's angels to cover them and hide them from the demons ahead. Laura was praying for all five of them to be so much in Yahveh's will that the enemy wouldn't want to bother them. Jack was praying that the team could accomplish what Yahveh wanted them to do in this evil situation. Mark was praying for understanding and the heavenly power to accomplish the mission. Sarah was praying that they could bring the Father's love to any who survived the slaughter in the area they were beginning to enter. General Serakov was seriously hoping that this Western religion would continue to protect him.

As the tram crossed into the "death zone" it quickly became obvious that a mighty evil was a work within this world. The grass was a sickly gray-brown and the few bushes they could see were withered and oozed a black fluid that didn't look like sap.

A hundred feet into the zone a chill invaded all of the passengers on the tram. It was already fifteen below zero to start with, but this was a spiritual chill that struck all the way to the soul. They encountered a gray, sticky mist that seemed to cling to everything and obscured sight beyond a few feet. The mists grew higher and blotted out the weak sunlight of the Siberian wilderness. It was as if they were in fog at late twilight and as the tram moved forward things would suddenly appear ahead and disappear behind them.

Mark was talking quietly to Charlie in the backup control truck. "Give me a description of what we are about to encounter. This ugly soup is so thick we hardly have time to react when something appears."

Charlie was watching the screen ahead of him with two of the Russian soldiers watching in fascination over his shoulders. The tram was visible to the satellite systems watching their progress. They would have another ninety minutes of coverage before the satellite passed out of sight. The tram was moving slowly on the narrow tracks toward the buildings about a half of a mile ahead. The GPS and locator chips were superimposed on the screen at the location of all five people.

Naturally the satellite vision couldn't see demons or anything else spiritual but it could see the natural things. Charlie keyed his mic, "You are about to encounter several bodies on the right side of the tram. There seem to be three men."

The bodies appeared out of the darkening mist. The one face they could see was frozen in death with a horrified look, eyes wide open, mouth open as if the person died screaming. The tram left the bodies behind and continued its slow progress forward.

Four hundred yards from the fence Charlie warned them at the satellite was tracking a half a dozen energy sources directly ahead of them but had no visual of what was causing them.

Several minutes went by with nothing but the mists flowing by. Suddenly forms began to appear. There were demonic forms that only resembled man in that they had a head, two arms and two legs. At least several of them had those amounts. Ugly was a useless term for these evil creatures, they went far beyond ugly. General Serakov was even more terrified by these demons and was about to raise his rifle to fire when Laura gently put her hand on his arm.

The peace and power that flooded the General's mind stunned him. The demons weren't frightening anymore. Dangerous, yes, but scaring him so bad he could not think, no.

The demons studied the tram as it slid between them but saw nothing but the mechanical device. They lost interest and moved away to seek human targets.

Laura was thanking the Father for the coverage when the tram started to pick up speed. The General leaned down to Mark and whispered, "There is a slight grade here, and it will flatten out just before we get to the fence."

Several hundred feet later the tram slowed down and resumed its normal speed. Then it started slowing down again as the fence appeared out of the mist. The little tram came to a stop several feet from the fence.

No one moved as Mark checked with Charlie to see if any more of the "energy sources" were anywhere near. Getting an all-clear the team unhooked their oxygen hoses from the big tank and went on their individual bottles.

Sarah looked at the analysis screen she had on her mini-computer. Selecting the "ALL-TEAM" position on her comm gear she announced. "The air right here is quite deadly. It is full of toxins, decomposing bodies, and radioactive particles. Try not to get a leak in your breathing gear, my friends."

Mark moved to the fence and slowly snipped a large hole in the wire with the cutters he had. The General and Mark moved the cut out section to the side and the whole team went through the hole and moved toward the nearest building. Staying near the wall they walked along until they reached the loading dock area. Everything here was covered in a slimy coating of the mist. Moving close to the entrance Mark signaled stop.

Everyone crouched behind boxes and barrels in the loading area and watched as two, even bigger, demons seemed to float out of the movable doors of the dock and come toward them.

Again the demons didn't see them and passed on into the mist. Inside the backup truck Charlie called Mark. "You got a problem buddy. There are at least a hundred or two hundred of those energy sources inside the building you're next to and many of them are near the end you're at right now. I can't see any way you can get in there without bumping into those things."

There was a loud bump as the biggest demon they'd seen yet came out onto the dock. The worse thing was that this one was looking right at them as if he could see them.

Laura prayed that Yahveh would give them the means to do his will because if the demons came at them now there was no way her little sword would stop them.

The big demon screeched something and dozens of demons flooded out onto the dock. The big demon pointed at the team and started to command the lesser demons to attack them when something even more unusual happened.

In the blink of an eye everything changed. The demons were gone, the slime was gone, the mist and the foul odor were gone. The door to the dock opened and two Russians walked out in heavy weather gear talking between themselves about something on a clipboard one of them was holding. They walked by the team, their breath fogging the air, and didn't see them. One of them climbed into the cab of a forklift and drove away towards a semitrailer truck a few hundred feet away with the other man following. The sky was gray but then it's always gray in Siberia.

Everyone looked at each other in amazement. Jack said, "Could this whole thing be an illusion that the people here have developed?"

Mark was even more puzzled, He couldn't raise Charlie or anyone at the backup truck.

Laura noticed that the miasma and icy dread they had been feeling was gone. It was cold, but it was a normal, clean, natural cold.

General Serakov looked at Sarah, "Could this all of been a nightmare of some kind?"

Mark checked his personal computer and whistled. Everyone looked at him, "What is it?" Sarah asked.

Mark shook his head. "According to this it's Wednesday afternoon, fifteen days ago."

CHAPTER THIRTY-SEVEN

At the back-up command post Charlie was startled when all the markers and GPS signals for the penetration team disappeared suddenly. He checked all of his signal equipment but it was working correctly. He spoke to Linda back in Colorado. "Babe, what happened to them? I can't spot them anywhere near the plant. Could they have gone inside and the building is cutting off the signals?"

Linda came back quickly. "No, the signals for other sources were always available even when they went into the lab buildings."

The two Russians standing next to Charlie exchanged looks. Charlie thought for a few seconds. "Linda, have Crayton do an extensive search for the signals."

Linda keyed in the request. Thirty seconds later she had an answer. But the answer didn't make sense. So she ran the program again with stricter limits. Same reply. Shaken she reverted to Charlie's Chinese name. "Zhijian! I don't understand this but Crayton has confirmed it twice. All five of their markers and their GPS signals are working as they should, and they are being shown at the lab site but instead of now they are shown as of fifteen days ago. The problem is that some of them are also showing as being in Israel at the same time."

Charlie thought very hard about that and then prayed for wisdom. He got an insight and told Linda to keep tracking both sets of signals. Taking a deep breath he asked the one Russian soldier who spoke English. "How long ago did this problem start?"

The soldier thought for a few seconds, "I think it started about two weeks ago but I only heard about it in the last week."

Charlie nodded and looked at David, Su Li, and Alexis. "Yahveh has translated them back to the beginning of this problem fifteen days ago."

David frowned, "But doesn't that mean they are alive in the world in two different places at the same time?"

Alexis's analytical brain had raced ahead of David's. "Yeah, but the key is in the fact that they are in two different places. The question we really face is this. What if they stop the blight before it began? What will happen to them, and us? If it didn't start, then we would never have travelled here. Think that one over!"

At the lab, the same thoughts were going through the team there. Having ascertained the same information that Charlie and the others had, the penetration team discerned the same problems, plus a different one.

Mark looked at General Serakov. "If this is real, then we're in Russia, at one of their most secret labs, without a leg to stand on. If they see us, and you, then we will have a fight on our hands that we may not be able to win."

Demetri was still struggling to understand their relocation into the past. His military thinking dominated his concern for his safety. "True, but it also means we have a chance to stop this terrible thing before it starts!"

Laura chuckled, "The solution to the problem is in its creation. Well, we're here at the time of creation at Yahveh's doing. So, I think He wants us to do our job and not worry about the interdimensional timing problems."

Jack asked the General, "Demetri, can you get us to the person directing the research? He could lead us to the team or group that is responsible for the demonic involvement."

The scowl on the General's face was grim. "Da, follow me!" Without another word he stood up, took off his gas mask, threw it in a trash container and started walking toward the dock doors.

Regardless of the implications and possibilities Mark decided, "What the heck, come on gang, let's make them think we are in charge." He got up and followed the Russian General. The other three fell in behind him after dumping their masks.

Busting through the dock doors the General was somewhat staggered by the heat inside the building. They had become acclimated to the frigid weather outside and the heat was a shock. Looking around Demetri found a lab worker and grabbed him by the neck. In stern Russian he told the man, "You will take me to the lab director immediately. Is that clear?"

The frightened young man nodded and led them off at a brisk pace. He climbed a flight of stairs on the wall of the dock area and opened a door to a hall. Pointing at a polished wooden door he told the General the director was in there.

The General told the man to stand guard at the door until he returned. Striding through the stairway door he made a bee-line for the Director's door followed by the other team members. Reaching the door the General turned the knob and walked into the office.

Sitting in the office was the Director and two military officers. They jumped to their feet and saluted the General as he strode across the room. Spotting the Americans with him they both grabbed for their sidearms.

Mark leveled his M8 at them and asked them to put their guns on the floor. He kicked the guns away and told them to sit down. Being very much out gunned they did as they were told.

The General stopped at the Director's desk and eyed the man for a few seconds. What he saw he didn't like. The man was a human weasel. A political brown noser who would go whichever way the wind blew.

"Which team is using this facility for unauthorized religious research? I want an answer now!" Taking his rifle he pointed at the Director's chest. "If you don't give me the correct information I will kill you and ask your second in command, are we clear on this?"

The Director blanched and almost threw up in fear. "Yes, yes, we are clear but I don't know what religious research you're referring to."

While this was transpiring, one of the officers reached into his pocket and keyed an alarm button. Suddenly a blaring horn resounded throughout the building. Seeing the motion, Sarah used a butt-stroke of her rifle to knock the man unconscious and out of his chair. Jack lowered his rifle on the other officer who raised his hands but sneered at Jack.

"You will never leave this room alive."

The General turned around and told the officer. "You will unleash a horror on our country that you can't imagine if these people can't stop this experiment! Are you so crazy that you would stop the only hope we've got?"

The officer studied the General. "These Americans have either bought your loyalty or have confused you General. We are in the right and they are the invaders. Whose side are you on?"

The General frowned one of his monumental frowns. "You are an uninformed idiot and I will see that you are broken in rank and will continue to serve in the real Siberia for the rest of your short years. The disaster I speak of is real and is about to happen. Now shut up until I can tend to you."

The man fell quiet. The General looked at Mark, "If he doesn't know which one what do we do?"

Mark had been praying and had a sudden thought. Tell him to eliminate all research not having to do with the nuclear power plant and see if there is one near completion.

Translating the information to the Director, Demetri was rewarded with an answer he could work with. "There is only one that meets those two conditions. Follow me."

Mark put up his hand, "I'd kinda check the lay of the land outside this office Demetri. The alarm has been silenced and I think that button the guy pushed has a locator on it."

The General agreed and carefully opened the door a crack. Then he shut it again. "Good guess. I think a whole platoon is out there. All crack Rangers if I'm not mistaken."

Mark nodded, "I doubt that they are going to listen to you right now and I don't think we have the firepower to make it through them. So ask the Director where his rabbit hole is."

Several minutes later the team and the Director exited an elevator on the ground floor leaving two unconscious military officers to greet the troops. Running through a mostly deserted building emptied by the alarm they came to a large doorway that was bolted closed and marked with a variety of warnings including a radiation warning. Sarah smiled, "Looks like the right place."

The Director was encouraged by the General to open the door and they entered. They were on an elevated balcony overlooking the research lab. Directly in the center of the floor space a huge pentagram was drawn and three men were reading aloud from some ancient texts.

In the center of the pentagram a mist was forming. Laura said to Jack and Mark. "Take them out, now!"

The two men lined up the shots and took them. All three men were knocked to the floor in a bloody splatter. But the mist continued to thicken and evil things could be seen moving in the mist.

Suddenly a demonic form appeared on the balcony and advanced on the little group there. The Director screamed and fainted. Laura's golden armor and sword appeared and she stood forth to do battle with the demon as she prayed. The demon swung his black sword at Laura. She parried the swipe and tried to run the demon through but it moved quickly to the side and made its own thrust which evaded Laura's blade and punched through the side of her armor. Laura's eyes widened as she crumpled to the balcony floor still holding her sword. The armor and the sword faded slowly from sight as Laura locked her gaze on Jack's eyes. Jack jumped to her side and covered her with his body as the demon raised its sword for the final blow.

Sarah was still watching the mist as it thickened and darkened. She realized this demon's attack was a delaying tactic. It was to keep them busy until the nuclear-powered interdimensional rift was complete and hordes of bullet-proof demons could come through and attack them.

Grabbing the small pack off of Mark's back she primed the ten-pound charge of C4 and threw it directly at the pentagram.

The demon screamed and threw itself off the balcony to stop the charge. Mark had flipped his M8 to full automatic and emptied the entire magazine into the demon. Because the demon had stepped into our dimension before whatever protection he would have had from the rift in the lab, the rounds tore great gaping holes in him and the demon disappeared into red smoke just as the C4 reached the mist.

Sarah yelled, "Fire in the hole!" and everyone that could throw themselves away from the edge of the balcony did that just as the C4 exploded.

The blast tore the lab to pieces and destroyed the connections to the nuclear power plant. The mist suddenly snapped into a pinpoint and disappeared completely.

A huge chunk of the balcony snapped off and fell into the fire on the floor of the lab. Jack held his wife as they fell toward the fire.

Buffeted by the chaotic forces of the blast the team held on to each other and the doorway to the hall. Dragging themselves out of the destruction of the lab they counted bodies and realized that the Director wasn't with them anymore and neither were Jack and Laura.

General Demetri Serakov shook his head to clear his hearing and struggled to his feet. Two rifle bullets slammed into his chest and blew holes out his back. Mortally injured he turned to warn the team as the Russian Rangers came running at them. Sarah took a round through the neck which robbed her of her strength and she fell to one knee. Mark had reloaded his rifle and poured a full magazine out the door at the rangers causing them to fall back. He turned and put his arm around Sarah and kissed her forehead. There was nowhere to go and no hope this time.

General Serakov fired his last rounds down the hall and turned for one last look at the valiant warriors that had given their all to save his country. He was surprised as he watched Mark and Sarah disappear before his eyes. Then the lab disappeared too.

The General sat up suddenly in his bed in his home in Moscow. His adrenaline was rushing through his body and his heart was racing. He felt his chest and didn't find any damage. He lay back down as his autonomic system realized there was no threat and the adrenaline ebbed slowly away.

The dream had been so vivid and real! He knew what he'd seen and done ever since the emergency call had pulled him from Moscow fifteen days ago. Even as the details began to fade in his mind he knew it was a warning and one he was going to listen to. He knew some good people that had talked about a supreme being and now he thought he might look them up, really soon.

He got up quickly and found a miniature digital recorder. He started with the emergency call and dictated his memories all the way until the lab disappeared before him. He was confident that it hadn't been a dream.

CHAPTER THIRTY-EIGHT

As his mortally wounded wife and the burning lab vanished Mark sank under the water in shock. Hitting the bottom of the pool he kicked his way back to the surface and looked into the wide eyes of his wife that looked paradoxically serene and panicked at the same time.

Sarah grabbed the side of the pool and tried to get her bearings. She felt her neck where the Russian bullet had sliced through her throat. She felt nothing but smooth skin. Shaking her head she noted that the Russian Siberian laboratory was gone along with the frigid temperatures of that region. The heat of the desert in Israel soaked into her cold body and added to the confusion. Seeing the same expression on Mark's face she shook her head again and pulled herself up out of the water.

Mark swam to the side of the pool and easily pulled his body out of the pool and started toweling himself off. Plopping into a lounge chair beside the pool he looked at the skyline view of Tel Aviv in the early afternoon. Gone were the icy tundra and the thin gray skies of Siberia. The deep blue skies over Israel disregarded his confusion and remained as they were.

David climbed out of the pool and grabbed a towel. Drying off he came over and sat next to Mark. Studying his friend's faces he said, "That was real you know."

Sarah pulled her towel around her. "I think so. I think it was real for then, but when we changed things by destroying the experiment in the lab, it became unreal and we were never there, really."

She hoped that didn't sound as stupid as it felt.

Mark contemplated the memories he had and smiled. "Do you think it was an obedience run?"

Sarah thought about that and prayed in her mind. "No. That was a possible future and Yahveh didn't want it to happen. Our actions just eliminated that possibility. That timeline no longer exists and that's why we are back where we were before it affected us."

Above them in their suite, Alexis's quick mind had accepted the time shift and realized that it was real yet it would never happen. She watched the conversation between her friends at poolside and knew the call from Jack wasn't coming. She sat on a bed and considered other things that had happened and couldn't be explained that were similar to this. She had been riding back from the death zone since the penetration team was no longer in there when she found herself back in the Israeli hotel room.

David decided he needed to get his memories onto some kind of electronic media before they faded away.

In a Boeing 777 flying toward Denver, the same type of thoughts were being discussed by Su Li, Charlie, and Linda.

In the Fortress, Laura staggered and almost fell. She put her hand to her side where the evil blade had penetrated her armor and felt nothing except her normal skin. She stared at the cold kitchen stove and realized she was back where she had been before the call from General Miles. She sought out a seat and collapsed into the cushions and started praying for understanding.

Jack's heart was beating fast as he clung tightly to the door frame he had been going through as if he had been clinging to his wife as the balcony in the Siberian lab was crashing downward to the floor of the lab.

Looking around at the familiar surroundings of the fortress he realized that they had done the Father's will and now had a second chance at the same time. "Weird". Jack's analytical mind didn't deny the dual time dimensions and he was confident that Yahveh could handle things like that easily. He thought back to the thoughts he'd had after seeing Laura struck down by the demon and the bomb going off. As he clung to his mortally wounded wife and they plummeted to the floor thirty feet below he had been happy that they had done what their heavenly Father had put before them. Their imminent death didn't bother him at all. He knew he would see Laura soon and there would be no more tears.

Then another thought hit him. Rose had told Laura that she would have children who would be warriors for Yahveh. "Hmmm!"

In Moscow, General Demetri Serakov was summoned before a three-member tribunal. The Commissar chairing the committee stared at him and read a charge against him. "General Serakov, you are charged with destruction of a major portion of our nuclear laboratory in Siberia."

"Many witnesses state that you and a force of Americans forced your way into the facility, killed the Director and set off a major explosion which killed at least three of the scientists working there. How do you explain this?"

The memories were still fairly fresh in Demetri's mind but he knew he could never explain time shifting, God, Satan, demons, and a nuclear-enhanced death zone because they never happened. He looked at the three men deciding his fate. "I have no idea what you're talking about. When did this happen?"

The Commissar looked at the papers in his hand, "At precisely four o'clock yesterday evening."

Demetri smiled inside but his face was stoic. "Sir, I was here in Moscow last evening and have an impeachable witness to that fact."

The older man stared at him. "And who is this "impeachable" witness that we need to believe?"

Demetri acted a little taken aback. "Why, it is you Commissar. We had coffee in your office yesterday about that time."

The Commissar nodded slowly, "Then how would you explain the witnesses to this crime against the state? Two of the injured officers in the Director's office spoke to you and one of them knew you from before. They swear that it was you."

"That is patently impossible even just considering the time of travel between here and there. I could not have travelled there and back since last evening. I suggest that it was an American imposter. Someone the CIA has created to resemble and act like me. Were the American's killed or captured by our forces there?"

The official shook his head. "No, they escaped somehow. We will continue to investigate this matter. I agree that it would have been impossible for you to be here and there at the same time. You may go."

As Demetri exited the massive building in Moscow his thoughts were turning toward a phone call he needed to make to a friend outside Russia. The omens were becoming clear and his time here was quickly coming to an end as a soldier to Mother Russia.

He remembered Mark's handshake and the look in his eyes. Demetri realized that honesty had an endearing quality that rank and power couldn't match.

CHAPTER THIRTY-NINE

Two weeks later it was a sober group that sat around the conference room table and discussed the recent non-action in Siberia.

Jack asked Charlie, "What did your computers record of the entire action?"

Charlie shrugged, "Absolutely nothing. As far as the digital and time records go, it never happened. The only knowledge of the event is what is in the minds of the nine of us. I'm including Linda and excluding General Serakov because we haven't heard from him and I don't know what he remembers."

Laura made a small face, "I think he'll remember it because we were there with him and Yahveh was blessing him with the same coverage we were being blessed with at the time."

Mark nodded, "Actually, I heard from Demetri three days after the event, or non-event, or whatever that was. He has seen the handwriting on the wall in Moscow and is interested in relocating to a safer climate and for some reason he has developed a new interest in a supreme being."

Jack thought about that. "I think Yahveh will reward him for his part in doing the Kingdom service he did in Siberia. I for one like his zeal and his military capabilities. But, he is not a believer and I don't get the leading that we need to ask him to join the Crossfire Team. At least, not now."

Mark chuckled, "Not to worry. I hooked him up with Army Intelligence and they are very interested in acquiring his knowledge and abilities. I doubt that he will be stressed to give up anything he doesn't feel he should. They have a pretty good idea of everything he's been doing and has been involved in. It will be more of a confirmation grilling than anything else. I put in a good word for him and they'll treat him as a friendly source rather than a hostile witness. Army Intelligence won't misuse him and will probably find a good fit for him in their operations. I doubt that they'll ever let him near the Russian group, more likely he'll be an advisor in other areas such as Iran and North Korea."

David raised an eyebrow at that. "I would think that it would be interesting to follow his contributions in those areas."

Sarah sighed, "I'm glad for him, but I'm still at a loss as to how to integrate this action into our history. I know what I did and what happened, at least to me. I know I was probably fatally wounded but am fine. I know that Laura and Jack were in a similar condition as well as General Serakov. Yet, here we are, sitting around the table talking about it as if it was a dream. How do you handle it?"

Laura smiled at her friend. "It's simple, really. You take it in prayer to Yahveh and ask Him to give you peace over it. It was His leading that we followed and it was His alteration of time that put us there to do His work. He can do anything as He wishes. Who are we to act as if this was an affront to us because it was outside our normal understanding and control? You gave your life to Him, trust him to show you new things always."

Laura looked at the rest of the people in the room. She realized that her "teaching" had prepared her for this type of action by opening up her understanding of reality. "Besides the four we are familiar with, Yahveh has seven dimensions that we are barely aware of as existing. The things that go on in those dimensions are so alien to our comfortable world that it is unsettling, unsure, and even scary. Still, He can give us understanding and peace about those things we don't understand because He does understand them. Our trust in Him means we don't have to understand it. We just need to walk as close to Him and His ways as possible."

Sarah sat there and stared in amazement at her best friend next to Mark in the world. Laura was right! All Sarah had to do is let go of her ego and pride at not being the one in control and trust Yahveh. She sat back and prayed for forgiveness for her pridefulness and His mercy to give her confidence in following Him. The change in her outlook was immediate and a major relief. She smiled back at Laura. "Touché!"

Laura laughed and the others joined in as the relief spread throughout the group.

Alexis let her gaze glide over the group and come to rest on David. She found him looking at her, smiling. She winked and got up out of her chair. "I'm starved; let us find something to eat."

The rest of the group joined her in attacking the kitchen and making a haphazard but hearty lunch for all of them. While they were eating a call came in from General Miles for Mark. To their credit, no one looked up in alarm or concern.

Mark answered the phone, "Yes General?"

The General was concerned but he hid it well in his conversation. Mark was becoming an expert at detecting the nuances of people's speech and their way of beating around the subject if they were less than confident. "Mark, I have a question about some things I think happened between us but now don't seem to have actually happened. Can you shed some light on this for me?"

Mark prayed for the right answer as he listened to the Chairman of the Joint Chiefs of Staff of the most powerful nation on Earth. "Yes sir, I think we can, but what I suggest we is that we do it in person rather than over the phone?"

There was a pause while the General thought of the capabilities of the alphabet organizations such as the NSA and said, "You've got a point there. I have a few days off and I've wanted to see your place there in Colorado anyway. I'll be there sometime in the next couple of days."

Mark hung up and thought about the conversation. "Okay, ladies and gentlemen, we are going to have a state visit soon. Let's see if we can coordinate our memories so that the General feels less like he's going crazy and more like a part of our group."

Jack smiled, "What's the difference? This group thrives on crazy anyway."

There was a laughing agreement with that thought and the discussions began.

CHAPTER FORTY

After General Miles had the grand tour of the fortress and the military establishments above and below it, he was ready to sit down and talk.

Looking at the members of the team he prefaced his comments with, "If there is any group on this planet that won't think I'm crazy it will probably be you people."

The discussion covered his memories of the initial warnings, meetings, and trip to Israel, including the attacks in the hotel and outside.

Mark gave him an abbreviated version of the Siberian action and their thoughts on the matter. When everyone that wanted to had shared their thoughts, the General sat back and nodded. "Then what I thought happened wasn't a dream or a fantasy of any kind?"

Jack shook his head. "No Sir. But, to anyone who had not been involved, it would certainly seem like one."

Howard Miles agreed with that assessment and he wasn't going to try to sell it to anyone. "Thank you all for standing firm in the Father and doing His will even though only a few will ever know it happened." Then he got serious again. "This matter is only half of the reason I came out here today."

He watched the team settle into a listening mode. "I have been given some research by several different heads of departments, primarily the FBI, DIA, CIA, and OCS." He smiled and tipped his head to Alexis in acknowledgement of her group.

"It seems that two of the groups you guys have exposed to the world have remnants that have gotten together with the express purpose of putting the Crossfire Team out of business for good. These are comprised of the surviving members of the OC that have escaped the dragnet and are apparently led by this person. He laid a photograph on the table of a very beautiful red head. "Her name is Raisia Ivanova, and..."

Mark held up his hand. "We've crossed blades with Raisia before and she will be a handful."

The General continued. "The Omicron Cartel and the Arab Strike Force have reached out to each other drawn by their mutual hatred of you. It appears that for the sole reason of eliminating the Crossfire Team the OC contingent is doing the planning and has resources, to the tune of forty million dollars, US. The ASF has the manpower due to major new recruiting of glory-hungry terrorists. According to the Homeland Security oversight committee, all of this money and manpower is geared expressly for the destruction of your team."

Jack asked, "Have they gotten organized and trained yet?"

The General nodded, "Oh yeah! And, they have already gotten into trouble. Spain found that out after the fact by computer identification of some of the members of this new group which calls itself "Istihla-k". The general use of the term means "death". According to our experts in the field, this is a rare naming as it expresses a singular goal rather than an ideal. You can understand the problem when a multinational, multi-cartel group is formed and named with only one task. That task is your elimination as a force."

Mark asked, "Do we have any idea where these forces are?"

The General frowned, "No, but everybody is looking for them with all their resources. The major opinion is that they are planning a strike here in the U.S. with this mountain as the likely site. After touring it, I doubt that they'll have the means to attack you here. My staff thinks they'll try to draw you out into a trap somewhere."

Sarah locked eyes with Laura and saw her understanding. Laura nodded. Sarah spoke up. "General, I think I can speak for the team in this. The more the enemy lines up their focus and aims at us the more Yahveh grants us grace and wisdom. The fact that this "Istihla-k" has been reformed with the express purpose of eliminating the Crossfire Team shows that Yahveh has restrained their assassinations and grossly destructive plans for His children that cannot fight back. If you'll pray for wisdom on this you'll see that this is His plan and we will be obedient and fight it His way. He doesn't lose."

Howard Miles did stop and pray for wisdom concerning this group he had come to respect as friends. He felt the huge black chasm below him and the tremendous forces that sought his life. It seemed hopeless as the wind over the depths tore at him. Then a small ray of light pierced the darkness and illuminated him. The peace and power that filled him made the power of the darkness diminish until it was nothing but an afterthought. There was absolutely nothing that could stop the light or the one that sent it.

He opened his eyes with a new understanding of the meaning of life. Like these people here, he too was tasked with doing Yahveh's will and had tried to walk that out. The vision he had just had convinced him that he was doing as the Father wished and that suddenly meant more to him than any rank or position ever could. It also gave him understanding of the team that he had only guessed at before. He looked at all of them. "I see", is all he said. He stood up and shook hands with each one. As he turned to go he said, "I'm counting on hearing how Yahveh takes care of this new group."

Mark saw the General back to his vehicle and his Marine escort. He came back to the room and stood there in contemplation. Looking up he smiled. "Okay gang; let's find the bad girl and her group."

CHAPTER FORTY-ONE

As her husband Stan guided their car expertly through the north-bound crush of cars on I-25 from Colorado Springs, Debbie wondered about the call from Mark asking them to come "equipped" to a meeting at the fortress. That meant bring weapons, especially her weapons. She looked into the back seat to see the two pebble-finished plastic carrying cases.

Stan was occupied with thoughts of his own while driving so Debbie let her mind recall earlier episodes in her life. A small-framed woman, she had never let size intimidate her. She had a youth and quiet beauty about her that immediately attracted men. To look at her you would have easily been led to believe that she was a young, busy housewife that had a nice home in a bedroom community and spent her time, cooking, cleaning, and taking care of her family and her home.

Truth was, Stan was much better at cooking and cleaning than she was and they shared the home duties such as laundry, dishes, and cleaning. She did have her hobbies but most people would never guess the clandestine life that was hidden in the housewife exterior.

As they passed by the weigh station at the foot of Monument Hill and started to climb up toward Denver from Castle Rock she thought about an earlier time in her life. The sky had been clear and blue then too.

-----------------------******-----------------------

The old bus labored up the unpaved road from one nameless village in South America to another. Most of the passengers were simple laborers and housewives coming back from their menial jobs or from the markets. Debbie sat alone with her big purse and watched the jungle bounce by. This was the sixth trip she was making on this particular bus.

Two weeks in the tropics had left her hair a mess and everything she had was sweat soaked or damp from the frequent rains.

As the bus neared the crest of the hill the driver brought the bus to a squealing, jarring halt just a foot from a tree lying across the road. He pulled on the big hand brake and then opened the door and he and several of the passengers got out to move the tree. They had scarcely moved the obstacle when armed men came out of the jungle and surrounded the bus. There were eight of them, rough men that had lived a hard life and had lost their jobs and homes to deforestation. Frustrated and angry they decided from now on they would take what they wanted. This particular group didn't have a name but had become feared in the area in the hills south of Asuncion in Paraguay.

Most of the people on the bus had less than a Guarani which equaled 100 Centimos on them. Debbie found it funny that while the people in the capitol spoke Spanish, most of the people in the rural areas spoke Guarani which was the name of the language as well as the name of the currency.

Debbie spoke Spanish which she had learned in high school and college as well as several trips to Mexico. She had crammed a complete course in Guarani before this trip and in the last two weeks she had plenty of time to practice it with the people she met. When the rebels, as they called themselves, demanded everyone get off the bus in their language she understood them. They threatened the driver and all the others with their rifles and knives. No one gave them trouble and no one got hurt.

As the sole American on the bus Debbie got special attention from the robbers. They took everything they could find from the locals and then the leader, a big, smelly, and overweight man, centered his attention on her. She kept quiet and tried not to seem afraid. He ripped her purse away from her and went through it. Not finding much other than a purse with ten Guarani in it, he turned to her and pawed her looking for a money belt or hidden funds. It was crude and embarrassing the way he used his hands all over her but she kept her silence and didn't resist.

Not finding any more money he ordered the other people back on the bus. Then he turned away from her to the men in the group and started debating whether to hold her for ransom or to take her back to their camp as entertainment. They left her standing there because she was unarmed and seemed totally harmless.

Picking her moment, Debbie stepped closer to the back of the leader and quickly raised her right foot and stomped on the top of his right calf just below the knee. As he fell to his knees she pulled the large knife out of his belt with her left hand and cut the strap of his assault rifle, freeing the weapon which had been hanging over his shoulder. As she grabbed the rifle in her right hand she slammed the knife into, and through the neck of the big man from his right to his left. Stepping back to avoid the spray of blood she raised the Kalashnikov rifle and rapidly started firing single shots. Before anyone could register what was happening she had killed all eight of the rebels.

It was over before any of them got a shot off. As the last man fell with a bullet in his brain, the leader fell forward with a strangled moan and didn't move. Debbie said a quick prayer of thankfulness and proceeded to pick up the rifles and stack them near the bus. She also took the handguns and knives she found.

She called two men out of the bus who quickly did as she asked. The locals on the bus couldn't believe the death and destruction she had dealt out so quickly and professionally. That didn't prevent the other people from getting out of the bus and stripping the rebels of anything of worthwhile getting their money back.

Debbie had them roll the leader's body over and she searched his pockets and the bag he had been carrying. In the bag she found what she had been tasked to find. A courier's bag with extremely sensitive papers in it. This little group had killed the courier last week and led to her assignment. The courier bag had been opened but everything was there and she doubted that they had a copier or a fax machine out here.

In fact, she doubted that the rebels had any clue to the potential damage these papers could do to the American efforts in Paraguay if they fell into the wrong hands.

Instructing the locals to load the weapons into the luggage rack of the bus she got back on and told the driver to drive the bus to the next village. He gestured to the men outside on the ground. He asked, "Aren't we going to give them a decent burial?"

Looking at him she asked, "Do you want to be here when the rest of his gang show up?"

The driver's face took on a worried look. That had not crossed his mind. He hastily shook his head and put in the clutch and shoved the bus into gear. Debbie sat down in a front seat which the two women who had been sitting there had vacated. One old woman got up in the swaying bus and came over to her. She smiled a toothless grin and said, "Thank you, you did what we could not do." Debbie smiled back at her.

As the bus lumbered on down the ridge toward the next village Debbie pulled out the satellite phone she had hidden on the bus earlier and moved over by the window to get a better signal. Making contact she asked for a ride home and named the village they were headed for.

After the bus came to a halt in the center of town, Debbie got off and walked to the large clearing at one end of the village. The passengers were quickly retrieving the rifles and other weapons and moving them out of sight in one of the dwellings. Many of the passengers were telling the towns people about what she had done and pointing her out. Debbie wasn't worried about reprisals because most of these poor people didn't like the rebels one little bit

A thunderous roar accompanied the sudden appearance of a military helicopter with Paraguayan markings on it. The helicopter caused the villagers to flee in terror. It flared out as it reached the ground and the door on the side opened. Debbie ran lightly to the aircraft and was pulled aboard by waiting arms. The door shut and the helicopter lifted off quickly and flew away from the little village.

Debbie recalled an interesting fact about the one-sided fight. When she had taken the leader's rifle she knew the weapon so well that she could tell from the weight of the rifle that it had enough rounds to take out all the rebels. She also remembered that after her last shot the slide had locked back indicating she was out of ammo. Good thing she had been a good shot. But then, the U.S. Government had spent a lot of money training her talents.

--------------------------*****--------------------------

Coming back the present she realized that they had reached the southern part of Denver on their trip and watched the city grow around her. They would be at the fortress in less than thirty minutes.

CHAPTER FORTY-TWO

After Stan and Debbie Hargrove arrived and had grabbed some seats in the expansive living area, Mark called the session to order. "As members of the Crossfire Team each of you have repeatedly put your life on the line for the things Yahveh wanted us to do."

Mark's craggy features and set jaw gave evidence to the fact that he took this new threat seriously. He looked the group over, categorizing their strengths and unique abilities.

Jack had his command of martial arts and weapons. Laura had her unique faith, grit, and Yahveh's armor and sword. Sarah was another great fighter with her years of spy craft and innate ability to understand an enemy. David was just like Sarah but with more years of experience and management in the world of espionage. Alexis who brought with her an excellent mixture of all of the talents the others had and an inside knowledge of the clandestine world. Su Li, good fighter, great pilot. Jim Grady, crafty martial arts master with guts to go around. Charlie and Linda Wu, both top spies and fighters with computer knowledge that was uncanny. Stan had years of police work and administration and a knack for investigation. Debbie was a good fighter and an excellent sniper. And, of course, himself. Well, let others judge his abilities. That made twelve companions of the highest order and twelve that lived to serve the Father of the universe. The odd thought ran through his mind from the "Lord of the Ring" series, "You shall be the Fellowship of The Ring"."

Silently praying for guidance in not only his planning but in his words he laid out his strategy for combating their renewed and united enemies.

"After analyzing the known tactics and capabilities of both of these groups we have come up with a plan to counteract their desire to destroy the team. First, we need to find them. Charlie and Linda, Sarah, Alexis, and David are tasked with that effort. The rest of us will train in everything we have time to, from nighttime HALO jumps into the ocean in Navy SEAL gear to hand-to-hand combat in preparation for meeting these forces on our timetable, not theirs.Once we locate them, and we will, I assure you, then, hopefully, we can attack them before they can set a trap or attack us. I already have your normal assignments for the order of battle but I want to make some critical detail orders for each of you so that we can finish it once and for all. Let's get started."

The Wus, Sarah, Alexis, and David headed for the elevator to the computer center to start their search for Raisia Ivanova and her troops. Entering the spacious computer center with its ceiling to floor viewports made Alexis feel like the center was on top of the mountain with an open-air atmosphere. Nothing could have been farther from the truth as ComSec, as the communications and security section was known, was buried under a half mile of granite mountain.

Charlie assigned computer consoles for each of them in a quiet section of the center and let them follow their own leads. David immediately started a world-wide security camera review from all the police and investigative groups he could access. That was almost all of them since he had done similar things before as a manager for the Mossad. Actually, he realized he had access to many more cameras than he did at the Mossad. He put Raisia's likeness into the face-matching software and let the system do the heavy lifting part of his job.

Alexis started a computer search for any references to Raisia Ivanova in any context.

Sarah tracked weapons transports over any national borders that had been detected.

Linda worked to crack the various Russian agencies that had trained Raisia and had continued to track her progress.

Charlie used the Crayton meta personality in an attempt to track Raisia since her release from a Spanish interrogation center several months before.

The efforts continued non-stop for the next six hours. Linda contacted the SOG personnel that had kitchen duty this week and had a lunch prepared and brought in so that everyone could keep working without breaking their train of thought by going to dinner.

Charlie, David, and Alexis were following clues to Raisia's whereabouts for the last sixty days and drawing closer to her present position when David grabbed the gold ring. "I've got her!" He said,

"Yesterday morning she passed a street cam in Omaha, Nebraska."

David called Mark and told him the news. Mark came up to the ComSec center and examined the photo of Raisia walking down the street with her head bare except for sunglasses.

Nodding his head he said, "Yep, that's her alright. I wonder why she wants to draw us to Omaha."

David studied the picture and thought about Mark's comment. "Rats! You're right. She's far too well trained to forgetfully walk in front of an obvious camera with little or no camouflage to hide her identity."

Mark slapped the older man on the shoulder. "She's definitely one step ahead of us at this point. So, go ahead and track her to whatever trap she wants us to rush into. It should be difficult but not impossible. She'll make sure there is enough information available to lead us to her lair."

It only took two hours to trace her from the camera to a ranch on 240th Street near Military Road, west of the city proper. Charlie did a detailed satellite scan of the three buildings and the outlying area with a variety of satellites and came up with several conclusions.

Before he could tell Mark what they were, Mark held up his hand and silenced the group crowding in to hear about their target. The counter-terrorism expert said, "Remember, this woman is very smart. Anything we find will be stage dressing for us to find. I'm fairly sure she is aware of our satellite capabilities so she will have set things up so that we see what she wants us to see." He indicated that Charlie could continue.

Charlie pointed out the first of the three buildings. "This building seems to be empty but there are sniper's nests on the top by these two turrets. There is a large vehicle in each of the other two buildings. My guess is that they are either small tanks or large personnel carriers. The scan shows roughly twenty people in and around the buildings. Between the buildings there are five concealed positions and FLIR readings are that there are two people in each one."

Mark nodded, "That is a classic suck arrangement. Your forces race to the first building and find it empty. Moving on the next two buildings you face the armed men in the ground level pits, probably machine gun emplacements, and the vehicles and men in the back buildings. Just as the forces clash, the snipers on the top of building one weigh in with precision fire to take out the leaders and rear-most forces." He stared at it for a minute. "Okay, since we know she knows we know, then it's all a sham and something altogether different. My guess is that the heat sources that FLIR is reading is mechanical heat and dummies. Probably one of the pits contains a major explosive, like a huge Claymore mine with a shaped charge, 270-degree spread and pointed backwards. There are probably cameras so that remote operators can fire individual weapons to simulate reality until we're committed and then they set off the bomb."

Jack shook his head. "So, we don't go there?"

Mark smiled, "Actually, we do. But, only two of us and in a way she may not expect. That is, assuming I can figure out a way she hasn't prepared for by then."

Jack thought for a second, "Let me make a call. I might have something that we can use."

Mark raised an eyebrow. "Oh, that would be great. I would be interested in knowing what that would be."

Jack walked away from the group for a minute as he used his cell phone. After a brief discussion he closed the phone and came back to Mark. "Come on, I want you to see something."

CHAPTER FORTY-THREE

Jack and Mark left the fortress in Jack's armored SUV and drove to the southeast section of Denver. Pulling into his Technology Alternatives Company parking area he was met with a series of concrete bunkers and two security personnel in body armor and carrying automatic weapons.

Looking at Mark he smiled, "Well, it looks like Will Conners is taking his job seriously."

Mark examined the outer defenses for the quiet Denver suburban business and was impressed. There were hidden automatic weapons positions, bunkers, and triple-layered Concertina wire on top of a dynamic steel and concrete wall surrounding the entire plant. Everything was styled and hidden so that it wasn't there to the casual eye. But it looked a lot stronger than some of the bases in Viet Nam had been.

Passing through security they drove up to the parking area only to find it covered and impassable except for two entries. Pulling into his spot marked President/CEO Jack parked the SUV and they walked up to the front entrance. Mark nudged Jack and tipped his head to indicate the smaller version of the vehicle/personnel scanning system that they had at the fortress. Mark was sure there was a Planax weapon back there too.

Once inside the building things became more familiar with the exception of the use of Viewports rather than windows in the lobby. The receptionist was glad to see them and announced them to Will Conners and Bob Wexler.

Bob Wexler was taken aback by the change in his partner's looks since he had left to run the Crossfire Team. He was still a commanding and handsome man but he had toughness about him and he had filled out in the arms and chest considerably. The fact that both he and Mark were wearing military fatigues and sidearms didn't do anything to soften the image. His handshake was firm as always but Bob noticed the calluses caused by carrying weapons and hand-to-hand combat. Still, the gleam was still in his eyes and the grin was the same.

Bob gave him and Mark a hug and told Jack he was glad to see them. Jack asked how things were going and how Dr. Clashire was doing.

Bob smiled, "Everything is ramping up and our production on the LifeCape is far exceeding our capacity. I'm glad that Victor was able to build new manufacturing facilities in Israel and Spain to meet the demand. You know the rest of it from the email reports and Dr. Clashire is ahead of schedule."

Jack asked how the new VP was doing and Bob smiled. "He's settling in and if I didn't know better, I would have thought it was you again. He's off at rehab right now and I know he'll be sorry he missed your visit."

Jack Mark and Bob headed off for the new building on the east side of the huge land area Jack had picked up for a song ten years before. Today the land values had multiplied greatly. Bob showed them up to the security entrance to the building and they worked their way in through the various identification checks and searches. Jack and Mark were required to leave their weapons at a check station manned by a flinty-eyed ex-Marine who knew his business. Jack wasn't surprised when Mark gave up three handguns and two knives.

Finally they got into the office and met Dr. Clashire. Mark was impressed with the seriousness of the man. It seemed he was on a mission and nothing else mattered to him. At six foot two inches of height the scientist matched Mark in height but weighed forty pounds lighter. It showed in the broad chest and thick arms Mark had developed. Still, Mark felt a camaraderie with the physics man.

Jack asked, "How's the project coming along?"

Dr. Clashire smiled a tight smile, "Come along and I'll show you."

They walked for several hundred yards through a long hall and exited into a large open space. Centered in the space was a squat building that radiated solidness. They went to one wall and entered the flush door. It was a massive door that slid to the side and sealed behind them. Mark estimated the wall thickness at no less than twenty feet of concrete and probably steel reinforced concrete at that. They walked the ten feet to a viewport window and stared inside the building that was inside the original building. The inner building was mostly open space roughly eight hundred feet square with dirt and various logs, bricks, and debris scattered over the surface. There was another massive wall on the far side and five viewport window sources faced them.

Dr. Clashire gestured to the enclosed space. This is our test room. As you requested I have set up a field test of the shield device for your review." He turned and picked up a microphone and spoke into it. "Sandra, please enter."

A good-looking brunette walked into the open space wearing a pair of jeans and a pull-over shirt, and flip-flops. She walked out to the space and stood there smiling. On her right hip was sort of a fanny-pack with electrical wiring and a plug on the top.

Dr. Clashire spoke into the microphone again. "Okay, run the test please."

Mark looked at Jack with a question on his face. Jack nodded back to the viewport, "Watch."

A few seconds went by and then, without warning, five Claymore mines exploded in rapid sequence with Sandra as their target. Mark was very familiar with these ball-bearing explosive devices. They could tear men to shreds at three times the distance they were from the girl. He stood there amazed as the balls all slammed into her and she never lost her smile. He watched the balls that hit her fall from her to the ground. The ones that missed her did a lot of damage to the debris around her. Then a two-pound block of C4 exploded four feet in front of the woman. The inner building shook and vibrated from the force of the explosion. When the dust cleared there wasn't a speck of dirt left in the area of the young lady but she hadn't moved. Mark felt the force of the explosion and he knew it was real. He looked at Jack, "Is that just a hologram standing there?"

Dr. Clashire watched the high-speed fans suck the sand and grit out of the air in the inner room. He then motioned for the two men to follow him. They walked around the perimeter of the room and watched Sandraas she turned to watch them. A massively thick door was released and opened and they were able to walk inside the space and over to the girl.

Mark stuck out his hand and shook hands with her. Her voice was soft and delicate. "Hello Mr. Connelly. Did you and Mr. Malone like the demonstration?"

Jack was smiling. Mark was stunned. "How did you survive those charges?"

Sandra laughed, "I just stood there. You'll have to ask Dr. Clashire about the "how" of the thing."

Before the doctor could respond, Mark said, "I want to try it myself."

Jack laughed. "You don't even know what it is but you're willing to risk your life on it?"

Mark leaned close to Jack and whispered, "Man, my pride is hurt. I can't let a little girl like this be braver than me." Then he stepped back and winked.

Jack looked at the doctor. "Have you got two of them?"

The doctor nodded and went out of the room. When he came back he had two more of the shield generators. He handed one to each of the men and then took Sandra's and put it on his own hip.

Sandra walked out of the room and the massive door shut and sealed. Dr. Clashire told both of them. "Make sure the operating switch is on and you have a green light." The doctor watched them carefully.

Both Jack and Mark pushed the only switch on the top of the generator and a small green LED lit up. Mark felt a tingling on his skin and the air had a fresher odor.

The doctor checked both of their shield generators for a green light and then checked his own unit. The doctor then raised his right hand and signaled the control room. A few seconds later another block of C4 detonated a few feet from the three men. Mark watched the blast shatter rocks near his feet but felt absolutely nothing. After the fans pulled the sand and grit out of the air, Dr.Clashire walked over to a pile of rocks that were still standing and climbed on top of them. Another massive explosion rocked the building as another block of C4 exploded directly under the doctor. Mark watched as everything under the doctor was vaporized and blown away. The doctor didn't move even after the explosion was over and the air cleared. He was essentially hovering three feet above the ground which had a nine-foot crater blown in it directly below the man. As the dust settled in the room so did the doctor. All the way down to the bottom of the crater. Then he walked to the side and climbed out. He motioned to the two men to follow him over to a concrete wall that was far enough away that it was still standing. He waved his hand again and two men came out with machine guns. They had Lexan shields to protect them from ricochets. They took a stance and fired their weapons at the three men. Bullets stuck all three of them and stopped and then fell to the floor. Jack didn't feel anything when they hit. The wall behind them was pock marked by the armor piercing rounds and some of them even went through the wall. The men ran out of ammo and stopped firing. One of them walked over to the three men and tried to stab them with a bayonet. No matter how hard he tried it didn't penetrate the shield. Then everyone left the room with the three men turning off their shield generators.

When they were seated in the Doctor's office and had some refreshments Mark finally exhaled. He felt like he had held his breath the whole time they were in the room. Taking a deep breath he looked at Jack. "Okay, I'm convinced, what was that?"

Jack laughed. "Several dozen months ago, Yahveh gave me a design for a personal device that could protect a person from any explosive force. I brought Dr. Clashire in as a partner to do the development and he has exceeded even my wildest imagination." Jack bowed his head to the doctor.

Doctor Clashire waved his hand as if to wave off the honors. "I merely did as you suggested and prayed about it. Yahveh led me step by step and this is the result. Actually my services were negligible. Any first rate scientist could have done this with the input you were given. I think my biggest contribution was believing you and Him and doing it His way.

Jack smiled, "Byron, it would not have happened any other way. Believe me when I say that you were the one He picked."

After that the doctor described in general terms the physics of what was happening. After about five minutes Mark waved his hand in the air. "I was lost in the first two sentences. Just tell me what limitations there are to the device and get me a dozen of them."

Doctor Clashire looked at Jack and gestured with his hand for Jack to field this one.

Jack looked at Mark and smiled a tight smile. "This device could revolutionize the world of war and the rest of the world at the same time. It would quickly destroy any balance of power or cause a huge new arms race to control the technology or find a way to defeat it. We were given this to use in Yahveh's service and it is not something that we can let the world know about. If the team wore these all the time it wouldn't be long before the knowledge of our invulnerability spread too far and the world, including our own government would be hounding us to give it to them. That we can't do. But, we can use it selectively and when Yahveh tells us to do it. Can you live with that?"

Mark realized that what Jack said was true. No one could be trusted with this technology, especially a government, even the U.S. Government.

Doctor Clashire shook his head. "Gentlemen, I need to tell you that the majority of the world will never control or use this development."

At Jack's frown the doctor continued. "You see, I had the physical device finished in less than two months. But it wouldn't work, even though I tried everything known to science to make it function. Exasperated and more than frustrated I finally turned to the path that Jack suggested in the first place, prayer. I realized all my scientific training and my experience weren't enough to make this work and that I needed a higher power than myself. Once I had become humble enough to realize how insignificant I was, and how great the Father is, things fell into place. He showed me that only a true believer in His Son, Yahshua, could use the device. If you don't have Yahveh's spirit in you and faithfully follow Yahveh's prototype, Yahshua, the shield generator is nothing but a bunch of wires and circuit boards.

That caused a silence to fall in the room for a while. Then Mark smiled and asked Jack, "Could this be the reason the Christians remaining on Earth during the Tribulations won't be hurt or killed?"

Jack just pointed upward. "Ask Him"

CHAPTER FORTY-FOUR

Mark's eyebrows rose. Turning back to the doctor he asked, "You mean that it was our faith in Yahshua that allowed us to survive those explosions and other attacks?"

The doctor nodded.

Jack laughed a hearty laugh. "Now, I understand how He could give us such a device. The enemies of Yahveh will never get it to work. Only the faithful can use it. Wow! I continue to underestimate Him. If you are not truly doing His will and His work it won't help you. If you are, then you're doing His Kingdom work. How perfect is that as a solution." He looked at Mark, "Even if you are a believer but decide to take revenge on someone this thing won't help you do it. Or, if you think you know better than Elohim and set out to do His work your way, same thing. I can't wait to tell the troops about this."

Mark was still stunned by the realization that he really did have enough faith to make the thing work for him. Then he realized that it worked for him not because of his faith but rather it worked because Yahveh had enough faith in Mark's walk to allow it. He grinned. "I think I see the application you had in mind for Raisia's Omaha site."

Jack nodded, "Although I never expected it to be ready on a personal level, I thought it might be functional in something a car could carry, but each of us?"

Doctor Clashire smiled something Jack had never seen him do before. "I assure you that the size is not important. It's the power behind it that provides the protection. All of the energy in the universe is under His control and He has simply given us a way to redirect certain orders of that power. I hope this "Raisia" isn't too beautiful. I wouldn't want to have impure thoughts about the time a bomb goes off."

The two warriors looked at each other and grinned. Mark said, "Not to worry doctor, she is only a snake in a woman's skin. Nothing to be interested in no matter how sexy she acts. Deadly, deadly, and not nice about it either."

The doctor sighed, "Well Jack, it seems my work here is almost completed."

Jack prayed for an answer and then grinned. "No, Byron, I'm afraid not. Your real work is just beginning. Pray about what Yahveh wants you to develop next. I think you'll be asking for new funding soon."

Dr. Clashire smiled and looked absolutely happy at the thought.

After taking their farewells, Jack and Mark headed back to the fortress with two of the shield generators and a promise of ten more in the next sixty days.

Once back at the Fortress, they told the assembled team what had happened and what it meant for their operations. Two by two the rest of the team tried on the generators and got green lights. There were a number of very grateful prayers said silently as the little green LEDs lit up confirming the faith of the wearer.

Later, after dinner, Jack, Laura, Mark, and Sarah were relaxing over coffee and discussing their response to Raisia's trap. Jack had been thinking and voiced his conclusions. "You guys know that these generators can only protect the wearer. We will still have to do everything we can to protect the innocents around us in a combat situation."

Mark nodded, "I have the feeling that if we, and I'm talking to myself in particular, get big-headed about our new toy then it won't work for us. So, really nothing has changed except our ability to do Yahveh's work as He directs us to do it in some very specialized areas."

Sarah chuckled, "So, if the green light goes out, stop. Sort of like a traffic signal, huh?"

That got a lot of smiles and some dry laughter.

The four of them finished their plans and packed their tools of the trade into the SUV for the trip to DIA to meet Su Li and the Citation X for the trip to Omaha.

Three hours later in a rented SUV they approached their target in the pre-dawn hour of two a.m.

All was quiet as it would be in rural Nebraska at that hour. The air was heavy with moisture from an evening rainstorm and the ground was muddy.

Jack and Mark strapped on the shield generators and checked for green lights. They had on the camera/audio units they had developed based on the ones the Mossad had provided them back in Tel Aviv. This allowed Laura and Sarah to monitor events as the men moved through them. Sarah's laptop gave a good color rendition of what was seen by Mark's camera perched over his left shoulder. Everything was being relayed to the fortress and Charlie was recording. They approached the buildings from the front rather than sneaking in from the back. Jack watched the front building and the three buildings in a U-shaped arrangement, behind and on either side of the front building, for any signs of enemy action. Mark was concentrating, for the first time, on what Yahveh wanted him to see.

As they skirted the front building, the darkness was shattered by a series of bright floodlights that lit up the area between the four buildings. Caught in the glare the two men waited until their eyes adjusted before continuing on into the trap.

The first rounds were almost tentative in nature, impacting on the shields with no effect. Then, a maelstrom of gunfire erupted and everything around the two men was shredded and re-shredded. Mark took aim at the blinking muzzle flashes and returned the fire. Some of the weapons were silenced by his shots and then they all fell silent. Most of the floodlights went out leaving only one small one on and that one illuminated a small stone column standing in the middle of the area. Both Mark and Jack walked over to it and read the note left there. Mark made sure the camera recorded it.

Then they turned and walked away. As they left Jack asked Mark, "Do you think we should disable those automatic weapons so that nobody else gets hurt?"

Mark shook his head, "No, I think everything here will be gone by dawn unless she is less competent than we think she is. They won't leave evidence behind."

Jack shook his head, "No explosion, kind of anticlimactic." Mark shrugged his shoulders, "The reason for this setup was to get us to read that note if we were smart enough to survive the trap."

Jack called Charlie and told him to keep a watch on the place to see if anyone showed to dismantle it. If so, find out where they went.

When they got back in the SUV, Sarah showed them the video they'd recorded. The hailstorm of bullets shredding everything around Mark as seen by Jack's camera was impressive. They all watched it several times.

Sixty miles away in a secure building, Raisia was watching a similar video. She shook her head and asked her two bosses who were sharing the video from much farther away. "How is that possible?"

Mr. Alpha's bass voice rumbled through her headset. "It's not possible. I would expect that they were some kind of hologram or video image. No one could withstand that much firepower and live."

Raisia stared at the scene and wondered.

CHAPTER FORTY-FIVE

Two days later Su Li fielded a call from Gary Rhodes of the FBI. She listened for a minute and told him to wait one. Keying the locator she found Jack in gym working out. Using the intercom she paged him to answer his cell phone.

Jack answered, "Yes Su Li, what is it?" He sounded perfectly normal and not out of breath.

Su Li smiled, "I've got Gary Rhodes on line two, and I'll transfer him."

She pressed the button and sent the call to Jack's cell phone. Jack flipped open the phone, "Hello Gary, how are you?"

Gary's normally cheerful voice sounded strained. "I'm doing okay Jack but I've got some bad news for you. It seems someone that doesn't like you is sitting in a very public place with an explosive device control and says she will detonate it if she doesn't hear from you in the next ten minutes."

Jack thought the situation through and held the phone away from his face. "Laura, will you get the group together in the War Room immediately?"

Laura nodded and keyed the "All call" button on her phone.

Jack asked Gary, "What number does Raisia want me to call her on?"

Gary chuckled, "Obviously you've had dealings with this woman?"

Jack laughed back, "Oh yeah, we've run into her before. She is very lethal. What is the FBI doing about this?"

Gary sighed, "Well, we've got two teams observing her at this point. Raisia is one very cool redhead. Since you guys are involved I haven't made any moves as yet. What do you want to do?"

Jack had an idea what the woman wanted. He got the number from Gary and memorized it. "Let me call her and I'll get back to you."

Gary spoke with the firmness of a senior FBI agent. "Jack, make it a three way. I'll mute my end but I need to understand what she wants."

Jack smiled to himself. "Okay, hang on."

When Raisia answered it was the first time Jack had heard her voice. "Mr. Malone? My name is Raisia and I want to meet with you. Be in the food courtyard of the Cherry Creek Mall in exactly fifty minutes. I'm sure you know what I look like. I'll be sitting at a table. If you're not here, well, you can guess the results." She hung up.

Jack told Gary, "I'll make the meeting and I'll wear a transmitter that Charlie can hook you into so that you can listen to our conversation."

Jack hung up, took a quick shower and dressed for the street. He ran to the War Room and gave the assembled cast a quick update. Then he said, "Mark, Sarah, you two are my backup. Su Li, I want you to take us almost there in a chopper and then go high and keep an eye on this witch. David, go with her to help. When we part, try to track her. My guess is that she'll go into a store to shake any surveillance. If she does, then Mark and or Sarah will stay with her. Track their GPS signals so that there are no communications between you guys."

Su Li called ahead to the chopper bay for the crew to warm up a bird and get it ready to launch.

Laura grabbed Jack's arm and gave him a kiss before he took off. She said, "Aren't you going to take the shield generator?"

Jack shook his head, "No. I think that is what she wants more than me." Then all four of them were gone, running hard on Su Li's heels for the elevator. They only had thirty two minutes left. Twenty minutes later Su Li's MH-60 PaveHawk armed helicopter dropped Jack, Mark, and Sarah off in a park two blocks from the mall and immediately lifted back off from the grass. Dozens of people stood around in surprise as Jack started trotting towards the mall. One man said, "Now that's how I want to shop."

Ignoring the people, Jack made it to the food court with three minutes to spare. Looking around he spotted the OC woman sitting alone at a table to his left. He walked over and sat down across from her.

Sizing her up Jack realized she was everything Mark warned him about on the ride to Cherry Creek. She was obviously cold, calculating, and in control. Physically she was quite similar to Sarah's athletic build. Her flame red hair contrasted with the lightly tanned skin of her face. Normally, red-haired people are fairly pasty white in color.

Raisia also evaluated Jack. Looking directly at his eyes she said, "I have been tasked with destroying you and your little band of troublemakers, which I will accomplish fairly soon. But, I am curious. How did you and your friend Mark Connelly survive the rifle fire I left for you in Omaha?"

Jack smiled, "Trade secret. Explain to me how a terrorist such as you expects to ever win at anything. Knowing that even if you accomplish a little bit, the whole world will work together to destroy you?"

Raisia smiled a cool smile. "Not my problem. I do what I need to. When the day comes for me to die, I'm ready and willing."

Jack was praying silently for the right words Yahveh wanted to give to this very lost child. "Raisia, there is a next life and you're capable of finding peace and love rather than death, destruction, and hopelessness."

The woman laughed. "Don't try to evangelize me Jack, I know the game. I've made my choices and am comfortable with them. Now tell me how you weren't killed by those bullets." Her voice had taken on a hard edge.

"Or what Raisia? You'll set off a bomb and kill a bunch of innocents? I don't think that will get you what you want. I am willing to deal with you but not with you threatening me."

Raisia got up and walked away from the table. Jack got up and followed her into the mall entrance. Walking quickly she turned into a wide, long hall that led to the bathrooms. Jack turned the corner and immediately picked up on the three hard guys standing there to block his path.

Raisia stopped just past them and said, "I think we need to talk at my place, Mr. Malone." She said to the men, "Bring him."

The three men advanced on Jack, two of them pulling out Automatic Police Batons. These are known as Tokusha Keibo in the martial art world and Jack was very, very familiar with them and the defenses against them. The steel sticks were only 8-1/2" long when carried but spring-loaded to extend them to 20-1/2" for use. The third man had brass knuckles on his right hand.

Moving to the wall to his right to limit access Jack took a fighting stance and waited for them to come for him. The two men with the batons attacked as a team, one from his left and one from his right. Turning to his left he did a full power side kick to the man on his right with his right leg. The baton struck his leg a glancing blow. At the same time Jack blocked the baton on his left with his hands crossed in an X shape. Twisting the man's wrist backwards Jack acquired the baton into his own right hand and struck the man forcefully on the forehead, knocking him out.

Without looking Jack swung the baton back and to his right as he started to turn back. Striking what he expected would be the man with the brass knuckles he was surprised to see an electronic stun gun fly out of Raisia's right hand as the bones in that hand broke from the power of the stroke. Her surprise was even greater than Jack's.

Jack continued to turn back to his right as the man on his left fell to the floor unconscious. The first man Jack had kicked was still falling backwards and had lost his baton. Raisia was clutching her right hand in her left as the pain of the damage hit her. To eliminate any more attacks from her, Jack brought the baton back up and struck her on the right side of her head hard enough to knock her out. Raisia fell to the floor, which left the man with the brass knuckles that stood there undecided how to attack Jack and defend Raisia.

Mark's distinctive bass tones joined the fray. "Put your hands on your head, and get on your knees NOW! No second chances!" The man did as he was told. Sarah ran up to the fight scene and surveyed the damage. Mark removed the man's brass knuckles and had him lie on the floor with his hands on his head, his fingers interlaced and his ankles crossed to limit his mobility.

Mark was impressed by Jack's response to the attack. "Remind me to have you teach me some more of that."

The two FBI teams ran up to the group. One of them was talking to Gary Rhodes on a cell phone. They quickly frisked the man lying face down on the floor and picked up the brass knuckles. They cuffed and thoroughly searched the other three people lying on the ground. Coming up with a small electronic transmitter they quickly placed it in an RF-proof container and carefully handcuffed Raisia's good hand and broken hand behind her.

Mark tipped his head towards the unconscious woman and looked at Sarah. Sarah shooed the FBI back and did a quick strip search on the Russian assassin. Coming up with three more weapons and four lock picks she gave them to the amazed FBI agents. Mark told them, "This woman is probably the deadliest creature I've run into in all my years. Take every precaution you can think of and then double them. Don't give her any rights or freedoms. She will kill you with her bare hands in less time than you can realize she's done it. I've seen her do it in combat to four armed men who were ex-military. Very sneaky and underhanded. You give her a food tray and she'll use it to kill you."

Jack asked for the cell phone and talked to Gary Rhodes. Then he handed it back and the Agent in Charge who listened for several seconds and nodded. He told the other agents to collect the three men.

Looking at Mark he said, "I've been instructed to leave this woman with you under existing terroristic charges against her."

Mark nodded and confiscated the gurney that an approaching EMS team was bringing with them. Sarah took the handcuffs off of Raisia at

Jack's command. Then Jack and Sarah lifted Raisia up on the stretcher and carefully strapped her on with no give for her legs or arms. He asked the EMS tech to immobilize her right hand in a temporary cast until they could get medical treatment for her. The team then used riot cuffs to strap her arms and hands to the rails on the gurney.

Raisia's eyes fluttered open and she groggily looked around. Sizing up the situation she said, "Let me go, now or that bomb will go off and the lives of those . . . "That was all she got to say before Sarah taped her mouth shut with medical tape. Patting her on the non-damaged hand Sarah told her. "That's all right honey. We'll take care of it. You just shut up and lie still."

The three Crossfire Team members rolled the Russian woman out of the hall, through the crowd of by-standers and quickly took her out of the mall. They loaded her into the ambulance and had the EMS team take them to the park two blocks away.

Su Li landed the helicopter and the team loaded the stretcher with Raisia on it into the craft and jumped on themselves. Su Li lifted off and headed for the fortress.

Jack looked at the angry eyes of Raisia and said to Mark. "I've got a bad feeling about taking her into the fortress. For all we know, that is exactly what she wanted in the first place."

Mark thought about that and agreed. "Okay, then let's take her to our other site." He winked at Jack out of Raisia's sight. Mark moved to the copilot's seat and made a phone call. Then he gave Su Li new directions. Su Li called the ATC and got permission to alter the flight path. Turning to the left she took them deeper into the Rocky Mountains until she got a homing beacon. Following the beacon she was contacted by a terse military voice warning her off. Mark spoke into the hush microphone on the copilot's side of the craft. "This is General Connelly, Alpha, Alpha, Zulu, nine, seven, three, two. I have priority traffic from General Markus Harrington for you." He switched the call to conference and listened to General Harrington's orders for the security at the base.

Su Li was given clearance to land. Bringing the chopper to the deck outside a large opening in the granite she was instructed to lift off less than two feet and fly into the opening. Following the instruction she flew into the dark. Told to set the chopper down and shut the engines off she did so. A rumbling was heard and all light from the outside was cut off by massive steel doors.

Arc lamps came on and illuminated the cavern. There were at least eight guards with automatic weapons pointed at the helicopter. Mark also noted the Planax weapon aimed at them from the wall. These guys weren't taking any risks.

Exiting from the chopper they brought out Raisia with a cloth tied over her head so that she couldn't see anything.

A Captain came out and met with them. Mark had a full ten minute talk with him which included a great deal of pointing at Raisia's stretcher. Apparently he was quite convincing.

The Captain called four of the Marines guarding the entrance over to the group by the chopper. "I want two of you to carry this stretcher into ward C and call the doctor to look at her hand and head. Do not let her see anything until you're in Ward C. Is that clear?" The men said, "Yes Sir." Then the Captain continued. "The other two of you are to have your handguns aimed at her at all times. If she does anything other than what she is told to do, you are to terminate her life immediately. Do not assume anything whatsoever. Is that clear?" These two men also said, "Yes Sir."

Following their orders the men picked up the stretcher and left for the far wall. The Captain looked at the five team members and nodded with his head towards the same wall. "If you and your team will follow me General Connelly, I'll see what I can do to facilitate General Harrington's orders to extend full service to you while you're here."

They walked to another steel door in the granite wall and stepped through. Jack was surprised that there wasn't a huge space and it didn't contain any machines, any laboratory or lab. It was basically a large office space with hundreds of computer servers and technicians.

CHAPTER FORTY-SIX

The team accompanied Captain Brubell back to the dispensary. They watched as an accomplished surgeon X-rayed and set Raisia's hand. After he cast it in a soft plaster cast that couldn't be used as a weapon, the doctor came over to them. "I've given her an injection to limit the pain while I reset her hand. I expect that she'll be conscious in the next fifteen minutes." He then left the room.

While they waited for Raisia to regain consciousness Mark shook his head, "I doubt that we can pry anything out of this female weapon. But, we can try."

Sarah frowned, "I agree with you. It would take an expert days to get anything of value out of her. And then I would doubt that it would be true. She's is a finely honed weapon and has been since her youth. I'm not sure she would survive interrogation."

Back at the fortress Laura was praying for the team and their new captive. Laura was very aware that Yahveh doesn't accept bitterness and anger towards an enemy. He told us to pray for them and that was what Laura was doing. She got a leading and asked a question. Sensing an affirmation she picked up her cell phone and called Jack. Not getting a response she called Charlie. He told her that normal cell phone signals couldn't get to where Jack was at the moment. But, he could hook her up. Several minutes later Jack answered his phone.

Laura asked how he was and if everyone was all right. Jack replied in the affirmative. Then Laura told him that Yahveh let her know that Raisia was dead.

Jack walked over to the stretcher and felt for a pulse. There was none. He looked at the others and shook his head. Sarah didn't trust Raisia even if she was dead. She called the doctor back in to confirm the death. He checked with his stethoscope and confirmed she wasn't breathing and that there was no pulse. Sarah knew of some Eastern techniques that allowed a person to effectively stop their heart for a short period of time. Looking at the doctor she

215

said, "This woman is trickiest person I've ever met. I don't really know that she's dead or faking it."

The doctor looked into Sarah's eyes and realized she was being straight with him. He undid the blouse on the Russian woman and bared her chest. He walked over to a cart and rolled it over to the operating table. "Okay, let's see if she is alive or dead." He fired up the defibrillator and ran the power up to half. Rubbing the paddles together with a cream he said "Clear!" He said this to make sure no one else would be in contact with the charge. He put the paddles to Raisia's chest and pushed the button. The body jumped in a muscular response but when he had hooked up the monitor to her heart it was still a straight line indicating no heartbeat.

He shook his head, "She is verifiably quite dead."

Sarah nodded, "Okay, if she's dead then I can't hurt her, right?" The doctor frowned, "What are you planning to do?"

Sarah walked around the table and moved the doctor to the side. Reaching across she ran the setting on the defibrillator to "MAX" and waited until it reached full power. Sarah then applied the paddles to both sides of the Russian woman's head and pushed the button. The whole body convulsed and seemed to collapse somewhat into itself, the eyes no longer looked the same direction. Sarah reached up and closed the eyelids.

Turning off the power to the defibrillator Sarah smiled at the doctor as she replaced the paddles. "You're right, she's definitely dead."

The very stunned doctor looked at the body. "If she had been alive you would have destroyed her brain by short circuiting every neuron in there at that setting."

Sarah looked at the man. "Exactly!" Then she walked back to Mark who was thinking that he was very glad that Sarah wasn't mad at him.

The trip back to the fortress was quiet and contemplative for each of them. Mark left Raisia's body at the Navy site to be turned over to the FBI.

Laura met them at the elevator and hugged Jack, and then each of the others. Walking into the living area they sat down and the other members of the team present at the fortress quickly showed up. Jack and Mark described the action as it unfolded up to their return including the death of Raisia.

Afterward they all discussed what it all meant. Alexis asked, "Do you think that Raisia was working for OC or meeting with you on her own?"

Jack had gone down that road of thought. "I think she was doing her own thing in trying to find out how we were able to live through the hailstorm of bullets. It went wrong so badly that we captured all of the OC people on that operation, including Raisia. The look of surprise on her face when I knocked the stun gun out of her hand was real and she didn't expect it. I don't think the new Mr. Alpha would have mounted such a mediocre op. I think Raisia was too confident in her own abilities and underestimated us."

Mark said, "I concur with Jack. This wasn't a well-prepared trap. She had to suspect we had more agents there than she could handle. Her whole trap doesn't really make a lot of sense. I think the use of the shield generators threw her such a curve she wasn't thinking proactively concerning nabbing Jack."

Alexis nodded, "Sounds right. I wonder what the reaction will be from the OC group."

Everyone sat there considering the implications in that thought.

CHAPTER FORTY-SEVEN

Four days later Jack got a call from Gary Rhodes. "Jack, we got the coroner's inquest results on Raisia Ivanova. It seems she died from the anesthetic the doctor at the Navy Data Center gave her to set her hand. Apparently she had something in her bloodstream that reacted to the anesthetic shot and turned into poison. It stopped her heart less than five minutes after the shot."

Jack thanked the FBI man. "Thanks Gary. Listen, I want you to have them pretty the body up and put it on cold ice for a while. I may need proof of her demise fairly soon."

Gary promised he would handle it and hung up.

Jack walked into the rifle range and found Mark and Sarah teaching both Laura and Su Li off-hand rapid fire with a variety of handguns. He told them about the coroner's findings. Mark nodded, "Yep that is a Russian trick for their spies. They take annual shots to keep a level of specialized formula in their bloodstreams so that if an anesthetic is administered, by hypodermic or inhaled, that it will mix with the anesthetic to become a potent poison." Seeing the questions on the other faces he was about to explain when David interrupted.

David held up his hand to get attention. "The concept is simple. If the agent is caught and administered an intravenous shot of many things, including anesthetic or subjected to a certain type of gas, the poison will be created and fatal. The reason behind it is that if the agent is in control they won't allow such a shot. If they have been captured and are not in control then they need to die anyway."

Su Li said, "That's horrible!"

Sarah laughed a quiet laugh at the girl's naiveté. "That's only a little sample of the twisted thinking in the world of espionage."

David looked contemplative. "But, what about the time we used a knock-out dart to subdue her````` in the airport in Spain? She didn't die then."

Sarah smiled, "Different drugs, different results I suppose. It really doesn't matter anymore."

That afternoon they got another call from Gary Rhodes. "Jack, it looks like your hunch about the body was right on. We just got an anonymous email that was for your team. It was in code but we were able to break it easily. I'll send it to you both ways but in essence it says, Crossfire Team, we know you have our female agent and we are willing to trade for her. We will trade the location of six, class 1 explosive devices in heavy traffic areas for the return of our agent. If you agree, call 303 555-0100 by noon today. Otherwise, we will detonate all six devices one by one between noon and three o'clock today. OC."

Jack relayed the information to Mark who suggested that they agree with the OC to return Raisia by six p.m. but only after they were given two locations of devices that they could confirm the threat.

Jack relayed what they planned to Gary and asked him to come to the fortress before they called the OC. Gary agreed and hung up. Three hours later the FBI verified two large bombs, one in a shopping center and one in an office complex. Both bombs were disarmed and removed.

Mark thought about the message they'd been given and suggested to Gary that they do a quiet evacuation of the area schools on a pretext.

Gary asked, "Why the schools?"

Mark pointed out that the OC were going to detonate between noon and three o'clock. The only crowded areas that would be empty after three were schools.

Bomb sniffing dogs were rushed to area schools as quickly as they could be evacuated. All four of the other bombs were found and disarmed before the body of Raisia was finally delivered to the location specified by the OC.

Less than ten minutes later all four of the detonators were set off by remote control.

Jack shook his head at the end of that period. "How are we going to protect the public from these monsters? They seem to be able to set up bombs anywhere without anybody noticing."

Sarah quietly said, "We find them and kill them. Then, and only then, will they stop killing innocents."

That evening, Jack and Laura were settling down to bed and Laura snuggled up to Jack and asked, "Shall we find these people by prayer?"

Jack hugged his wife and then kissed her. Smiling he said, "It can wait until morning."

The Crossfire Team will return in ***"Violent Crossfire"***.

If this story has awakened your spirit or moved you to seek the love of Christ and His power for your life, whether you've never accepted Jesus as your savior or you've fallen away, repeat the following prayer and begin a most wonderful journey into eternal life with Him today.

Father God in heaven, As You said in Your Holy Word, (Romans 10:9) that if we confess the Lord our God and believe in our hearts that God raised Jesus from the dead, we shall be saved.

(The prayer on the next page is a sample prayer when asking Jesus into your heart as your Savior. You can also pray this in your own words.)

Salvation Prayer

Dear God in heaven, I come to you in the name of Jesus. I confess to You that I am a sinner, and I am sorry for my sins and the life that I have lived; I need your forgiveness. I believe that your only begotten Son Jesus Christ shed His precious blood on the cross at Calvary and died for my sins, and I am now willing to turn from my sin.

Right now I confess Jesus as the Lord of my life and my soul. With all my heart, I truly believe that your Holy Spirit raised Jesus from the dead. Today I accept Jesus Christ as my personal Savior and according to Your Word, right now I am saved.

I thank you Jesus, for your unlimited grace which has saved me from my sins. I thank you Jesus that your grace that never leads to license, but rather it always leads to repentance. Therefore Lord Jesus, transform my life so that I may bring glory and honor to you alone and not to myself.

I thank you Lord Jesus, for dying for me at Calvary and giving me eternal life.

Amen.

If you just said this prayer and you meant it with all your heart, believe that you are now saved and have been born again.

You may ask, "Now that I am saved, what do I do next?" First of all you need to get into a spirit-filled, bible-based church that teaches the Scriptures, and you need to study God's Word.

Once you have found a church home, you will want to become water-baptized. By accepting Christ you are baptized in the spirit, but it is through water-baptism that you publically announce your obedience to the Lord Jesus. Water baptism is a symbol of your salvation from the dead. You were dead but now you live, for Jesus Christ has redeemed you for a price! The price was His atoning death on the cross. May God Bless You!

www.ingramcontent.com/pod-product-compliance
Lightning Source LLC
Chambersburg PA
CBHW071326250626
47159CB00004B/1479